WITHDRAWN

D0955754

Endure

Also by Carrie Jones
Need
Captivate
Entice

ೞ

With Steven E. Wedel
After Obsession

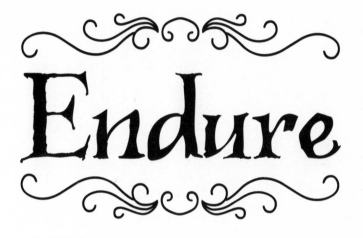

Endure

Carrie Jones

Columbia County Rural
Library District
P.O. Box 74
Dayton, WA 99328
(509) 382-4131

BLOOMSBURY

NEW YORK BERLIN LONDON SYDNEY

Copyright © 2012 by Carrie Jones
All rights reserved. No part of this book may be reproduced or transmitted in any form
or by any means, electronic or mechanical, including photocopying, recording, or by any
information storage and retrieval system, without permission in writing from the publisher.

First published in the United States of America in May 2012
by Bloomsbury Books for Young Readers
www.bloomsburyteens.com

For information about permission to reproduce selections from this book, write to
Permissions, Bloomsbury BFYR, 175 Fifth Avenue, New York, New York 10010

Library of Congress Cataloging-in-Publication Data
available upon request
ISBN: 978-1-59990-554-9

Book design by Nicole Gastonguay
Typeset by Westchester Book Composition
Printed in the U.S.A. by Quad/Graphics, Fairfield, Pennsylvania
2 4 6 8 10 9 7 5 3 1

All papers used by Bloomsbury Publishing, Inc., are natural, recyclable products
made from wood grown in well-managed forests. The manufacturing processes
conform to the environmental regulations of the country of origin.

To the fans of Zara who stuck with her for so long despite her flaws. You are all made of awesome sauce.

And to my daughter, Emily, because every book I write, I write for her. "Remember upon the conduct of each depends the fate of all." —*Alexander the Great*

Endure

ITEMS OF INTEREST TO LOCAL AGENCIES:

12/14: Trooper David Seacreast responded to a theft complaint in Brooklin regarding metal stolen from a rental property. Investigation continues.

Trooper Jennifer Roberts responded to a missing-persons complaint in Bedford concerning a fifteen-year-old male last seen at the YMCA. FBI took over investigation, which continues.

"Do you want some more spaghetti?"

Nick's voice is so abrupt and unexpected that it actually makes me jump in the dining room chair. As he pulls a hand through his snow-wet dark hair, I try to pretend like I wasn't startled and everything is all fine and normal. This is a big lie. Even the weather isn't normal. December in Downeast Maine isn't usually this overwhelmingly snowy, but we're battling a potential apocalypse and one of the signs is a "lovely" nonstop snow. That's why there's a plow attached to the front of my grandmother's truck, and that's why I have blisters on my hands from shoveling, and that's why Nick's hair is wet from snow that's melted in the warmth of the house.

"I'm good for now, thanks," I say to him, and for a second I feel like we're an old married couple that's had some fight over shopping money or something, but it isn't that easy. We aren't old or married. He is my ex-boyfriend, I think. We never officially broke up and now the air between us is awkward with this crazy undercurrent of tension.

He twists some more spaghetti around his fork and sort of grunts to acknowledge that I spoke.

One of the conditions of my mom leaving me in Maine and finishing up her work contract in South Carolina was that Nick had to stay here in my missing grandmother's house with me. Under normal circumstances a mother (especially a Southern mother—especially *my* mother) wouldn't leave a teenage male and a teenage female in the same house together at night unsupervised, but these aren't normal circumstances. Let me detail why:

1. Evil human-sized pixies led by a pixie king named Frank/Belial are attacking us. They have additional help from Isla, Astley's freaky mom. Astley is a good pixie king. Yes, there is such a thing.
2. Frank and his evil pixies are kidnapping young guys and killing them, draining them of their souls and torturing them in the process.
3. They have also just started kidnapping girls.
4. This same evil pixie killed Nick, sending him to a mythical place called Valhalla where only fae can go.
5. I had to turn pixie to go there.
6. Nick hates pixies.
7. Therefore Nick now hates me, even though I rescued him.

Nick doesn't actually *say* that he hates me, but he doesn't really say anything to me. Even right now, he looks away while I push spaghetti around my plate. He stares down so intently at his food that it's like he's memorizing every single strand of pasta. The silence is a painful, solid thing that crackles the air between us.

I push my bright yellow plate away, force myself to look at his rugged boy face: the stubble on his cheeks, the dark smudges beneath his eyes, the tight line of his mouth that makes his lips disappear.

Flipping my fork over, I put it on the side of my plate and steel myself for whatever comes next, but seriously, anything has to be better than this silence.

"You know," I say. "You can hate me *and* still talk to me."

His eyes flick up and meet mine for a second, just a second.

"I mean, you hated Ian and you talked to him. I hated Megan and I talked to her," I say, referencing two evil pixies who posed as high school humans before they were killed in this escalating war. "Hate and rudeness don't have to go hand in hand."

Ugh. I can't believe I said "hand in hand." I sound like my mother.

My bamboo fork falls off the plate with a clacking noise. I didn't balance it well, I guess. I pick it up again. I could kill Nick with this fork. That's how strong I am now. Well, maybe not kill him, because he is one tough shape-shifting wolf, but I could hurt him. Not that I'd ever want to.

"I don't hate you, Zara. I hate this situation. I hate that when you first got here you were this normal, depressed, pacifist girl who cared about human rights and peace and now you're this . . . Now you spend your nights hunting down evil. Now you kill without blinking an eye and it's just part of your routine. I hate what you've become." His voice cracks the tension between us, evaporates my random thoughts, and before I can even answer him, he stands up and heads to the sink, bringing his plate with him.

My adrenaline pulses and I will myself to be calm, to not cry or fill up too much with the anger that comes from being offended.

His metal fork rubs across the ceramic surface as he scrapes off the remnants of the meal. "I'll clean up. You go get ready. It's our night to patrol."

I know that. I know that it's our team's turn to look for pixies, but it doesn't make me happy. I never imagined that I would dread spending time with Nick, yet I do. I wish Astley were here. He wouldn't say he hated what I've become if I magically turned back to human, I don't think. And what have I become that's so hate worthy? A pixie. A killing machine who wears jeans with peace signs on them. A protector of my friends and this crazy town. Someone who eats spaghetti way too often. But that's my life now and I'm totally okay with it. I just wish Nick was too. He's the real killing machine around here, the big were warrior, and now that I can protect people too he gets all uptight about it. I think it's because I lack testosterone. Just thinking about the whole double standard of it makes me cranky.

"We need more people to help us patrol," I say. I've said it about a dozen times in the last two days.

"It would just put them at risk. Humans can't fight pixies."

"We could make an army, train them. Devyn and I have been talking about it a lot."

"You'd be sending them to slaughter."

The argument is pointless. We've had it before. Standing up, I stare at Nick's broad back as he faces the sink. The muscles of his shoulders work as he moves his arms to turn on the faucet. The water runs down the drain, swirling the spaghetti bits into the trash compactor, where they'll be ground into nothing. Everything leaves so easily. It is there and seems so real and then it can just get washed away. I miss my grandmother, Betty. She's run off, turned into a tiger and left. Every patrol I look for her. She's never there. And I miss Nick. He's here but he's always angry, nothing like the old Nick.

I put my plate on the counter next to him and say, "It feels like you hate me."

"Well," he says as he grabs the plate, runs it beneath the hot water. "I don't."

Three words. He gave me three sort of positive words.

That has to be enough for now, I guess, so I say, "Let's go patrol."

He nods.

Well, I don't.

That's what he said. Usually when people hang on to three little words, those words are "I love you," but for me it's "Well, I don't." That's pretty sad, even I know it, but as I get dressed to go outside, I still hold on to those words like they are some magic lifeline to happiness.

We have to replow the driveway first because of the snow that keeps trucking down, but once that is done we drive out toward the high school and the YMCA to hunt. Neither of us talks as we pass the First Baptist Church, which is currently a trailer because the real church burned down in the summer and they still have to rebuild. It's hard to rebuild a church when people keep vanishing. We sludge past the self-storage place that has a big barbed-wire fence around it, past the Bedford Falls Minimart where they make the super-good butter rolls, the gas pumps where a state trooper is filling up his cruiser, all the little houses sided with aluminum and clapboard. Windows squared with light brighten up the night and the snowy scene. The world is quiet. Most people are too afraid to leave their homes after dark now. There used to be a curfew for everyone under eighteen, but things have gotten so bad that hardly anybody is around to break it.

Nick doesn't say anything as I park my grandmother's truck in the school lot. We'll head down the railroad tracks and into the forest, which is where we've found the biggest clusters. Frank's pixies must be living back there or something. Tonight, Astley and Becca, and another all-pixie team of Amelie and Garret, will be hunting in town. They are stealthier, less likely to be seen than me and a giant wolf, which is why I've assigned us the woods. It made sense before, but right now it just makes me feel lonelier to face all these trees and the snow-closed sky.

Nick turns wolf the moment he steps out of the truck. I pick up his clothes and put them on the seat before locking up. He takes off down the tracks and I follow. He always has to be alpha and tonight I'm too sad and stressed to really mind like I normally would.

I'm barely out of the truck when I sense something. It's a smell that I don't recognize—rotting flesh, but that's not it. There is vanilla mixed in. I stand still, completely creeped out. This is something different, something powerful. I survey around me, slowly turning three hundred and sixty degrees. The sensation that I'm being watched makes me hold my breath. I get back to my original position. The smell dissipates and I lope down the track after Nick, catching up pretty quickly.

It's dark and cloudy and snow is booming down out of the sky like it's on some sort of world-freezing mission. I can still feel that something, somehow, is not right tonight, even though the rotting smell is gone.

"Please let it be a wimpy pixie," I mutter. "One that's easy to fight."

My muscles rigid up while the wolf next to me pricks his ears, lifts his head, and growls. I reach out to touch his neck, to feel the fur bristle, but he moves away from my touch like he has over and over again these last few days. Something in my heart cinches up. Truth is, this is the only form where he'll get even slightly close to me.

It's been half a week since I rescued this wolf/man from Valhalla, half a week since he lost his memory of what I did there to save him, almost a week since I turned from human to pixie. Just one week and my heart has been broken over and over again. My heart must hate me, because I swear it would almost be easier to die than to have to face Nick blowing me off again, turning away.

No, not tonight. I'm not about to wallow in oh-my-boyfriend-doesn't-love-me-anymore self-pity tonight. And I'm not about to die either. I've already hesitated too much, distracted by Nick. I'm off my game.

I put my gloved hand on my knife, pull it out from the sheath thingy that's attached to the belt on my jeans, and press my back into the tree, waiting, breathing as shallowly as possible.

Nick doesn't move either. He waits in wolf silence. Dawn is still hours away. The closest road is about a mile behind us. It's just us and the woods. It would be the perfect time to make Nick listen. When he's wolf, he can't talk, but he still understands.

No, I will not be distracted.

I will focus. Nick paws the ground once, but doesn't leave his spot.

The fear of loneliness is eremophobia.

I will not be eremophobic.

My thoughts and mind will be still.

Still.

Still . . .

"Nick," I start. "I know that you are mad at me because I'm a pixie and that makes you think—"

He growls. It's soft and low at first. I glare at him, will him to be silent and just listen to me, but he's either not psychic or he doesn't pay attention, most likely both. I squat down, tap him on the flank.

"Hey. I know you don't want to hear this, but I need you to listen."

His eye flits toward me to see what I want. I raise a finger to my lips and then point at him to be silent. He growls again and that's when I realize that he's not growling because he's trying to ignore me and make me shut up, which would be totally rude. He's growling because he senses something.

I groan. I've lost my focus. Again.

"What is it?" I whisper far too quietly for human ears, but I know Nick can hear me. "How many?"

Suddenly, I can sense it again too. Something heavy moves

through the woods behind us. There's a rasping noise to the footsteps, almost like the sound of paper on fire. Nick's body tenses. Then to our left is another noise. Something else creeps through the trees. I sniff, trying to smell something, but all I know is that it's not pixie or human or a wild animal or what I smelled before in the parking lot. I stand again, step forward as gently as I can on the snow. The air smells of burning and frost and snow-wet dog, balsam and spruce. Fire. I think that's what it is. Whatever is coming behind us smells of fire.

Nick and I turn simultaneously. I peer around the tree. An orange glow creeps closer. It smells of death, burning, anger. It takes the shape of a man, a man twice the size of a normal man. He marches in a straight line right toward us. His sword burns with flame and he holds it in one hand as he walks. He's getting close, maybe thirty feet away from us.

What the hell is he?

This is not a pixie. I still don't know a lot about us but I know that we can't change into this form. We aren't so tall. We aren't made of fire but instead, like humans, we are made of flesh and bone and need.

I swallow hard and grab Nick's fur to keep him from lunging forward. He doesn't pull away because he probably knows that to pull away would give us up for attack. He grunts softly just as another giant man-thing steps into the first one's path. This one's not on fire but he's just as huge. Blue hair hangs from his head. Bare forearms that are larger than my thighs ripple with the movement of his muscles. His boots strap up his legs and seem to be made of fur. His skin is as white as the snow and a helmet obscures most of his head. He raises a two-headed ax thing that's covered with ice. He roars.

The woods bristle.

These things are way worse than pixies.

Way.

Worse.

I will not be afraid of monsters . . . I will not be afraid of monsters . . . I will not be afraid . . .

But fear overtakes me. It's like a punch that comes from the inside and tries to pound its way out. One second passes. It is the longest second in the universe. Nick's muscles tighten the way they do right before he attacks. I drop to the ground and wrap my arms around him. He struggles against me halfheartedly, I think, and then gives up just as the first giant man, the red-hot one, swings his sword toward the icy guy. They clash. The sound is almost as loud as thunder, but more metallic. Steam rises from where their weapons meet.

I think my mouth drops open, because my teeth suddenly hurt from the cold and snow is falling on my tongue. The orange giant raises his sword above his head and charges. The frosty one lifts his ax and deflects the blow. Metal hits metal. Again, steam rises from where their weapons meet. One of them, the fiery one, roars and the trees shake. A branch above our heads catches fire, it pops and sizzles and then the entire thing is engulfed, flames raging high.

I stagger backward, pulling Nick with me. And he actually lets me. He would never do that before; he'd be surging forward, joining in the fight or guarding me. Now he is just as scared as I am, I think. The fire sizzles above us and to the left, and suddenly the air is much warmer. The branch cracks off the tree and falls to the snow, smoldering. It's black and twisted.

That's when it hits me: they really are giants, not just giant men, but giants. Both warriors wear chain mail; links and links of it surround their massive chests. Weapons slash against each other, and the mail seems to withstand it until . . . They both thrust forward. The ax cleaves down on the frosty one's shoulder and neck. The movement leaves the fire giant open for a thrust to his chest. The sword sticks into his pecs and stays. Steam flies up to the air as the fire giant falls to the ground. One second later the frosty giant slumps to his knees and then keels over backward. Blood gushes out of his neck.

The world is quiet except for the frosty giant's harsh, gurgling breaths. Nick whimpers. I let go of my hold around his neck. "Okay. Be careful though."

He rushes forward, sniffs cautiously at the fire giant and abandons him. He must be dead. He is still. I don't hear him breathing. But the other one?

"Pixie." The icy giant gasps out the word. "Zara of the willow, the stars, the White."

My name. He knows my name. I look to Nick, who has rushed to the frosty giant's side and is sniffing at the ax, at his wound. Nick makes a soft whining noise into the still-burning air. I move forward, finally no longer frozen. The giant is sprawled across the snow. His beard is icy in some places, singed in others.

"We'll get you help," I say, grabbing his hand. It is like touching frozen metal. My skin adheres to it almost. His eyes are ice, dying and unfeeling. His muscles limp. We both know it's too late for help. Plus, what kind of help could I even get? An ambulance? For a giant man of frost?

I maneuver myself so I can lift his head up off the ground a little bit, but the blood just rushes out more. Which is a good thing, I think, because taking a long time to die a painful death could never be right.

"How do you know my name?" I blurt.

He doesn't answer that.

"What can I do?" I beg him. "Tell me how to help you."

His breath shallows. Beyond us, the fire giant's body hisses in the snow. This one's mouth moves and each word seems a tremendous exertion of will, of effort. "Loki will escape the cavern. You will die. Must. Stop."

I will die? Me specifically?

"Loki?" I search for answers in the empty eyes. "The Norse god, Loki?"

His nod is just the tiniest of movements. His voice is so quiet I have to lean closer and cock my ear to hear him. "Ragnarok will come. Here to warn the king . . . He must not . . ."

"Must not what? What?" My voice begs, pleads, is a cry into the night, but it doesn't matter. His head falls into my lap. His body stills. There will be no more answers from him; not tonight, not ever.

"Thank you," I whisper. My hands move to close his eyes. For a moment it is as if all his power, his cold will, echoes through me. The shock of it leaves me still. Frozen.

Then it is gone.

I don't know what to do. Do I leave him here? What about the other one? Nick whines and paws the ground. I wipe my hand in the snow to try to get off the blood and then flip open my cell phone. No signal. Of course. I make an executive decision.

"We'll go back. We'll get help to move the bodies, then bury them. They'll be okay here for a minute, right?" I ask Nick.

He pants, which I'm going to decide means yes.

I gently take the giant's head out of my lap and place it on the ground. I kiss his cheek. "Good passage."

It is all I can think to say. The snow behind me sizzles from the smoldering branch next to the other giant's body. Something is off here. As I turn to look, the giant himself suddenly bursts into flames. Nick yelps and scrambles backward, paws sliding on the earth. Then, just as quickly as it started, the fire is gone and the giant is gone with it. All that's left is a black smudge on the ground. When I turn back to look at the frosty giant, he's gone too. There's just a pile of snow. I reach through it, feel for him, but there's only vapor.

"This. Is. So. Weird," I mumble. "This is *Twilight Zone* weird, freaky sci-fi weird. I'm not hallucinating, am I?"

Nick rolls his wolf eyes, which is pretty impressive, albeit annoying.

"Nice," I say. "Very supportive of you. Thanks."

He barks a short retort.

"You are so lucky I don't understand wolf," I tell him.

It takes us about twenty minutes to get back to the parking lot between Bedford High School and the softball field. Nick stays in wolf form the entire way so I can't bounce ideas off of him about whether or not we were hallucinating or if we really just saw giants. I can't ask him why I rarely see him in human form since he came back despite the fact that we're living in the same house. Seeing him at school hardly counts since he avoids me and doesn't even come to lunch. In this form, I can't ask him one freaking thing, which is probably why he's like this—all wolf and quiet.

When we get to my car he just turns around. He doesn't even give a nice bark or anything like a dog in a Disney movie would. Then again, he's not a dog and this is not Disney. Disney pixies are decidedly different. Nick just takes off into the woods without looking back.

"Yeah," I mutter, "nice seeing you too. You want to go get some pizza, 'cause I'm sick of spaghetti? Maybe thank me for bringing you back to the world of the living? Yeah . . . awesome."

I open the door to the truck, sighing, even though sighing is cliché. I sigh because there is nothing else to do. I sigh because sighing about Nick is all I have left in me right now. Just that. A sigh.

I start the engine right away because if some evil pixie is going to sneak attack me it's best to be able to drive away super-fast. But when I let my brain relax for a second it's not evil pixies I think about or even Nick. It's what just happened in the woods—the fight.

Images of the ax wound in the ice giant's neck and the fire giant erupting into flames flash into my brain, searing themselves there, and I shudder as I grab my phone and text our friend Devyn because Devyn is brainy and research oriented and occasionally a bird. It's too late to call.

Giants? One icy. One fire. Signs of Ragnarok?

In Norse mythology, Ragnarok is this ancient prophesized end of the gods and of humans, which a year ago I would have rolled my eyes at but now . . . now . . . Well, I've met Odin and Thor and been to Valhalla. It's hard to really roll my eyes at anything.

Air starts blasting in through the heaters. I hold my breath. Something is watching me again. I can feel it, a nasty darkness that shouldn't be there. The tiny hairs on my arms stand up and brush against the fabric of my shirt. I don't have to move my sleeve to know that I have goose bumps.

"Astley?" My voice whispers into the truck. It's pretty pathetic that when I get creeped out I automatically hope that Astley's close by, or Amelie, his kick-butt second in command.

"Betty?" Maybe my grandmother is nearby, stalking, protecting? Maybe she's found me while I've been looking for her.

She doesn't answer. Nothing answers, which is a good thing. Bad pixies aren't known for being silent.

Resisting the urge to just give in to nerves and play damsel in distress, I don't call Astley for backup, don't call Issie for moral support. I focus instead on my own power. I'm a pixie queen. I'm powerful now. I have to remember that.

I haul in a big breath and put the truck in reverse. That's when the smell comes again, hard and true, a rotting smell like dead mice in a hot attic—only magnified about twenty times. Gagging, I put my gloved hand over my mouth and pull out of the parking space, then put it in forward so I can get out of the lot. Then I think better of it and brake. If there's something dead in my grandmother's truck, I'd like to get the darn thing out before we get home.

"Why me?" I mutter. Sure I'm a warrior and all that, but I'm not so good at actually looking for dead things, especially in my truck. Just as I'm unbuckling the seat belt and twisting around to check behind the seats, my phone beeps. I shriek because I'm so on edge. My in-box icon flashes that there is one new text from Devyn.

I keep holding my breath while I read it.

It's just two words: Why? and Yes.

I don't answer right then. I just can't. Closing my eyes, I lean my head back against the headrest and pray. The smell is gone again, the feeling vanished with it. My flesh has lost its goose bumps, but the worry about us and the future makes my skin terribly cold. I reach over, turn the heat up past eighty, and head home.

When I get there I finally text back, We need to talk about Loki. I send it to all of our crew.

The moment I step out of the truck, I notice the wolf tracks that head up the porch steps. Nick is already back. As I slam the car door shut, he steps out of the house, a bag slung over his shoulder, looking human—sad and human.

"What are you doing?" The words are out of my mouth before I can stop them.

He steps closer, one step, another. It's like it's all happening in slow motion. The snow swirls around us, tiny specks of fluff stick to his hair, his cheeks. His voice is hoarse and tired. "Zara . . ."

All he says is my name, but it rips me apart anyway because he fills my name with pain and regret.

I step toward him, raise my hands, cover his lips. An ache of sorrow threatens to take over me, rising up from my stomach. "Don't say anything."

He can't. He can't say anything because I can't hear anything bad, anything . . .

"You feel so different," he murmurs. His lips move beneath my fingers, forming syllables of hurt. "You don't feel like Zara anymore."

My fingers drop from his lips. My fingers did nothing to stop him from saying it. My changing did nothing to stop me from losing him. I lift my hand again to touch his face, to say good-bye, but a muscle in his cheek twitches and instead my hand just hangs in the air, not sure where to go.

"You said you would love me, that you would always love me, no matter what," I say, reminding him of right before he died. "Do you remember that?"

His lower lip sucks in toward his teeth for a second. His voice is broken and weak. "I remember, Zara, but—"

My heart collapses in on itself. "But what?"

"You aren't *you* anymore. The Zara I loved—the human Zara—is gone."

I whirl away because honestly I can't stand to look at him, can't stand to have him look at me, look at my face crumpling or my eyes getting mad—so mad. My hands shake as I cover my face and give in, just for a second, I give in to the sorrow; let it take me down into some place that's dark and desperate. I'm so familiar with that place from when Nick died, when my dad died, when Mrs. Nix died, when I lost my humanity. I know it so well and I know that if you stay there too long, it is so very hard to get free. The sorrow never wants to let you go.

I can't let that happen again. I don't have time to let that happen again, so I battle my way out before I get stuck there forever.

"I am still *me*, Nick." I groan. "Even Devyn admits that now. I am a different species, but I'm the same person—my soul—the Zara part of me is the same. Only my body is different."

17

I pull at my skin, which is kind of dramatic. "That's all that's changed."

He takes a step toward me and then stops himself. "No. No, that's not quite true."

I force myself to stand still, to not go to him. "What do you mean?"

"It's more than that, Zara." He looks at the sky like he's searching for help from the stars. "You smell different. Not as bad as the other pixies, for some reason, but not like you."

I actually laugh—a short sputter of a laugh, bitter and hard. "So you don't love me anymore because I *smell* different? That's not shallow or anything, right? What? Like if I buy some new nice-smelling body lotion from Sephora, we'll be all good again?"

"Zara, don't be ridiculous." He coughs, almost a bark. "It isn't shallow. We read about this, remember? Pixies don't have souls."

"I have a soul." I cross my arms over my chest. My foot taps on the ground the same way my mother's does when she's beyond mad.

The wind gusts, smashes against us. A wind like this used to just about knock me over, but now that I'm a pixie I can withstand it. I brace myself until the worst of it passes, just staring up at Nick. I say it again because it's important. "I have a soul, Nick."

This is ridiculous, ridiculous and awful. I am standing in the cold, telling my supposed boyfriend that I have a soul when *he's* the one who came back from the dead. The irony of the situation isn't lost on me.

Tears spring into his eyes, eyes that refuse to look down and meet my own. Instead he stares ahead into the snow.

"I have to go," he says.

"You're just giving up on us?" My voice squeaks. I hate it for squeaking, for the weakness there, and then I can't hold in my emotions any longer. "I changed for *you*. I changed because I had to save you. I changed because I loved you—and you don't even think I have a soul." My voice breaks. "You don't even love me anymore."

"Zara . . ." His face softens a tiny bit. "I never said I didn't love you anymore."

Something frees up inside my chest. "You didn't?"

"No." He shakes his head. "It's just— Agh!"

Instead of finishing his sentence, he sticks his hands in his hair and actually pulls at it for a second. It stands up in crazy bunches. If things were normal I would reach over and smooth it back down.

He does what Issie calls the Captain Kirk move. He grabs me by the shoulders—not too hard, but like he's trying to make sure I'm paying attention—which is what Kirk did on all those old *Star Trek* episodes from the 1960s or something. I don't care whose patented move it is. I just like the fact that his hands are touching my arms, that his face has lowered toward mine, that he's making eye contact, finally. Talking to me, finally.

"Zara." His voice is deep, impassioned, and slower than normal. "You need to understand that you are not the same. It's not just your smell. You kill things. You *kill*. You are . . . entwined . . . with that king now."

"Astley?" I think of how there are two branches that repre-sent our souls and how they really are entwined. Could Nick somehow know that? Just instinctively maybe?

He nods. "Devyn told me how he pretty much magically

appeared when you were shot in that bar. He knew you were in danger. You and I? We never had that link. Not like that."

"It's just because he's my king," I start to explain.

"Exactly!"

I step away, pivot, stop, force myself to turn back at him, to really look at him. He's so tall and strong looking. His tan boots plant his feet firmly on the ground, but he's not confident about us anymore. My best friend, Issie, may be goofy but she is good when it comes to human psychology, and she was right—he is jealous.

"Astley being my king is not the same thing, Nick. It's just—" I realize then that I don't know what it is. I don't even know if I'm telling the truth. I can't imagine a world without Astley in it. He calms me down. He lets me be me without criticizing. "We are connected, yes. But everyone who is his subject is connected."

"Do you realize what you just said? You just called yourself his *subject*. The Zara you once were would never be anyone's subject. She would die before she'd be someone's subject."

I swallow. It's true.

Nick's hand touches my chin. "He has some sort of power over you, some sort of hold, doesn't he?"

I break eye contact and whisper, "He's my king. I couldn't have saved you without him. He . . . he helped me."

"That doesn't make it right." Nick bites his lip as I look at him again. "I hate that you did this for me, Zara, that you are one of them now."

I shake my head. "Didn't you see any pixies in Valhalla? Weren't any of them good?"

"You know I don't remember anything. Why do you even ask me?"

"It would be easier if you remembered," I sputter. If he remembered he would know we went through this already, that we kissed, that . . . And where would that leave Astley? I don't even know. I mutter, "So much easier."

"Obviously."

"Okay. Think of it this way. Some of the pixies had to be good if they were in Valhalla." I push on, voice rising with each word. "I am one of those. Astley is one of those."

Nick cringes when I say Astley's name, which is beyond annoying but understandable. "How do you know he is, Zara? How do you actually know he hasn't been manipulating you this entire time for his own reasons? How do you know?"

"I know because it has to be true," I whisper.

"Because?" Nick urges.

"Because if it isn't I don't know how I'll survive. I can't survive if I don't have a soul, Nick. I can't survive if I don't think I'm essentially good. Flawed, obviously, but good."

The sorrow threatens again. It's not just sorrow. It's despair and desperation and a host of other horrible emotions that make my skin shiver. Nick's thumb brushes against my cheek.

"I've changed too, Zara. I've changed," he says, and repeats it like he's only just realizing it himself. I can see the fear in those dark brown eyes of his.

"How?" I ask.

He shakes his head, unlocks his MINI, and throws the bag in. The shovel leaning up against the porch falls over into the snow. "We can't pretend to be a couple anymore. We've just—we've changed too much."

"Nick?" His name is a plea that won't stop. "You're just leaving? You're leaving me alone?"

"I have to get out of the house for a while, just a couple hours, maybe the night." He actually snickers as he folds his long body into the small car. "You aren't alone."

"Yes, I am. Without you, I'm alone."

He pushes the key fob into the ignition hole. "That is the weakest, least Zara White thing I think you've ever said."

And then he shuts the door.

And then he backs around.

And then he drives away from the house, through the trees, and onto the main road.

And then he is gone.

Again.

I growl, an inhuman, angry growl. The snow muffles it. I give up, grab the shovel, and stake it into a snowbank. Just like me, it will have to wait there until someone wants it again.

WEEKLY REPORT: 12/14 TO 12/21
TROOP/UNIT: Troop J

ITEMS OF INTEREST TO LOCAL AGENCIES:

12/15: Trooper David Seacreast responded to a report of suspicious activity off Surry Road. Juvenile complainant reported hearing his name whispered in woods outside his home. When Trooper Seacreast responded he found no tracks but did hear laughter in the woods. Possible radio transmitter in trees as part of a prank? Investigation continues.

I drop into bed, dead tired. The house smells different without anybody else here. It doesn't have that same alive smell, that same good toughness of bad cooking, burned spaghetti, tiger fur. A couple months ago, my mom sent me up here to Maine to live. I grew up in Charleston, South Carolina, where the world is much warmer and full of flowers, but when my dad— technically my stepdad—died I became pretty depressed and my mom sent me to live with his mom, Grandma Betty, who is a paramedic/EMT. Really my mom sent me here because she was worried that my biological pixie king father might track me down and try to kidnap me or something. She had seen him in Charleston. She thought I'd be safer with Betty because Betty is a weretiger. Weird, I know, but in the last couple months I've gotten pretty used to weird.

Using my foot, I push my Amnesty International reports off my bed, along with a couple airmail envelopes that my mom bought me at the post office before she left. They plop on the floor in a messy unpile of papers. The selfish part of me wishes that my mom could just appear at my door wearing some flannel plaid pajama bottoms and a Flogging Molly T-shirt so we could talk. She can't, and she goes to bed early, so I call Issie instead.

"Did you have a rough time of it tonight?" she asks.

"No pixies," I say, "except me, of course. But great weirdness ensued."

"What was up with the Loki thing?" she whispers. Her mom doesn't like late-night phone calls.

I ignore the question about Loki and blurt, "Nick left."

"What?"

"He left, Issie. He told me I had no soul and he left." The words come out with a sob. I lose my phone a little bit. It slides down my shoulder.

"He did not!" She yells it and a second later she goes, "Crap. My mom heard. I'll call you back as soon as I can."

There's a rustle of noise as she hangs up the phone. I stare at my cell screen: CALL ENDED. The screen goes dark, but I keep staring at it, willing it to ring. Three long minutes later she calls back.

Her voice is an exasperated hush as she says, "I'm back. I have to be super-quiet."

I settle into the bed, stare at the ceiling, and quickly tell her about what happened, about how Nick said I wasn't quote-unquote me anymore.

There's an awkward pause before Issie says, "It's just hard to get used to."

"I'm still me. I'm not suddenly evil."

"But you *are* different."

I sit up and stare at my feet. "How? How am I different?"

"You're tougher, more assertive," she says.

"Those are bad things?"

"No . . ." She fumbles for words.

"How do you know that I'm not different because I've been through some serious crises? Because of Mrs. Nix dying or watching Nick die or even Gram taking off and going all MIA? How do you know it's not just because of struggling to save people?"

"I don't. I just know that you've changed and it's for the better. It doesn't matter what the reason is. I am almost jealous—not of the blue, sharp-toothed way you look when your glamour is gone—I think it would be nice to be better than I am, you know? Devyn says I'm having an identity crisis because I'm human. But wait! This is not about me. I'm so sorry. Oh, I totally suck as a friend. This is about you. Let me tell you: you, Zara White, are made of the sauce of awesomeness." She was whispering but then her voice shifts into a louder, exasperated, Issie-lying voice. "No! You took my phone, Mom. Maybe I was sleep-talking."

Click.

End of conversation. Poor Issie. Her mom totally controls her.

I nod my head back at the cell phone, trying to let it all register. "Okay."

After I've shut off the light, for a second I pretend that it *is* all okay, that Nick's words didn't hurt me, that Grandma Betty will come back, that we'll kick all the evil pixies' butts, that the whole apocalypse-coming thing was a big lie, and that my insides won't feel like oatmeal left on the counter all day.

Columbia County Rural
Library District
P.O. Box 74
Dayton, WA 99328

It doesn't work, and instead of being brave and stoic, my face starts to pucker up like all the sadness is sucking it in. I wonder if I even still have my glamour on, if I still look human, and then I realize I don't care. It's just me here in the dark, sobbing, and there's nobody else to see me, nobody else to tell me I'm ugly or monstrous or soulless or anything. I am alone, terribly alone. That's when I realize how much I don't want to be alone, how sobbing should not be a solitary sport, how I wish my mom or Grandma Betty were here to hold me and rock me in her arms and lie to me that everything is going to be okay. That's what people who love you do: they hold you and lie. They tell you that you're worthy, that everything will be all right, and they do that even when you both know without a doubt that this is not true, that it is nowhere near truth.

Something knocks on the window. Wiping at my eyes, I stumble over to see, pulling aside the shade to reveal Astley, his face a hollow slate of concern.

"Let me in," he says, hovering there in the snowy sky. Flakes drip down his face, melting as they touch the warmth of his skin.

I open the blind and the window, struggling to even stay upright. It's like sobbing has taken away all my energy, all my will, so much so that it's hard just to stand. He hops through the window immediately, closing the blind and window behind him, blocking out the cold. He grabs me by the arms, stares into my eyes.

"What's happened?"

It takes me a minute. I can't say it aloud again. I just can't. I should tell him about the giants anyway, not about Nick.

"Nick left?" he asks before I can speak.

Columbia County Rural
Library District
P.O. Box 74
Dayton, WA 99328

I manage to nod and then I pull away from his arms and flop back on my bed.

"Oh, Zara . . ." Astley takes off his snowy coat, drapes it on my chair, and comes and sits next to where I've gone fetal again. He rubs at my shoulder a bit awkwardly and says, "He is a fool."

"He thinks I'm a monster." My voice sounds tiny. I clear my throat.

"Because you are a pixie?" He sounds so tired and angry. All his words are tight little pieces of sound.

I sniff in and start full-body sobbing again. He bundles me into his arms just like I'd been hoping someone would.

He mumbles into my hair. "Bigotry is the only monster here."

"He's scared," I say, trying to defend him. "He's been through a lot."

"So have we all," Astley says. "But that does not make us all into bigots. It did not make you into that."

"Because you showed me I was wrong," I say, hiccupping, too tired to think, to do anything except clutch at Astley's sweater, to hang on to the one warm thing left.

He pulls me in closer, stretching his legs out to either side of me. He smells of cold night air and some sort of nice deodorant. "You did not need me to show you. You already knew."

And then he rocks me against him, a slow, sweet movement that's as comforting as when I was little and my stepdad did it because I'd fallen and hurt myself or because someone had told me my hair was ugly or that I was too pale or some other little-girl-mean nonsense. And it feels good, just like then. It feels comfortable and safe and so I just let go, clutching on to him, hanging on to him, to him, Astley, the pixie king, and cry and sob and sniff until my lungs want to explode from the sorrow of it, and my eyes can no longer see because the tears are so thick and heavy, clouding out the world, my room, everything.

I ache.

"It will be all right," he lies, breathing the words against the hair at the top of my head. "We will be safe and you will be loved."

I want so badly to believe him that I almost actually do, but instead I say, "You will be loved too, and you'll be okay."

He laughs. "Are you trying to comfort me? I am not the one who needs comforting at the moment."

This is true, but I worry about him. I worry about what will happen to his pixies if he loses his good, or gets hurt. Pixies are tied to their king's well-being. If the king is weak, then the pixies go wild, sucking energy out of boys that they torture, caring only about their own needs. Knowing that his health and well-being is so important has to be a lot of pressure for a guy like Astley, especially in a time like now. I want to take all that away from him, let him have a life where he can relax and smile all the time. He has the best smile.

"Tell me a fairy tale," I whisper. "Tell me about something good, something I can look forward to when this is all over."

The muscles in his chest tighten up. "Have I ever told you about our home on the Isle of Skye?"

I shake my head no.

"When this is all over, I shall bring you there. It was once a castle, passed along via my father's line, and the castle is still on the property, but the place you would like is much warmer. It is more of a manor home. There is a garden of azaleas there that stretch around grassy paths and stonewalls. You can smell the sea. Seals come bark on the shore."

"It sounds nice," I murmur. "No snow?"

"No snow." He laughs. "It is lovely. There are no battles, no war."

"Is the food good?" I ask, stomach grumbling.

"Very. No spaghetti."

"And are we happy?"

"Completely."

"And we have souls?"

"Absolutely. We have perfect, unblemished souls."

"I like this."

His voice is so mellow and beautiful. "I thought you would."

Astley leaves sometime before my alarm goes off. I can still smell him, so I know he hasn't been gone long, and I can also smell Nick's absence. It is like a slap of cold water against my heart.

There are texts on my cell phone.

Issie: Zara? I am so sorry. U OK?

Devyn: Loki? Why Loki?

Cassidy: U must text me! Something is wrong. ♥ U R 1 big mass of sorrow.

Issie: Don't b mad.

Astley: We need to talk as soon as you are able.

I text them back as quickly as possible and it's not until I'm in the shower that I feel it: a darkness. Again, no smell. Again, no actual person, just this feeling of being watched by something icky. I rinse the conditioner out of my hair and reach for a towel because I don't want to have to step out of the shower naked. That is how freaked I am. Just to the left of the shower is a polished boat oar that's been bolted into the wall as a towel rack. Grandma Betty does not have the best taste in home décor.

My hands clutch the soft cotton. Wrapping it around me, I relive every horror-movie shower scene I've ever witnessed—the psycho with the knife, the blood running down the drain . . . Shuddering, I step into the well-lit bathroom where no psycho killers lurk. Still, I feel something.

"Pshaw," I say, using one of Grandma Betty's words to make me feel tougher, because honestly, as if my life wasn't scary enough? What? Now I'm getting freaked out by things that aren't even there. Lovely.

School isn't exactly a hopping place today. Bedford High School has about six hundred students and only about four hundred have been showing up this past week. Some parents are too frightened by all the missing-teen incidents to let their kids out of the house now, even for school. So the halls are full of a weird buzz that's fueled by fear. I hold my breath as I walk into the front hall, try not to look through the glass windows to the left and into the office where Mrs. Nix would be if I hadn't gotten her killed. Nick is somewhere in this building; I can smell him.

Issie hops up beside me and puts an arm around my waist. "So, how is my favorite warrior woman doing today?" she chirps. "Saved humanity yet?"

"I wish." I adjust my backpack and bump my hip into hers.

She bumps me back. "I thought we should put up a brave

front about the whole Nick thing. Is that okay? Because if it's not okay, I'm totally okay with not being okay, okay? Did that make sense?"

"Sort of," I say.

"When I thought that Devyn liked Cassidy I had to be brave, because if I wasn't brave then I would just sob all the time, which was not very rah-rah feminist of me, you know?"

"Girls are allowed to be sad about boys," I say. "Boys get sad about girls."

"True . . . true." Issie is thoughtful for a moment. "I just don't know how it fits in with girl power to sob uncontrollably over a guy. It's a dilemma."

People nod when we walk by. Some talk.

"*I am so scared.*"

"*I think my mom is figuring something out.*"

"*I heard my name last night. Someone was whispering it when I went into the driveway.*"

"*I like meatballs. There is nothing wrong with a good meatball.*"

"Crap, this sucks," Issie says as we catch up to Cassidy, whose braids are adorned with black and white beads today. She smiles and waits for us.

"What sucks?" she asks.

"Boys," I say.

"And all the typical doom-and-gloom, end-of-the-world stuff," Issie adds.

"Know it," Cassidy says. She starts trying to smooth down my hair as we head toward class. "Hey, Zara, I was wondering about what the giant said . . ."

We talk about it, ponder, go to class, try to focus. I have

e-mails about SAT test dates, ACT test dates, college recruiting things. We go to lunch. Nick is nowhere. I make it through another school day. Somehow.

Most of our school is a cell-free zone. The school system hired a contractor to wrap some weird mesh conducting material in the school when it was built ten years ago because they were worried about people using their cell phones to cheat. According to Devyn, the material blocks static-electricity fields or something. They call it a Faraday cage, named after this English scientist who invented it way before cell phones and who has been dead for over a hundred years. According to Issie, there was also a really cool Daniel Faraday character on the television show *Lost*. I don't know. Anyway, everywhere in our school the signal is pretty much jammed except for the library.

So when Issie and I step outside, my cell phone starts beeping that I've missed ten text messages.

"Wow. Popular," Issie teases as we head down the sidewalk toward the parking lot. A man is working in a bucket that a truck has lifted up to the electric wires. He wears a white hard hat, gloves, and a coat; working with all that voltage, all that danger. He looks fragile despite his rugged body.

I check the phone. "They're all from Astley."

Issie doesn't say anything. I'm not sure how she feels about Astley, really. She used to be terrified of him, but I don't think she is anymore. She widens her eyes and says, "And they say?"

"That he wants to meet me."

"And?" she prompts.

"And he's worried about me."

"And?"

"And that's pretty much it," I say, shutting the phone and trying not to think about how weak I was last night and how impossibly kind he was during all of it, the way he just held me, rocking me back and forth, letting me cry, telling me about his house on some Scottish island. He was the best kind of friend last night.

I check out the man in the bucket. He works at a bolt, wrenching it. The sound of metal on metal grates against my teeth.

"Does he know about Nick?" Issie asks, pulling my attention back to earth.

"Yes." I grab the door handle of Grandma Betty's truck. It stings a bit. I need another anti-iron pill. "He . . . um . . ."

"So you told him?"

As I'm thinking about how I didn't actually, technically tell him, his voice comes from my left and he walks around the back of the truck. I didn't even smell him I'm so distracted.

"Tell me what?"

"Astley," I say, watching his face move from something bland into concerned lines. He reaches past Issie, nodding at her, and moves his hand up to touch my arm as I say, "Hi."

The touch is at once comfortable and uncomfortable. It's just a tiny brush of fingers to arm through layers of fabric, but it feels excessive somehow and charged, probably because of the whole pixie thing and possibly because I feel awkward about how much I cried last night.

"Hi," he says back, and he must realize that he's blocking my view of Issie or something, because he moves aside a bit, mumbles an apology to her, and then says, "I have been trying to get you all day. I was wondering what happened last night that made you so sad and so scared. Would you like to tell me?"

"Oh boy . . . ," Issie mutters. She straightens her hat over her ears as I explain to Astley what Nick and I saw last night in the woods. As I do, his expression goes from concern to agitation.

"Zara, why did you fail to tell me this before?"

"I was tired . . ." I search for reasons that don't involve explaining the truth: that I was moping about Nick and simultaneously distracted by Astley's niceness. "I'm not sure."

Conflict-averse Issie interrupts the silence. "Zara sometimes has issues remembering the big picture when human elements are involved—like emotions and stuff. It's part of what makes her lovable."

We both stare at Issie. My mouth must drop open, because she gently touches the bottom of her chin as a signal to shut it again. I resist the urge to hug her crazy self.

Apparently so does Astley, who lets out an exasperated sentence. "How angry would you have been if I saw this and did not tell you?"

"Pretty ballistic," I admit. I rub my hands across my eyes. "I'm so sorry."

"I do not need you to apologize—"

"I know." I interrupt him and pull my gaze away, staring again at the man working on the wires. He plays with currents of electricity, things that will never end, things that make our world work. We even have electricity inside of us. It's everywhere.

Astley's voice is calm but strong, a current all in itself. "I just need you to trust me. We are a team, Zara. You have all our people behind you and—"

"And us," Issie adds. Her arms cross in front of her parka and she rocks forward on her toes. But does "us" include Nick anymore? I don't know.

"This is a rather large development. It calls for an emergency meeting," Astley says, pulling his phone out of his pocket. "I'll contact Amelie and Becca. Call Devyn and Cassidy. Please have Devyn research as quickly as possible."

Issie and I give each other a look.

"He's already been researching," she says. "And Nick? Should we tell him?"

"Is he stable?" He looks up from his phone.

The word makes no sense, so I repeat it. "Stable?"

"As in mentally sound?" Astley clarifies.

"I think so. He's back from the dead. He's not in need of medication or anything." Pain wells up inside my stomach, but something else does too. It's a little knot of willpower or strength or something.

Astley nods. I let Issie text Nick because he obviously doesn't want me to have anything to do with him anymore. We all agree to meet up at the Maine Grind, this little coffee shop on Main Street that's all orange and purple funkiness. As soon as Astley leaves, Issie climbs into the truck and puts her hand on my arm.

"It'll be okay, Issie. Whatever those giant things mean, it'll be okay," I say as I turn on the ignition.

"That's not it. I mean, yeah, I'm freaked, but I wanted to tell you something." She pulls her hat down a little lower over her ears, but her door is still wide open.

"About Nick?"

She shakes her head. "About Astley."

I wait for it. People straggle to their cars. The parking lot is so empty.

"He's in love with you." She watches my face and says all mock angry, "Do not roll your eyes at me, young lady. He is. And it isn't some weird I-am-a-pixie-king-and-you're-my-queen love. It's like Willow and Tara kind of love, like Spock and Kirk, like Jack and Kate on *Lost*, like Princess Leia and Han Solo or Olivia and Peter on *Fringe*."

I have no clue about half of the characters she is referencing, so I close my eyes and lean my head on the steering wheel. "It doesn't matter."

"Because of Nick?"

I shrug. "Not even that. Because everything is insane. Because there are giants in the woods, monsters in closets, the end of the world waiting to happen. Boys do not matter now. Surviving matters."

She shuts the door, keeping out the cold air. "Zara White, since when has love ever not mattered?"

BEDFORD FIRE DEPARTMENT

Personnel responded to a reported fire in the woods near Bedford High School. Evidence of a fire was apparent, but the state fire warden will have to investigate due to no obvious incendiary devices in area. If you have information, please contact the office.

Like • Comment • Share

I have to drop off Issie at her house so her mom can verify she's in one piece and force her to do her homework for an hour. Then we all meet at the Maine Grind on Main Street. Main Street in Bedford is two blocks of mostly two-storied brick buildings, half of which are closed down with giant FOR LEASE signs on them. Insurance companies dominate one end. The other end has retail shops, nonfactory stores, a health food store, the Grand Theater, a diner, and the Maine Grind. The coffee shop used to be the Masonic temple and the new owner has tried to liven up the steady squareness of it by painting the pillars by the door purple and orange and funkifying the bricks with gold-foil stuff.

Cassidy and I drive over together and the whole way she keeps her hand on my forearm. I know this is her way of "reading" me, which is basically her psychic energy trying to see things through my energy. This sounds hokey, but it's actually pretty cool. Cassidy's whisper-small voice makes me turn the music way down because I don't want to miss anything she says. Right now it seems like she wants to say something important but can't gather up enough courage to do so. The cue to knowing this is how she keeps opening and closing her mouth.

It's not till I've made my fifth attempt at parallel parking Betty's truck that Cass inhales so loudly it makes me look at her. Tears are peeking out the corners of her eyes.

"What is it?" I ask, putting the truck in park and double-checking that there's enough space behind the hybrid in front of me. "Cassidy?"

She doesn't answer, just slowly moves her hand off my forearm and clasps it in her other hand, almost like it hurts her or something. "I don't want to tell you."

"Cass," I try again as her braids swing down, obscuring her face. I move them to the side and kind of hold them there so I can see her eyes. "What is it?"

Every motion she makes is tired, slow, like an elderly arthritic woman's or someone who has the flu. Her eyes meet my gaze and I swallow hard because her eyes are so terribly, terribly sad.

"Death."

"Mine?"

She nods.

I want to drop her braids. I want to scream in frustration or run or hide or something, but I just sit there and wait despite the fact that it feels like my stomach has transformed itself into a giant glob of mud.

Instead of doing any of that drama-queen stuff, I say, "Do you have any details?"

"They are horrible."

Snow trucks down out of the sky. Sometimes I forget to notice it—all the coldness, the way it's like a shroud. I notice it now.

"Tell me anyway, Cass," I say as the car engine makes a funny clicking noise, which is weird since I turned it off already. I don't understand cars. "I can take it, Cass. If you saw it, you saw it for a reason, so just tell me, okay? It'll be okay."

My reassurance sort of works, I think, because she nods fiercely like she's summoning up her will for real this time.

"There's blood. You're in Astley's arms and he's burning too, but just wounded, and you aren't you anymore. Curtains fall down." She closes her eyes. "I'm sorry. I shouldn't have told you."

"No," I offer. "No. You should. We need to know anything we can about what's happening. Any hints are good, even if it's a bad hint, you know?"

She nods quickly and I let go of her braids, unlock the doors to the truck. The mechanism makes a popping noise. I search for another one of Astley's iron-resistance pills and pop it in my mouth. Iron is poisonous to pixies. Just being near it—like in a car—gives us headaches. Luckily, Astley's people have developed a pill that lets us tolerate it. Still, my head hurts a bit and it's hard to focus for a second while the pill kicks in. Maybe it's the fact that people are predicting my death. It's only four o'clock, but the light is fading as a mom hurries down the street, clutching her toddler's hand. As we get out of the truck, the mom looks from one side to another like she's expecting to be killed right there. A white police car trolls down the road, snow flipping out from beneath its moving tires. It's Detective Small. She waves. We wave back. I can feel the pill reach my stomach and settle there, and I turn back to Cassidy as I press the fob to lock the truck.

"Is it soon?" I ask her as I step over some snow slush on the sidewalk. "Do I die soon?"

"Yeah," she says. "I think it's soon."

"Do you know where?"

She shakes her head. "It's dark. There's a curtain that hangs to the floor. Other than that, nothing."

"Well," I say trying to be lighthearted for her sake. "I'll avoid all places with curtains."

"Zara, this is serious."

I clear my throat. I know it's serious. "We aren't telling anyone else about this."

"But—"

I interrupt her. "Seriously, Cass, they'll freak. It will get us all unfocused. You know how we go off on tangents. The other day Issie talked for twenty minutes about what we should call ourselves. She wanted a group name, remember? And then there was that time that Devyn started explaining chaos theory."

She stops on the first step to the coffee shop. Her hands go to her waist and she glares at me, her voice hard to match her no-nonsense eyes. "You dying isn't a tangent."

"Well," I say, stepping around her to pull open the door, trying to ignore the horrible feeling of doom that seems to be crushing my kidneys into my spine, "yeah. Am I the only one?"

"What?"

"The only one who dies?"

"No." She sighs. "I don't think so."

Nick, Devyn, and Issie are already waiting inside the Grind, sitting on two leather couches, sipping drinks. Nick gives a little wave like he never told me I was soulless. I give a little wave back because it's more mature than giving him the finger. I'm a pixie queen now.

Is holds up two Super Juices, which she's already bought because she knows that Cassidy and I don't do coffee. It makes both of us wacky-hyper. While we wait for Astley and our pixies, we settle in and start talking about the giants, what Cass just saw, what steps we need to take to stop the apocalypse and deal with the crazy pixies who are tormenting our town.

It isn't nice coffee-house chatter. Throughout our entire conversation Jay Dahlberg keeps making eyes at us. He's sitting with Callie and Paul, Cierra, and some other people from school like Austin and Danielle, who I don't know that well. Callie's got her Mohawk bejeweled with some crystals and Paul's rocking a new surfer-boy haircut. Cierra's touched up her roots. For a second I'm almost jealous that they have time to deal with their hair, but that's just wrong of me. I'm happy for them.

"Something is going on over there," I whisper to Issie.

Nick looks up. His gaze meets Jay's and Jay stands.

Jay's blond hair flops over his eyes, shading them a little bit. He grew his hair out after he was kidnapped by evil pixies. It's hide-me hair, not teen-idol, pop-star hair, although it's the same kind of trendy cut. He walks over and leans on the coffee table, making direct eye contact with me now instead of Nick. "I remember things."

The air goes still. The only noise is some background hum of coffee and espresso machines, the mechanical droning of refrigerated display cases and the music. It feels like my entire body is shaking, but it isn't. My stomach lurches and I get this image of Astley grimacing. He's so late. I hope he's okay. It doesn't feel like he's okay, and I start thinking about Loki and frosty giants, Cassidy's prediction. That kidney-crushing feeling inside me gets worse.

Jay's voice snaps me out of my worries. It is low and urgent as he says it again. "I remember that you were there, Zara. You saved me from those—those things. You got me out of the house."

Issie's hand goes to my arm, and I think she's trying to be reassuring because we both know that now I *am* one of those things.

Earlier this year, Jay was kidnapped by my biological father. He was tortured and bound to a bed where pixies fed on his energy—his soul, basically. We rescued him from this hellish pixie house in the woods, Devyn and Issie, Betty, Nick, and me. He didn't remember any of it.

"It's not just that Jay is remembering what's happened to him." Callie clears her throat. She meets my gaze. I resist the urge to look away. "We saw you take that guy out the other night after the dance. That wasn't playacting and it wasn't because he hit on you. Those were mad fighting skills, Zara. Mad. Fighting. Skills."

Austin does this weird male-posturing thing where he lifts up one leg and puts it on the coffee table and then he goes,

"And that's just weird, Zara. You're all Miss Pacifism, Amnesty International, write letters for political prisoners, end all war, and there you are just whaling on somebody?"

None of us say anything. Cierra and Danielle hang back watching. Winking, Paul reaches over and takes a sip of Cassidy's drink. "You mind?"

She shakes her head.

"Thanks." Paul puts it back. He's like that—always in everybody else's stuff. Nobody thinks anything of it anymore. He crosses his arms over his chest. "If we're in danger, we should know. If you know something, you should tell us. It's your responsibility to tell us."

And it is. It is our responsibility. Would I want to be in the dark while pixies were running around? Is it fair to not tell them? Honestly, though, I'm not sure of the implications of telling. I'm not sure if it will make them safer or make them panic, and we don't even know for sure everything that's going on.

I look up at Dahlberg. He's so sweet looking still, but his eyes are wounded and half dead. When he couldn't remember what had happened to him I thought that was good, keeping him safe and sane, but maybe the not knowing is haunting him anyway, killing him slowly with partial images and questions. I touch the tip of my juice bottle with my finger for reassurance and then lock eyes with him. "Are you really starting to remember?"

He closes his eyes after a second and swallows so hard that his Adam's apple visibly moves up and down his throat. "I remember teeth, being trapped on a bed. I remember you bringing me down these ornate marble stairs through all these monsters. There was a wolf and a tiger out in the cold. I know it sounds crazy but I also know that you saved me from something, Zara. I am positive you did."

Devyn leans forward on the couch. I nod at him. Nick clears his throat and I can tell just by looking at him that he's okay with this. The decision is made. I wish Astley wasn't late so he could know too.

"Maybe they can help," I say to Nick, even as a knife seems to stab into my stomach. What is that? It's all I can do not to crumple over. I soldier through it and say, "We can't do it all by ourselves. Not even with Astley's people. It's just too big."

"I know." He motions for Paul and Cierra, Callie and Danielle, Dahlberg and Austin to pull up some chairs.

My stomach sort of flops around inside me. If we tell them, then their innocence is gone—just gone. Their entire perception of the world will be shattered. If we tell them, they could potentially tell other people, who could tell other people, and more and more regular human beings will know that the world isn't anything like they thought—that there are secrets lurking right next to them, predators that look human but have needs, horrible needs.

"Oh my gosh . . ." Issie looks at me. "Is this kosher?"

I nod. Cassie swallows hard. She grabs Issie's hand. "It's the right thing to do. It's better for them to know what they face."

"But it could go viral." Issie makes big eyes. "The whole world could know."

"That's the risk," I say. "It's a big risk."

They quickly pull the chairs up to the table and once they are settled it is Devyn's turn to clear his throat.

"Okay," he begins, "we don't know everything and it's

going to sound unbelievable but this is what's happening. There are these things called pixies . . ."

They listen. They gasp. But I know as I watch them that they believe.

There's a time when you're super-little when you don't really know yet that bad things exist. It's before that first bully pushes you down on the nursery-school floor and says something like "I'm a lion and I'm going to eat you up." It's before that first-grade teacher puts you in timeout for talking, even though you weren't talking and it was actually Stephen Sills. It's before you see your best friend's dad punch her mom. That's when you realize people aren't always good.

It is not a good realization. It is gaunt and tangled, a sucker punch to the stomach, the last breaths on Heartbreak Hill while running the Boston Marathon kind of realization, and it hurts and resonates all of your life and here we are—Nick, Devyn, Cassidy, Issie, and me—giving Jay and Paul and Austin, Cierra, Danielle, and Callie that same horrible sucker punch, watching them realize that the entire world is not what it seems, that there are secrets, dangerous secrets, out there lurking.

Sweat beads on Paul's forehead, Austin's face turns beet red, and poor Cierra is slowly rocking back and forth in her chair while Danielle pats her back. Callie looks like she wants to kill people. And Jay? His entire face is closed and hard.

Finally Devyn finishes our story, and we wait for their verbal reactions. Across the shop, some lawyer-type person orders a triple-shot espresso to go over at the counter.

"Well," Callie says as she leans back in her chair and fiddles with an earring but keeps her gaze strong and steady on us. "Wow."

Is blurts, "You're going to accept it, just like that?"

I open my eyes again. Paul lifts up his hands and sort of shrugs like he's already getting used to the idea. I wonder for a second what he'd think if Cassidy just told him he would die soon. Would he shrug then too?

Danielle speaks first. "All my life I've felt like there was something else going on. Something lurking. Something—oh, I don't know—something that was here that I just didn't know about. Now, I know."

"That's how I used to feel," Cassidy agrees. "I even told you that one time at the bowling alley. Remember, Zare?"

I nod and give her a smile. It seems like forever ago, and it was probably less than a month.

"It makes sense," Callie adds. "Seriously, this town is a freak zone of weird."

"Jay?" I ask him.

He's paler than normal. He looks up and meets my eyes. "I can't believe you didn't tell me before."

Jay repeats what he said while his feet twitch on the floor. The left foot. The right. It's like they want to run away from the truths of his kidnapping, our deception.

"We thought you'd been through enough," Issie starts, trying to explain as another pain stabs into my stomach. Where is Astley?

Jay's hands are shaking he's so upset, and I would be upset too. I rub my hand across my eyes. Every cell inside of me is tired and sad. And that's when I realize that this is really it. We are making an army. I have to be willing to lead them, willing to let them risk their lives fighting this. If we ever want life to return back to normal we have to fight for it, all of us.

"I deserve to know what happened to me." He shakes his head hard, brushing the hair out of his eyes.

"You do," I agree. "I'm sorry."

He nods sharply. "I want to know everything. All of it. We have to make plans. We can't let what happened to me happen to other people."

"No, we can't," I say, determination hitting me full scale. There is no turning back now. "Let me tell you about this thing Devyn and I have been writing. We call it the *How to Survive a Pixie Attack* manual. It's everything we know so far about fighting pixies. We'll make you all copies and then we'll start training—"

"Training?" Issie's eyebrow lifts up.

Callie says it for me. "There's no option, is there? You'll have to train us to fight."

"Not just us. Giselle too," Paul says. "She'd want in on this, and Andrew and Brad and Tyler and Blake . . ."

His list goes on for a while and Devyn starts typing the names into a file. I lean back and close my eyes. Fate feels like it comes spiraling in on me. I want to know where Astley is.

"Do we start today?" Callie interrupts Paul's never-ending list of names.

"Tomorrow," Nick says. "We'll start tomorrow afternoon, meet at the Y. They have free gym time at one. Nobody's ever in there."

And so our army begins.

We're gathering our things together when Becca explodes into the Grind and runs to me, looking like a frightened cheerleader, not the killing machine she is.

She grabs me by the arms. "It's Astley."

"What's happened?" I knew it. I knew something was wrong.

"They've poisoned him." Her face breaks into tears. "He's bad, really bad."

Running toward the doors, I yank her along with me, demanding, "Where? Where is he?"

"At the birds'."

WEEKLY REPORT: 12/14 TO 12/21
TROOP/UNIT: Troop J

ITEMS OF INTEREST TO LOCAL AGENCIES:

12/16: The Holiday Inn staff reported suspicious activity outside one of their guests' ground-floor bedrooms. A woman was reportedly standing in the snow, laughing for twenty minutes. Failed to locate upon arrival.

Becca gives me the lowdown as we rush to the car. She and Amelie had gone to meet Astley in his hotel room. He didn't answer when they knocked, but they could smell him inside, so they busted down the door and found him, unglamoured and unconscious on the floor.

"How did you know he was poisoned?" I ask, turning on the truck and yanking my seat belt into position.

"There was a note."

"A note?" I pull out of the parking space way too quickly and swerve on the slushy road. I just want to get to Devyn's house, get to Astley, find out what happened. Devyn is flying there. I wish I could turn bird and do that. It would be so much faster.

"Taped to the outside window. It said, *Poison is a fitting way for a weak-hearted king to die.*"

"Weak-hearted?"

She rubs at her eyes and says in a voice choked with venom, "Isla, his mother, always thought he was weak. Too willing to see the good in people, too hesitant to use his power, his authority on his subjects."

"So basically, he's not an evil tyrant." My foot pushes harder on the gas pedal and part of me wishes it was Isla's face.

"Exactly." Her tone is heavy and she presses her palm against the glass pane of the window like she is trying really hard not to break it.

The truck skids over the snow-slick road as I turn onto a side street. I ask, "And she's the one who poisoned him?"

"The note wasn't signed but the word choice makes it look that way."

"Why would she do that?"

"Million-dollar question," Becca says. "Can't you drive faster?"

I do, zooming dangerously over the freezing roads, passing a city plow truck. I think my questions are frustrating her, or maybe it's my ignorance plus the situation. I don't know. All I know is that Astley is hurt, really hurt. Maybe Astley is the key to everything somehow.

"If he dies—" Becca starts.

"He can't die," I blurt.

"If he dies, you will be our queen."

The thought of it makes me cringe. "A queen doesn't usually rule alone."

"Some do. You would."

There's a pause in her voice. "But?"

"But," she says, "I think this is part of the plan. Other than a few weres, we are the only ones protecting this town from Frank. If Astley is gone we weaken, especially if you are not strong enough to rule alone. If you are gone, then Astley weakens. It works either way. So, then there is an opening—"

"For an evil pixie king named Belial, also known as Frank." I pull into Devyn's driveway. "Not going to happen."

I shut off the truck, fly out, and race up the stairs. Becca rushes right behind me.

She grabs my arm just as I push open the door. "Promise me."

Even though it kills me to hesitate, I take the second required to appease her because that's what a leader does: she takes care of her people. "I promise. We won't let him die."

The house is full of noise and the agitated sound of intellectual scientists in crisis mode. I follow the debating voices to Devyn's bedroom, where they've laid Astley out on the twin bed. He's blue, but a horrifyingly pale blue that's turning white. His face is puffy and he's gasping for air. Devyn's mom stands over him with some sort of breathing tube. My heart stops for a moment, just stops, and breaks as I stare at him.

"Astley," I say his name in a whisper.

Nobody hears. I bolt forward, the pain in my stomach exploding, my own breath twirling around, gasping to get out. I feel what he is feeling.

"Put the tube in," I shout. "Get a shot of Benadryl. It's like asthma. Like shock. Trust me. It will help."

Devyn and his parents stop for a moment and then his dad

nods and races out of the room. His footsteps thunder down the staircase.

Devyn says, "A couple months ago, you panicked when Nick had an arrow in him, and called Betty, now you're giving commands."

"Maybe I have changed," I say, grabbing Astley's hand. It's limp in mine. "Someone talk to me."

Devyn swallows hard and pushes his glasses up his nose. I wonder why he's wearing them today. His voice is a worried monotone as he says, "It's bad."

Bad. The word just barely registers. There is no time to let it register.

"No death. You are not allowed," I order, and my voice is both frantic and strong. I turn to Becca. "Text Cassidy to come now. Tell Amelie to get the food in his room, anything near where you found his body. His toothbrush. Anything that could enter his mouth. Anything that could be poisoned. Bring it here. Maybe we can isolate what it is and get some kind of antidote. You can do that, right?"

Devyn's mom has tiny eyes and they close a little bit as she thinks. They almost disappear. "Possibly, but Zara . . ."

Possibly has to be good enough.

"That will take time," she says. "We don't have time."

We don't have time.

"Becca!" I call for her to come back into the room. "Is there anything I can do? As his queen?"

She swallows hard, but nods. "You can take half."

"Half what?" Devyn barks.

"His poison. The injury."

"How?"

"You can't, Zara!" Devyn throws up his hands, most likely in frustration. "Just once could you think something through? Just once, Zara. Do not be the martyr. We need you."

I silence him with a look and he clucks, angry, and turns back to Astley, feeling the pulse in his neck.

"You are entwined. There is a link between you that is stronger than the link between him and the rest of us," Becca quickly explains. She gets more animated as she talks, excited by the possibility. "If he were not the king, drawing on the health and power of the rest of us, he would already be dead. I have heard that a queen can help."

"How?"

Her emotions ooze out of her. It's all worry mixed with hope. "It's not good."

"Just tell me, Becca."

"It's like . . . Where's Amelie?"

Devyn's mom finishes taking blood from Astley's arm and hands it to Devyn. She says, "We don't have time to lollygag around. Tell her what it takes."

Becca goes flat. "He has to drain you."

I flash to what I saw my father's pixies doing to Jay Dahlberg. They bit him, kissed him, drained him of his energy somehow. I'm not sure how. I just know it almost killed him.

"Do you have to bite me or kiss me?" I ask.

"No, just lay hands on you," Becca says, "and on the king. The power should transfer. I've never done it, though. And it hurts. You should know that it hurts, Zara."

"It doesn't matter. Just do it." I squeeze onto the bed, close my eyes. "Just do it before I think about it."

I grab Astley's hand in mine. His whole body is burning up,

and his skin looks puffy and unnatural. I can feel the life ebbing out of him. Devyn's parents will never isolate the poison and find an antidote in time. There's no choice, really. Not for Astley. Not for me. He's given me so much. It's the least I can do.

"I don't know if he'd want you to do this," Becca says. She hovers over us and Devyn starts muttering objections too, and I get ready to shush them but his mom does it for me.

"Zara's choice, and we don't have much time," she says abruptly. "Devyn, take this to your father downstairs. See what's taking so long with the shot. You. Blond pixie. Get started."

Becca's face hovers over mine. Her hair flops onto my cheek. "I'm so sorry, Zara. Try to focus on Astley. Look at him, maybe, or something."

Turning my head, I do. He is so beautiful even when he's blue and his teeth are pointy. It's like all the good of him shines out even when he looks like a monster, bless his heart. I can't lose him. The world needs him so much.

"You will be okay," I tell him. "We'll make you okay and we'll go to that manor-house place and run through the gardens and bark back at the seals. I promise. You will not die like this."

I grab his hand more tightly and Becca whispers, "Try not to scream."

I wake up in Devyn's room in the bed next to Astley. Looking across him, I can see that the light through the window means it's morning and it's still snowing. Scanning the room quickly, I suppress a moan. It feels like I've had the flu. Every muscle aches. My head throbs. My throat seems to have closed up, parched and broken. I vaguely remember last night, how it felt like I was dying. Nightmare images of demons and teeth, of the life being yanked out of me until I felt like I was just a husk of skin with nothing underneath. I can still hear the echoes of my own screams that zing around in my memory like flies trapped in a glass jar. I try to shake it all away.

Cassidy's sleeping in a chair in the corner of the room. Her hand is clutching something, probably a crystal. Her braids dangle limply. Beyond her, Amelie and Becca pace the hallway. Devyn's snoring on the floor right below me. His laptop is flipped open and upside down on his stomach. Everyone looks like hell, especially Astley.

Propping myself up on an elbow, I tuck the sweat-caked strands of hair behind my ear and get a better look at my king. His chest moves up and down in a normal breathing pattern. I place my non-weight-bearing hand on his skin. It's warm, but not boiling hot anymore. The puffiness has faded away. His chin seems more pointy and his jawline seems sharper than I remember.

"He will be okay," Cassidy whispers from across the room.

I don't turn to look at her. "You're awake?"

"Barely." There's a sound of her stretching, of her vertebrae shifting into shape.

My hand moves from Astley's chest to his face. His skin is shiny from when he was feverish. His hair is mussed and sticking up everywhere. Even in sleep, he seems tense. There's a line in between his eyebrows, like he's thinking about horrible things.

Groaning as she stands up, Cassidy joins me. She is obviously trying really hard not to topple over. She doesn't look much better than Astley, really.

"Are you sure he'll be okay?" I ask. "Will *you* be okay?"

"It was very touch and go," Cass says. "But your energy saved him, and Devyn's mom isolated part of the poison. She treated both of you. You've bounced back more quickly, obviously. They had been developing a poison themselves, so that helped."

"And your magic helped." I state the obvious. Cassidy is part elf. She doesn't know how much or even really how her magic works. It's all trial and error, but it involves chanting and crystals and the elements. It also drains her energy. The bigger the magic, the worse she feels.

"A little bit." Her voice is so tired, and her face is too. Circles make themselves at home beneath her eyes and she looks like she's lost about twenty pounds.

"I worry about you, Cass."

She helps me sit up, stepping over Devyn to do so. "We all worry about each other. That's what friends do."

Later, I'm alone with Astley. I sit on the edge of the bed and then swing my legs up next to him. He looks so small, and he's normally so far from small.

Astley's eyes flutter open but he seems tired, and he can't quite focus. His eyes are silver. His skin is a sickly blue still, but better than yesterday. I touch his face.

"You will be okay," I whisper. "We will be okay."

His lips move but no sound comes out. Instead, he moves his hand and I grab it. Our fingers interlock.

"We will be strong together," I promise.

YAHOO! ANSWERS
Trey D
In the event of a pixie apocalypse?
So allegedly there's like a pixie invasion in my town and we're having this meet-up to learn how to fight them. So, um, yeah . . . any pointers or ARE WE DOOMED?

BEST ANSWER - CHOSEN BY VOTERS
Trap the little things in jars like fireflies. Totally worked for Peter Pan and Wendy. Also, lay off the bath salts.

1 hour ago
60% 2 Votes

I feel much better after a shower, and Astley is up and walking around. I get ready and head over to Issie's house so we can carpool to the training. We're late because Issie is taking for-freaking-ever to find appropriate "pixie war training" clothes. Issie deals with horrible situations by ignoring them. Instead of focusing on Astley's poisoning, she's focusing on clothes. It's a weird survival method, but it seems to work well for her because she's . . . um . . . surviving.

"I need something both war appropriate and cute," she explains as we finally get in the car. "Do you think this works?"

She's wearing yoga pants and a red T-shirt that they were selling at the Gap a while ago when it was cool to care about world hunger and things like that. She zips up her coat and adjusts her rainbow-striped hat. I'm wearing my favorite black running pants and an old rock band T-shirt.

As we drive to the YMCA, Issie babbles on about Devyn, her mom's new insistence that hairspray is an effective weapon against mass murderers, and how any of us will pass any of our advanced placement exams at the end of the year since school is so insane. Once we get there, she parks and I haul the box of *How to Survive a Pixie Attack* manuals out of the back of her car. Now that I'm pixie it's easier to carry things.

As we get out of the car, she squinches up her nose, tucks her hair behind her ear. There's a loose blue thread on her rainbow hat, sort of unraveling. It dangles and hangs out with her hair.

I tuck it into her hat. But as soon as we walk up the cement curb, the little blue thread has fallen out of her hat again, dangling there, homeless, as we walk in and veer to the left. The gym is on one side of the main hallway of the Y, set off by a big admission desk. The front-desk lady says, "Joining the fun?"

On the other side is a hallway to the weight room and the locker rooms. Issie grabs the door handle to the gym and stops.

"Holy—" she starts and then breaks off.

I peek around her to see what it is, ready to drop the box in case there are pixies or something awful and dangerous inside. I stagger back too. "Issie . . ."

"I know!"

"There are so many people here." I'm shaking. I can actually feel myself shaking.

"I know!"

"Is there a basketball game we didn't know about?" I ask.

"Okay. Fact check. The people aren't in the bleachers. There are no bouncing balls. No refs. No cheerleaders. No smell of popcorn. I think they are here for us."

For us. I swallow hard. "Okay. Okay. This is a good thing. Repeat after me: this is a good thing."

"This is a good thing," Issie whispers.

"The whole entire freaking world knowing that there are pixies is a good thing," I say, trying to convince myself. I stare up at the empty basketball hoops. The nets dangle off of little orange rims, waiting for the balls, waiting for the action. I toughen up and say to both Is and myself, "We can handle this."

"We totally can." She looks stunned, though.

I scan the crowd. "Is Nick coming?"

"I think so."

"Okay. We can do this." I stride into the room like I have done this a million times, like I'm not worried about Astley, like I'm a leader. I hold up the box. "Hey! People! Everybody! Let's get started!"

People stop talking except for Austin, who basically never stops talking. Everyone starts heading toward me. They are tall, short, skinny, not so skinny, and regular. They are younger and slightly older, but mostly all in high school, I think. Some have pimples. Some have glasses. Some look a little confused. Some look a little scared. And some, like Jay and Callie, look angry and determined. Jay nods at me. I nod back.

Cassidy grabs the box from me and smiles. It's a serious smile, but still a smile. I smile back. It's so good to see her here, so good that she is on our side. She's wearing a tracksuit that looks pure vintage 1970s, all orange and cotton. With her multiple braids she looks kind of Rastafarian, like she might start singing reggae or something. Maybe she's trying out a new identity. I can understand that.

I take one of the manuals out. "We've got some handbooks, but not enough, so you'll have to share!"

People hustle forward and grab the handbooks out of the box. Some people even say thank you, which is kind of astonishing. Anne Kat looks up at me. She clutches her manual to her chest. She's wearing a white T-shirt and jeans. Her hands shake.

"Is this for real, Zara?" she asks.

"Yeah," I say. "It's for real."

She sucks her lips in, nods just the tiniest bit, and turns around. I have no idea how she'll ever be able to fight. Her glasses always fall off in PE class every time she runs. She skitters into the crowd and disappears between the taller, broader people.

Paul grabs a handbook and says to me and Is, "Got a turnout, huh?"

"Did you tell the entire school?" Issie asks.

He shrugs and then reaches up absently to touch his hair. "Basically."

"Awesome sauce." Issie bounces on her toes and hands out some more handbooks, passing one to Tara Bogue. "People! Get your handbooks here. Step right up and get your handbooks."

She sounds almost like a circus barker or something and it makes me giggle. She giggles too. I turn into her and whisper, "I can't believe we are training people to fight pixies."

"I know!" She leans back a little and gives a handbook to Tonisha Walsh, who starts reading it before she even turns away. "Like, who would have ever believed it?"

She must see the doubt in my eyes, because she adds, "You'll do a good job, Zara. No worries."

"Yeah. We will," I say, and wink at Cassidy, but I'm still sort of wondering where Nick is.

She holds up the box and yells out, "All gone, people. We'll make some more for tomorrow. Share for now."

People stand in clumps and alone. Their body lotions and perfumed soaps and deodorant smell like lilacs and baby powder and musk. Some of them are flipping through the manual. It seems so skimpy, like there isn't nearly enough information in there to keep them safe. I blow the hair out of my face. It flops right back in it. I tuck it behind my ear and decide that this is it. It is time to take charge, time to prepare for war.

I clear my throat. People stare at me. Jay Dahlberg crosses his arms over his chest. He rocks a little backward and then comes up and stands right beside me. I resist the urge to grab his hand. Instead I give him a little sideways hug. He relaxes a tiny bit and I let go. Someone tosses his jacket into the basketball hoop. It hangs there and then drops hard to the floor.

I turn to the crowd and yell, "All right, everybody, let's learn how to kick some pixie butt."

First, Issie and I give a little introduction, explaining who the evil pixies are, what they are capable of doing. Then we go into the fitness drills, running the length of the gym, working on quick turns. I make them do sit-ups and push-ups and suicides. It's all about coordination and strength, and sadly, a lot of people have none of it. The basketball players do well. Yeah. That's about it.

Apparently, in every eighth-grade year the Bedford Middle School has a medieval fair. The boys make foam weapons and sell them to each other. Every guy here has about three swords made of gray foam that they've brought to practice with. We move into combat simulations and I watch them jump and lunge and parry, giving pointers where I can.

"Not something I'll be putting on my college application," I say as Callie totally beats down Paul with her foam saber.

Paul looks at me, momentarily distracted, and says, "You think we'll live till college?"

Callie smashes him in the gut with her elbow. He falls to his knees and covers his head. "I give up! I give up!"

She does a happy dance and Nick strides across the gym. He must have just gotten here.

Nick leans toward me, crossing his arms in front of his chest. He hems and haws but finally says, "Real pixies won't be this easy."

I nod as Callie helps Paul back up into standing position. "I know."

"And foam swords aren't real weapons," he adds.

Someone fake screams.

Someone else shouts, "Die, you pixie scum!"

"I know. We'll get real weapons," I say.

"How?" Nick scratches at his scalp, just above his ear.

"There's a Web site. It takes two days to ship. They have axes and swords and crossbows and stuff."

Nick nods. "Okay. Sorry I just got here. I was out hunting."

"I know." I don't add that he smells like death, which is good because until today he'd been coming back not smelling like anything, smelling like he maybe froze in the woods, like maybe he wasn't hunting at all. I think about how he didn't do anything at first when we saw those giants. Maybe death changed him. Maybe he's lost some of his bravery, but I don't push, don't ask like I would have before. Instead, I let him have his space.

"What about real weapons?" he asks.

It takes me a second. "You mean guns?"

"Yeah."

"Only the kids who hunt are any good," I explain, wishing he'd been with me and Dev when we talked all this out. "So there's no point in training them to work with them. They can't bring them to school, and legally they have to keep them locked up in their trucks when they're traveling."

"I doubt the law matters much anymore," Nick scoffs.

"Well, yeah. But anyway, you can't get handguns unless you're over eighteen and pass a background check, and that takes time. Guns aren't the most effective against pixies anyway, not unless you have iron bullets. Wait. What are bullets made out of?"

He shrugs. "It doesn't matter. It still slows them down at least."

"True," I agree.

We all stand there for a moment, a truce and trade-off, and then I decide enough is enough. Everyone is sparring, but it's all too slow motion. It's all too . . . human. I jump up onto the bleachers and yell, "Hey!"

Nobody notices.

I try again, cupping my hands around my mouth. "Hey!"

Nothing.

Issie rolls her eyes and scrambles up the bleachers next to me, nearly flopping sideways because she misjudges the distance between the steps. I catch her by the arm and she rights herself and murmurs, "Let me, 'kay?"

"Sure," I say. "Good luck."

"YO! PEOPLE! ZARA NEEDS YOUR ATTENTION!" Her voice is huge and powerful and not what I expect from super-quiet Issie.

"Wow, Is," I murmur as everyone turns to stare. "I didn't know you had it in you."

"Projection. Voice lessons in grade school." She beams and promptly sits down. "Plus, I was trying out the Loud Person in Charge identity."

Her sheer cuteness makes me want to hug her, but everyone is looking at me, expectant. I am the leader here right now. Me. Weird. I clear my throat.

"Look," I start. "You all are doing an amazing job, but pixies are faster than humans. Pixies are trickier. They are the predator and you all are the prey. You need to be ready for that."

"Who says we aren't ready?" Austin asks, all basketball-jock cocky with his foam sword by his side.

It strikes me the wrong way. I bristle. Issie murmurs something like "uh-oh" under her breath, and I leap off the risers in one massive jump, landing softly and catlike on both feet, my knees slightly bent. Someone gasps. I take two stealthy steps toward Austin.

"You ready?" I ask.

"You don't even have a weapon," he scoffs as some people giggle.

"The pixies won't need them," I explain.

"Show-off," Brianne Cox says.

"He'll totally take her," Paul says.

"Nope. I saw her fight the other night. She has mad skills," Callie insists.

I ignore them.

"Fine," Austin says. He raises his sword in front of him, all six feet, four inches of jock. "Show me."

"Be gentle, Zara!" Cassidy yells.

In less than a second, I zip toward him. He lifts the sword and makes to lower it on my skull, but my skull is already past him. I'm behind him. He turns, but I reach up and grab his sword arm, twist it, and at the same time kick at his knees. I make sure it's not too hard because I don't want to actually hurt him. It's just enough to make him lose his balance and fall. As he does, I snatch his sword away, flip it in the air, catch it again. By the time he hits the ground, I am pointing the weapon at his chest.

He swears. Sweat beads on his forehead.

"Holy . . . How did you do that?" Cierra is basically hero-worshipping me.

Flushed, I step away from Austin. I don't know how to answer as he scrambles up on his feet. He cringes like he's embarrassed. I can smell fear coming off of him too. It smells like steak, which makes me shudder. I toss the sword back to him.

"That's how pixies fight," I say, ignoring Cierra's question. "They don't fight fair. They fight for life or death. They fight for fun. They do not fight like you."

I back up, brush the hair out of my face.

"She's not even winded," someone whispers.

Sucking in my lips, I look to Issie. She takes the cue and claps her hands. "Okay. Everybody fight hard this time. Do not be afraid to bruise each other. These babies are foam. It won't really hurt . . . too much."

I walk back toward the bleachers and grab the training

notebook we worked on last night. It's time for drills. We get them to line up and I shout directions: lunge, extend your sword arm, recover. We do it again and again until people are rubbing their quads.

"With swords, when you want to kill, it's all about closing the distance and making multiple parries," I yell. "And when you want to survive, it is all about keeping that distance open, but always keeping your eyes on the predator. So, let's do backward lunges this time. Pick a partner. One side offense, one defense." I wait a second while they pair up. They are moving slowly, so tired from just a little bit of training. "Okay. Let's go. Left side, defense. Right side, offense. Lunge. Lunge. Swords up! Swords up! Eye on the target. Faster. Lunge. Parry. Lunge."

"Zara." Cassidy grabs me by the shoulders and then fixes my hair into my ponytail. She tugs at it pretty aggressively, but it feels good—like she's taking care of me.

"You have a visitor," she says. With her elbow she points at the gym doors while her hands tug the elastic and twist it around my hair. Looking up I see Astley in all his blond regalness standing there. His hands are braced against the doorframe in a cross-like pose. His mouth is pulled in and he's exuding the smell of pain.

"He doesn't look happy, does he?" I ask.

"Did you tell him we were doing this?" she asks.

"No. He was busy dying. I was busy helping him live. You know . . . priorities."

She pats my shoulder and pushes me toward the doors. I walk underneath the hoop, look up at its loops of yarn or netting or whatever it is. It's all one string but twisted and manipulated to look like a bunch of diamonds. It has a purpose. All of us here are like that net—we have a purpose. And judging by his face, Astley has a purpose too.

Nick catches up to me in three strides, touches my elbow, and says, "You okay?"

"I think he might be mad," I say.

"Good," he chuckles. "Good."

I could rush across the gymnasium in two seconds and get to him faster than the time it takes the humans to pull in a full breath. We both know that. But I don't. Instead I walk slowly and remember the first day I ever saw him. It wasn't long ago. I was running on the unused railroad tracks that cross the access road to the high school. I'd gone left toward Bedford Building Supply and the backwoods. There are cross-country trails in there. The snow covered everything but I had spikes on, which helped keep me from slipping. He'd been tied to a tree, dying and broken. I knew he was pixie, but I'd still let him go. Somehow I trusted him even back then.

Astley's wearing his cargo jacket again. His hands rest on his hips. He's got dark low-slung jeans on and he looks . . . he looks beyond mad and pale and not perfectly healthy.

"What is this?" he asks.

I stand close to him, right in his face so I can catch him if he wobbles or something. "We're training, and you should be in bed resting."

He ignores that. "Training for what?"

"To fight pixies."

There is this horrible pulse of anger that seems to fill the air. It's red and hard and I can almost smell it. His face hardens but he doesn't yell. Instead he just bangs out the words like bullets. "You cannot do things like this without telling me."

"Why not?"

"Because, Zara, this has broad implications." He turns his head away. A muscle in his jaw beats against his skin.

I wait for him to say more. He doesn't. There's a fire alarm on the wall. I resist the urge to smash the glass, pull the lever, and have the alarm sound just because I so badly want to rush out of here and away from this horrible tension. Instead I just say, "And . . . ?"

He groans, leaves the gym, and enters the corridor. I follow him as he paces away, flashes up the stairs to the second floor, and then jumps down to the ground next to me again in a total display of pixie speed, pixie power despite last night's near-death experience. "I have no desire to insist that you check with me before you do things, Zara, but this? This is huge. We will be sanctioned by the high council for this. You have revealed us to all these humans. You have no idea of the implications. We have hid our existence for centuries, Zara, centuries! And now you have undone all that hard work in a day." He pauses, sways a bit. "This is what occurs when I am poisoned."

"Times have changed," I say. There's blood on my lip. I must have been biting it. I wipe it away. It's the same color as the fire alarm and I breathe in, relieved. Every time I see my blood, I'm so glad it isn't blue.

He grabs my entire hand in his, swallowing it up.

"Astley, you are not acting like yourself." I start to pull my hand away but he holds it in his fingers. For a moment we just stand there. For a moment neither of us moves. I try to will him to calm down, to feel kind. Then his eyes soften and his hold on my hand lessens and I know that I could pull away now, but I don't. I force my anger into myself a little, force my voice into a kinder mode and then explain.

"I didn't 'out' the pixies. They've outed themselves with what they did to that bus of Sumner kids. They've outed themselves by taking the Beardsley boy and killing him, by kidnapping Jay. I didn't do that. My father did. Frank did. Your mother did. Not me. I have to keep these people safe. I have to, Astley. It isn't just about stopping the apocalypse. It's about empowering people to stand up for themselves, to fight, to know what is killing their friends. How can we not do this? How can you even be angry about this?"

"I cannot." Astley draws in a breath. His teeth appear at the corner of his mouth for a second and he looks so terribly young all of a sudden, young and vulnerable. His free hand reaches up and rubs behind his ear. That's when I notice his eyes.

"Your eyes are green." I'm trying to figure it out. "Your eyes change color. When I first saw you they were like this, but then—"

"They have been blue and silver. Yes."

"Why?"

"It has to do with you, my reactions to you, my energy."

I wait for him to explain more. He doesn't. The shouts of people in the gym echo into the hallway.

"They sound so innocent," he finally says. "They don't fully understand how feral we can be, how hungry."

"I know."

He lets go of my hand and reaches up to stroke my cheek before I can react. Then he pivots hard, paces away, looks inside the gym. I don't move, just watch the expressions twist across his face, the feelings flow off of him in colors. Resignation is blue. A deep yellow is the color of his pain. Despair is a dark, dark brown that almost looks black.

"You are just preparing them to be slaughtered." He turns and strides toward me, suddenly all powerful again. Nick had used the same word—slaughtered. His shoulders seem to have grown six inches wider and his face is rigid. "I apologize for saying that. You would not be my queen if you did not care for your people, and I have to recognize that humans are still your people just as much as pixies are your people."

I don't say anything. He lifts his hand up to touch my face again, but I step backward just enough for him to notice.

"You must learn to trust me. Tell me before you act on things with such colossal implications, please."

He is gone, striding out the glass front doors, leaving a trail of gold glitter behind him. I squat down and touch it with my finger. It sparkles and sticks to my skin. I wipe at the specks as I stand back up, but it clings to my finger. I rush out a text to Becca and Amelie and tell them to find him and protect him. He shouldn't be out gallivanting when he just almost died. He looks like he could pass out any second.

Issie flings open the door from the gym. Nick and Cassidy are a half step behind her. All their faces are frantic, tense.

"That didn't look right," Nick says. "He was bothering you. Wasn't he?"

Issie hiccups. I look over her head at Nick and Cassidy and right behind them is everyone else. They are staring. Jay Dahlberg is at the front. His mouth is tight but open and he asks, "That was one, wasn't it?"

I nod. "Yeah, but he's not bad. Let me explain."

They wait.

"Not all pixies are bad," I start. "The ones who can't control their needs are bad. They start to torture people, feed on their energy. I'm not sure what kind of energy. I think it's their life force or—"

"Soul," Nick interrupts. "They feed on people's souls, torment them, seem to get more energy and pleasure the more frightened and in pain the person is. Usually it is young men. But once things get truly out of hand, it can be anyone. That's what's happening now."

People sort of murmur. Some just look scared. Some look angry.

I take over again. "But not all pixies are like this. A lot of it depends on their king. They are somehow tied to the emotional stability of their king. The kings rely on queens to keep them in balance. They are all linked somehow. It's not telepathy, but more like they are one multifaceted entity."

Now people are looking blank. Worried that I lost them, I bluster on. "Anyway, the one you just saw, Astley, is not from here and he is a good king. He and his people are trying to help us get the bad pixies under control."

"And you know he's good how?" Jay asks.

"He just is," I say. "He's been trying really hard to help."

"And he's stable?" Austin asks, stepping closer.

"Super-stable," Issie answers. She smiles and bobs her head. "Really, really stable."

"So who is his queen?" I'm not sure who asked this. I didn't see. I open my mouth to answer.

Nick answers for me. "Zara is. Zara is a pixie now. And she is his queen."

There are more questions and lots of reassurances as what should have been a good training time becomes Pixie 101 and Zara interrogation. Cassidy and Is back me up and field a lot of the questions. Nick refers people to the handbook, and eventually they all head back inside the gym. I think about what both Nick and Astley have said, how I am just preparing them to be slaughtered, but I have to believe that it's better to know. Right? It has to be.

Standing at the door, holding it with one arm, Nick turns around and waves for me to come in and join them, to get ready for the war.

I do.

After a long day trying to train our friends and acquaintances, we've been trying to figure out why Astley's mom attempted to poison him, other than the obvious: she wants him dead.

"I want to understand the why," I keep saying.

Nick, Cassidy, Issie, and I are in the gym cleaning up. Pretty much everyone else has left. There are water bottles rolling around and paper scraps everywhere.

"Sometimes the whys aren't knowable," Nick says, tossing a tissue into the garbage. "So you just have to ignore the whys, and just focus on what *is* and move on."

I wonder if he's talking about the murder attempt or about us.

ITEMS OF INTEREST TO LOCAL AGENCIES:
12/16: Trooper Barnard responded to multiple reports of a
tiger seen roaming in the area adjacent to Leonard Lake.
Failed to locate.

After the training, even though I'm still sore from saving Astley
and feel like total crud, Issie and I do the task that everyone
hates. That's because the worst part of killing pixies isn't actually the killing, which is what I used to think. Believe it or not,
you get used to the sickening feeling of bones breaking or blood
spilling onto the snow or onto your nice flats, your *favorite* flats.
You get used to the responsibility of causing death, which seems
horrible, and let's face it: it *is* horrible. Still, that's not the worst
of it. The worst part of killing pixies is getting rid of the bodies.

We head to the river and pull down the back bumper of
Grandma Betty's truck. Issie holds the legs of a now-dead pixie
man. He's heroin-user skinny and wearing dad jeans, which are
pulled up way too high. It's like a casting director got two parts
confused and made a mishmash character called Heroin-Using,

Minivan-Driving Dad. Although in the credits it would probably be called Dead Evil Pixie #5.

As she stumbles beneath his weight, Issie's hair curls out from under her rainbow hat and she is shin deep in snow.

I hold the arms and shoulders and say, "On three. One . . . two . . . three!"

We throw him up and into the water. His body splashes into the dark gray river and sinks. Soon he will melt away like a marshmallow that's been sitting in hot chocolate too long. The water will take him. Astley told us that the bodies will become one with the water and the authorities won't find them, not ever. I cross my fingers that he's right about that as we go back to my grandmother's truck and take another body out from under the tarp, trudging through the snow.

"You know," Issie says, "I wish they were vampires. In TV shows vampires always explode or disintegrate. It seems so much easier for cleanup."

"Even the exploding?"

"Yep, just a little vacuuming up the dust, maybe a Clorox bleach wipe, and you're done."

"That would be nice," I admit. "This is a better workout, though. On three. One . . . two . . . three!"

We send a pixie girl splashing into the water. I recognize her from an earlier attack at a school dance. Nick killed her this morning, tearing her throat out as she stalked Paul Rasku leaving his house for the Y. I had let her go from the dance with a warning. I'm still soft even now that I've turned into one of them.

Issie's arms shake from the exertion. It's too much for her muscles. We'll have to make sure she doesn't get stuck doing this duty again, but she's not the best fighter and it seemed safer somehow.

The feeling comes back—cold, deathly, like someone is watching me. I pivot a full three hundred and sixty degrees, scanning the parking lot, the river, the old Community Health and Counseling building off to one side, the harbormaster's office off to the other. Nothing. I sniff and get only the faintest smell of death mixed with vanilla bean.

We hike back to the truck, secure the tarp with rocks so it won't blow away, and climb into the cab. I turn the heat on full blast so Issie doesn't freeze.

"We just threw bodies into a river," she says.

"I know." I put the truck in drive and edge it forward. I'm not too comfortable with driving it, so I take it slowly.

She pulls off her hat, revealing crazy hair frizz. Some of it actually sticks to the roof of the cab because of all the static electricity.

"It's just I know that this whole keep-people-safe-from-evil-pixies thing is of 'vital importance.'" She actually makes air quotes around the words "vital importance" and then continues, "But I would like to have a conversation without the words 'death,' 'corpses,' 'bodies,' or 'end of the world' in it, you know? And I'd like to be able to leave the house without my mom giving me pepper spray and taping knives to my forearm and acting like she's never going to see me again."

I pull the truck out onto the main road. "'End of the world' is a phrase, Is, it's not just a word."

We trundle toward Mike's, this corner store that's not actually on a corner. I pull into the parking lot of Mike's Store.

"Thank you, Miss Nitpicky," she says, and out of nowhere

goes, "Just remember at the end of the day it isn't boys that matter. It's your friends that matter."

"And whether or not you stop the apocalypse."

"Yeah," she says, leaning her head back into the headrest and closing her eyes for a second. "That too."

Mike's Store is small and sort of claustrophobic. It's known for having a penny candy section where you scoop candy out of glass jars, which is very retro. The other end of the square store has a little deli, which, according to Betty, is Food Poisoning Central. There are about three rows of wooden shelving with canned goods, dog food, and tampons. That sort of thing. A lot of stuff is covered with a thin layer of dust. Someone once said that's all people are: dust. But I can't believe that's true. I think we have souls and energy and that goes on even after our bodies die. Valhalla sort of proved that, actually, right? Still, the dust gives me a creepy feeling.

"Zare?" Issie nudges me with her hip as I stand there motionless in front of the spaghetti sauce. There are two options squeezed in between diapers and boxes of macaroni and cheese. One is Ragú. Nick loves Ragú.

"Yeah . . ." The word leaves my mouth super slowly. "I'm fine. Just . . . just tired of spaghetti, you know? And that whole draining-my-soul-energy thing last night to save Astley. I am fine."

She studies my face like she knows I'm lying. She throws her arm around my shoulders and gives me a one-armed bro hug since we're both carrying things. The door to the store opens, making a jingly bell noise. I can smell it's a pixie. Pushing Issie behind me, I stand up as straight as I can to see over the rows of flour and sugar and Maxwell House coffee. The moment I see him, I relax. I even smile.

"Hey, Astley!" Issie says, popping out from behind me. "Long time no see."

He tilts his head. His blondish hair flops a bit onto his forehead. "I saw you this morning, Isabelle."

She cringes at the use of her full name.

"It's an expression, dude. Geesh." She turns to me. "He is sweet but way behind the times."

"I know." I smile at Issie and then at Astley.

He's closed the distance between us. "Spaghetti? Again?"

I nod.

"You could have dinner with me," he offers.

"I would, but . . ."

His expression hardens just a little. Nobody else would notice it, but I do.

"But you have to feed him." Astley nods, grabs a water bottle out of the refrigeration unit, and then takes my spaghetti and sauce out of my arms. "Well, then at least let me pay."

I do because, since I am technically the queen to his king now, his money is half my money or something like that. I don't know. All I know is there's a bank account in Switzerland that has my name on it. Austin's working at the counter, and he's firing away eight thousand questions about training. As Astley pays, I read the flyers tacked up on the wall next to the checkout counter. There are old ones for spaghetti suppers. There are newer ones about grief.

MISSING LOVED ONES? JOIN US. If the mystery
and disappearances are getting you down, you aren't

alone. Come join others who share in your sorrow and long for answers. Don't grieve alone.

I touch the yellow piece of paper without even realizing it. It's only when skin meets paper that I know what I'm doing.

"Zara?" Astley's voice is at my ear. His breath rustles softly against my hair, the skin of my earlobe.

"Yeah?"

"Nick isn't dead anymore," he whispers low, calm. His voice is like a heater rumbling to life in a car. It holds the promise of comfort and warmth. I'm not sure if that promise is because he is my king and I am pixie-bound to him in ways I don't understand, or if it's just because he is nice.

Either way, he is right about Nick. I swallow hard. "I know. I know he's not dead."

And then Issie says the words that I can't say. "It just sometimes still feels like he is, right?"

Before I can respond Astley sniffs the air. "Zara . . ."

The way he says my name makes the tiny hairs on my arms bristle. I hand Issie the bag of food and step back from the wall, turning just as Frank comes in the door. He slams it open so hard that it hits the wall.

Austin curses behind us. "Dude, you've got to be more careful. The glass on that thing cracks."

Frank glares at him. "Shut up."

I don't know if there's something in his voice or his gaze, but the very talkative Austin actually stops talking, which is too bad, because he could have distracted him. I try to move in front of Issie and Astley, protecting them, but Astley makes the same move. We bump hips.

"Brilliant. You are so out of synch you collide," Frank snarks.

He starts laughing. It's a crazy person/pixie laugh, the kind that just rumbles through his chest and splurts out into the air, uncontrolled and revealing how wild he is inside.

"That's one of them, isn't it?" Austin says behind us. Austin wants to be a cop. He's gone to the junior trooper program in Vassalboro with state troopers and everything. He's pretty tough and calm in a crisis.

"Yep," Issie answers while taking a step forward.

I direct my attention to Frank. "You could at least shut the door behind you."

"My apologies." He kicks it shut with his foot and then looks Astley up and down like he's sizing up a piece of meat. "The question truly is: should I kill you now? It's a shame the poison didn't work, isn't it? Good waste of time. And time is ticking, isn't it? As your mother would say, Astley, 'Always ticking. Always ticking.'" He mimics Isla's demented singsong voice as he says it.

"Oh, I do not think that is the question," I say, stepping one more foot forward. "I think the question is should *I* kill *you?*"

"Crap. She's a badass," Austin says pretty admiringly, while both Issie and Astley say my name in a warning voice.

"So tough now. I miss the innocent, crying princess pining over her dead wolf." Frank tsks at me and then leaps, showing teeth. He hits me right in the stomach with his foot, but I grab it at the ankle, pulling him down with me and then pushing him back. His body arches and hits the jars of penny candy even as my own body thumps to the ground. Glass smashes on the floor. Gummy worms and fireballs free themselves and splat or roll across the wooden floor. I feel bad about that. Poor Austin. Poor gummies.

"Zara!" Astley roars, but instead of helping me up, he flings himself toward Frank. Frank's already standing and ready. He moves like he's going to rip Astley's neck out.

"No!" Everything that happened to Nick flashes back to me and I scream the word as I make a football-player tackle, hitting Frank midstomach. We both schlump into the edge of a row of shelves. The wood cracks and the shelf breaks, cans of corn and spinach topple onto us.

"Zara!" Astley yanks me backward by my legs. He must overestimate the amount of force needed, because I slide all the way across the snow-puddle-wet floor to the counter, bumping into Issie's boots.

As I scramble back up, Astley and Frank begin to fight with fists. Astley's obviously still weak. His blows aren't as powerful as Frank's. He's faster, but not full form. If this turns out to be a battle of pixie kings, Frank is going to win. I start to rush back over there, but Issie grabs me by the arm.

"Get out of the way, Zara," she says.

"But—"

She's holding a gun. A gun! Where did she get a freaking gun?

Austin yells at Issie, "Aim at his head."

Issie says, "Dude! Evil dude! Stop now or I'll shoot."

She looks at me for approval. For a second, I contemplate taking the gun out of her shaking hands. Astley roars in pain as Frank's fist comes at him.

"Astley, get back!" I yell.

And he leaps away, not asking why, just trusting.

And Issie pulls the trigger.

The noise is deafening and the recoil of the gun thrusts Issie back against the counter. Grabbing her by the waist, I make sure she doesn't fall over.

"I mean it. Next one is in your head, psycho pixie guy!" she yells.

"Just do it!" Austin's reaching for her. "Give me the gun, I'll do it. Issie!"

But she hesitates, and as she does Frank stands up, wipes off the front of his long leather coat. The bullet didn't hit him, at least not anywhere critical. He says, "The clock is ticking. Time is running out. Tick. Tock. Tick."

"What?" Astley starts for him again but he leaps out the now-broken window and rushes off.

I stare at the door blankly. "I should chase him."

"No." Astley shakes his head. "He was just toying with us. They do that. Try to make us afraid. It makes the death better."

"N-nice," Austin says. "Oh crap. I better go erase the video. We have a video camera up there."

He points to a blinking red light on the ceiling and leaps over the counter, rushing off to the back wall and a door marked EMPLOYEES ONLY, yelling at us to watch the register.

Issie plops the gun on the counter.

"Where did you get that?" I ask. "And awesome job, by the way."

"My mom. She bought it off some guy behind the library."

"Seriously?"

"Yeah."

We stand there for a second. I try to let everything that happened sink in. Some woman with mall hair comes to the door, peeks in, and backs right back out. Astley has grabbed a broom and is sweeping at the glass and gummies on the floor.

"That's kind of sexy, man doing domestic duties," Issie whispers. She turns and looks at me full-on. "I can't believe I fired a gun!"

"I can't believe you had a gun and didn't tell me."

"I know! My mom made me promise not to tell anyone. It's completely illegal to carry a concealed weapon without a permit. Plus, she's made me bring it to school."

Grabbing a dust pan so Astley can sweep the glass into it, I throw her a look, and she lifts her hands into the air in mock surrender. "I know! I know! I still should have told you, but did I or did I not rock back there? I missed his head, though. I was aiming for his head."

Astley has this terrified look on his face. "Have you ever shot a gun before?"

"No." Issie starts picking up fallen cans. "But I remembered how to get the safety off and everything. Go me."

The door slams open again and we all stop midcleanup, but it's just Nick, albeit Nick looking frantic and energized. He's so focused he doesn't even ask what we're doing and we're all so stunned we don't even ask how he found us.

"I saw the truck outside. I've been monitoring the police dispatches on my laptop," he says. "There's been another tiger sighting outside some woman's house on Elm Street by the river. I guess it happened last night. The state police came."

My stomach pits into something hard and I dump the glass from the dustpan into a trash can behind the counter, beneath the lottery tickets. "Did they find her?"

"No."

I'm not sure if that's good or bad. I hand Issie the dustpan for a second so I can fix my coat and I explain that to him. "It's like if they find her we know she's safe and out of the woods, but then you know—"

"They might put her down because she's an animal." He grimaces.

"Exactly." I shudder. "We should go look near there. I'll check the river through town. I'll start at the harbor park where the boats get put in and work up to the library and the jail. Can you go up past the dam? In the more wooded areas?"

He nods. "Of course."

Austin tells him what happened as I check with Astley and Issie that this is an okay plan, which it is, and Astley will come look too as soon as he's cleaned up and gets gun-toting Issie home. Nick and I actually walk out together and he tells me that Cassidy and Dev are running a training again early this evening. Two in one day may seem like a lot, but it's essential.

"It's nice to be on the same team," I blurt when we get to Gram's truck.

He nods and does this little half-smile thing. "Yeah. I figure there are bigger things going on here than our romantic issues and, um, my ego."

"And my ego."

"More my ego." He laughs. He runs a hand through his perpetually messed-up hair.

"I think so too," I quickly correct myself. "I think we need to focus on saving the world, getting things safe, you know?"

"I know." He looks around.

"But maybe after this, maybe we can figure things out again.

Make it so you can talk to me?" I hate how my voice lifts up at the end of that. I sound so weak.

"Maybe. Yeah." He shakes his head. "But we are talking now, Zara."

"Oh. True." But it isn't the same. I wave good-bye and then I open up the door, turn on the truck, and drive away.

I drive past the Y, and the tow-truck place where the guy puts anti-government stuff on his signs, the old school that's now a daycare center, and the lawyers' offices. I look for pixies and a tiger grandmother the entire time. It's late in the day. We aren't as active in the daytime because, like most predators, we like night. Still, I look for them and her, for signs of the apocalypse. And the signs are hard to see. You could fool yourself into thinking this is just any regular smallish Maine town in the winter. Houses line up in spaced-out rows along the three main streets. Sidewalks are shoveled or plowed. It looks so normal. Cold but normal.

Slush kicks up beneath my tires. The wipers slowly move back and forth across my windshield, pushing the snowflakes off the truck and back into the air, free for another second before they fall to the ground.

I stop at the red light, watch an oil truck slide through the intersection, think about my grandmother out there attacking pixies, out of her head with grief because of Mrs. Nix's death. The tip said that they saw her by the river, and they weren't wrong. As I drive into the harbor parking lot, she comes into view, prowling back and forth in a straight line by the metal docks. One lobsterman in a heavy gray coat and hat is stalled out in a dinghy that floats halfway between the land and a lobster boat. The little white boat bobs as he frantically tries to restart the outboard engine. The poor man probably thinks he's had so much coffee brandy that he's hallucinating a tiger.

I yank a blanket out of the truck.

"Gram?" I make my voice as nonconfrontational as possible, creeping forward across the snow.

Her tiger self turns and faces me, teeth bared, ears back. She doesn't recognize me, maybe? Maybe she's so far gone she doesn't recognize anyone? For a second I'm more scared than happy to see her. I feel like a corpse, just flesh and bone, waiting to be mauled by tiger teeth. But she's not just a tiger. She's my grandmother.

"It's me, Zara," I say, taking a tiny step forward. "I've brought a blanket."

I hold it in front of me.

"You must be kind of cold?" I add. "Plus, if you want to be human, I thought you'd rather not be naked out here where people could see you—like the lobster guy."

She sniffs the air. The dinghy's engine starts on the water. She does not look happy. She makes a little noise as her ears move forward into a slightly less confrontational stance.

"Right. That's right. Nobody's going to hurt you," I say.

Her muscles are rigid and tight, ready to pounce or run away.

"I'm your granddaughter. Um . . . I love you?"

The silence between us is like a broken chicken bone, jagged and thin. I am scared and tired and love her so terribly much, this massive predator of a grandmother. Her sorrow is my fault, because I wanted so badly to retrieve Nick that we fell into a trap. And Mrs. Nix died because of it.

"Please, Betty," I whisper her name. I squat down low, making myself small. The blanket twitches in my hands.

She lifts her head to stare into my eyes. I try to remember if I'm supposed to stare back or not, wondering what big cat behavior protocol is. I decide to screw that and just do what Zara behavior dictates; I stare back into her big, amazingly brown eyes. As I do, the pupils dilate, shifting into circles. This always happens when she's about to change. I stay in my squat but shuffle-turn and give her privacy. After a moment a hand reaches over my shoulder and yanks the blanket away.

"Good of you to bring a damn blanket. Nobody's going to want to see my ugly old ass," she says gruffly.

I give her a second, which is as long as I can manage, and turn around.

"Gram?"

No answer.

I try again, say the words that are the most important. "I'm so sorry."

"I know." She doesn't meet my eyes, but I don't care.

I hug her anyway.

"I missed you so much." I almost sob it out because it's so true.

She nods really quickly. The movement of her face against mine feels familiar and good. "I know. Missed you too."

After a couple of moments, I pull away to look at her. Her face is worn and tired and her eyes are dull, not half as spunky as normal. She smells of wood and blood and death. She turns away and watches the lobsterman's dinghy slowly move across the water.

Out of nowhere she says, "This is bigger than us. There is a giant out there against us, a literal giant, Zara."

Betty closes her eyes. I tuck the blanket around her a little more tightly. Her shoulders are gaunt now, not so ruggedly muscled.

"I brought your boots. Well, they were in the truck. Hold on. You have bare feet in the cold," I tell her as if she didn't know it. I jog to the truck, pull out the boots, and bring them back over, the whole time thinking, "Do *not* disappear again. Do *not* disappear again."

As soon as I put the boots on the ground, she slips each of her feet inside, not bothering to lace them up. She stands up again, but her posture isn't as straight as it's always been. Her shoulders aren't squared against the world.

Snow falls onto the harbor. Only a couple of lobster boats are still moored. Even the harbormaster's boat has been hauled out and put into dry dock, which is a trailer in the parking lot by his office.

Betty's voice flattens, cold as the blending snow. "Too many people, good people, have died."

She shudders, and Betty is not the kind of person who shudders, and I would bet a million dollars that she's remembering what happened here—how Mrs. Nix died in an explosion—how the grief and pain made Betty turn tiger, devour a pixie, and then disappear for days and days.

We stand there for another minute, even though she's shivering. And I tell her everything that's happened since she's turned. She knows some things already because she witnessed them while she was in tiger form. She knows that I got Nick back. She knows that my mom is gone again. I tell her the rest of it too, about how Nick is being a jerk a lot of the time, about Cassidy's visions, about the army we're trying to build. I expect her to argue with me about that one because she's always been pro-secrecy when it comes to regular people knowing about pixies and weres, but she just listens and takes it all in. She gives none of her wisdom, none of her sarcastic comments.

While I talk, the lobsterman ties the dinghy to his real boat, climbs aboard, and starts the engine. It sputters out. His swearing echoes across the water. Betty smiles at it.

"Some things don't change," she says. "When he does finally get that motor on, he'll have to run it a couple minutes so it doesn't keep stalling out."

I nod even though I'm not all that concerned with the lobsterman. Instead, I tighten my arm around Betty's waist.

"You can't leave again," I tell her.

She opens her mouth to say something, but an ambulance roars into the parking lot, lights on, no sirens though. Keith jumps out of the driver's seat.

"Betty!" He smiles and hollers but his eyes are concerned. "Betty! Holy God! What happened to you?"

She shoos him away. "I'm fine."

"You've been missing for days! You're at the city harbor, buck naked except for a blanket. You are hardly fine!" He insists that she sit in the back of the ambulance and she asks him why he's even here. He stares at her for a second while giving her another blanket and wrapping a blood-pressure cuff around her arm. "That guy on the lobster boat reported a tiger in the parking lot. Josie thought he was probably 10-44."

I must look confused, because Betty sighs out, "10-44 is the code for crazy person."

Dispatchers use "10" codes to talk on the radio to the cops and ambulance drivers.

"The cops are looking for a big cat," I say. "I, um, Keith, you must know that."

He just gives me a quick look and a nod while the boat tugs away, heading toward the bay. I can see it through the open door of the ambulance.

"Your vitals look good." Keith breathes deeply for a second, sits back on one of the built-in benches, and says, "Where the hell were you, Betty?"

She meets his eyes and lies without twitching. "I don't remember."

There's a pause. The sounds of the boat's motor fade.

"Nothing?" he asks.

She shakes her head. "Nothing. Just came to in the harbor, naked as the day as I was born."

"And you?" he asks me.

"Zara had a hunch," Betty says. "She's like that. Cop gut on that one. She's all instincts."

Keith shuts the door of the ambulance, closing out the cold, and gives Betty his own straight-on glare. His buzz cut is covered by a knit hat, but he has the attitude of a guy who has had enough. He says, "You are going to tell me and you are going to tell me right now, Betty White."

"Tell you what?" she asks, all innocent, crossing her arms in front of her.

"You're the damn tiger, aren't you?" he says. He actually points his finger at her.

"Why would you think that?"

"Because I'm a hamster."

He says it so deadpan that I don't know what to think. I have no idea if he's kidding or not, and neither does Gram, I don't think, because she snatches his sleeve and barks out, "Don't you mock me."

"Just tell me you aren't the one making all the kids go missing." He crosses his arms in front of his chest.

"You know that's not me," she snaps back. "I was with you when that call on the Sumner bus came in."

You can tell that she wants to call him an idiot, but she's holding back. Keith's focus seems to turn inward. The "accident" was really a pixie attack on a bus full of Sumner High School band kids. It was a blood bath.

"You're right," Keith finally says. "But I still think you're that tiger."

"You're crazy," Betty retorts, adjusting her blanket. "Zara, tell the man he's crazy."

"You're crazy," I say in a computerized, flat voice that hopefully shows I'm not supporting either side.

"I don't think so." He hands Betty another blanket. "You were standing out there buck naked in the cold. Your core temperature is still in normal range when you should be hypothermic. Your feet should be blue. You have been missing for days. You should have frostbite. Yet you're only shivering and only a tiny bit. That's not normal human behavior."

"So you think I'm a tiger."

"No, I know you're a tiger."

"And how do you know that, Mr. Delusional?" Betty asks.

He opens the ambulance door and points up at a telephone pole. "There's a camera there now, Betty. Josie monitors it at dispatch. It caught you turning back."

"Crap," Betty says, noticeably upset, which is unusual for her, but what's also unusual is how calm and accepting Keith is being, given the fact that his partner is a human who morphs into a large feline. Props to him. He's not even batting an eyelash.

"It's okay, Gram," I say, trying to soothe her by petting her knee. "It's just Josie and Keith. They're your friends. They won't tell anyone they saw you."

I fix Keith with a death glare, which hopefully conveys how I will kill him if he loses his mellow about this and tells.

"Ah, I know that, Zara. I'm not worried about that." She puts her head in her hands.

"Then what are you worried about?" Keith asks.

"That everyone saw me naked."

Keith mutters a curse and shuts the ambulance door, shaking his head like she's nuts, which maybe she is. Maybe we all are, but when Betty lifts up her head and starts laughing, Keith and I start laughing too.

Betty takes a long shower and I order pizza, which we gulp down in two bites. It's so good to have her back, even if her eyes are haunted and she seems older, more fragile.

"Why didn't you come back, Gram?" I whisper. We're sitting together on the couch, an empty pizza box in front of us.

Tears form at the edge of her eyes. After a few moments she turns and looks at me. "I thought I'd do more good killing than riding around in an ambulance most of the time. I don't know. I just . . . When she died . . . You have no idea how hard it was not staying tiger," she says. "I just wanted to stay feral and kill and not think. Still want to."

Sighing, I close the pizza box. "Not thinking sounds very nice."

"Not thinking is for wimps," she says after a moment. "I was a wimp."

"You were in pain."

She scoffs. "You're supposed to battle through it, not give in."

"Maybe that's how you had to battle through it," I say. "It wasn't the right way or the wrong way, just the Betty White way."

That's enough emotion for the both of us. Nick and I are scheduled to canvas again tonight, but he's not at the house at six, so I plow the driveway and shovel the steps for the eight thousandth time and head out alone. Then all hell breaks loose. Literally. It starts when I smell that same horrible smell—rotting and death. And it continues with a fist to my head and a fall into the snow.

FBI INTERNAL MEMO
The incidences of lost children seem to coincide with an influx of visitors to the town. All hotels are filled to capacity, which I have been assured is highly unusual for the month of December. Are these two things related? —AGENT WILLIS

"Get up!"

Broken and silent, I've fallen onto the snow, knocked down onto the ground between the tall pine trees. My vision blurs and shifts, but if I squint really hard I can see a half-rotting human foot as it gets ready to place another kick.

It smells of death.

It smells of vanilla.-

This is what's been following me, and this is not a pixie. This? I have no idea how to fight this. I don't know what this thing is and I don't have time to wonder about it because one more kick might kill me, break me forever. Blood gushes out of a cut on the back of my head, pooling into the snow. That's where it struck first. That's what knocked me down. It was a surprise attack. I must have twisted as I fell, because even in the moonlight, I can make out the rotting skin. The monstrous thing is standing on two legs, barefoot in the snow. It pulls the other foot back to kick me again. This foot isn't rotting at all. It looks female somehow. Maybe it's the black toenail polish and slender toes.

"You need to fear!" it/she roars at me. "How can I tell what you're made of if you are not afraid?"

I roll to the side. There's been another blow to my stomach. The knot of it slows me down. I lift my head an inch as the next kick goes just shy of my ribs. I have to get up. I have to . . .

Another kick knocks my breath away. I am dying. I must be. In the distance, a squirrel chatters its horror at the scene. The world smells of decay and pine, snow and blood. From somewhere far away comes the sound of a heavy animal running on the crisp snow.

I need to breathe, to live, to figure out what is happening, but I don't know how.

The creature pulls back her foot again, then pauses. If I could focus, I would maybe know what has caught her attention. I shift my gaze sideways. She is giant sized and definitely female, the kind of female that would star on naked Web sites if half of her body wasn't rotting like she was some sort of zombie. To make it weirder, half of her is pale and half is dark like she's two different races.

I must gasp or recoil or something, because her expression changes.

"I know. Not very attractive," she says.

I struggle, trying to get up while she snorts her disdain.

"You are so weak. Hardly a worthy opponent at all."

"Just kill me then," I mutter, and fall back into the snow, too tired to move, too tired to care.

She crouches down, stares into my face. Her eyes are a mere three inches from my own. The wind rushes by both of us, lifting a patch of skin from her cheek. "I do not want to kill you."

I swallow hard. "Just toy with me? Nice."

"Not toy with you. Test you." She sniffs the air. "You are destined to be part of the end, or perhaps you can stop it. You can end up with me in Hel or with them in Valhalla. When so much rests on the fate of one girl, how can I not test you?"

"I have no clue what you're talking about," I manage to say.

The snow has turned to icy pellets. They hit against both of us like weapons, reminders of the pain that exists.

She smiles, revealing broken teeth and perfect teeth, half and half. "Our destinies choose us. I was not always this way, Zara of the White. Destiny shaped me into a woman, half rotting, half whole. Despite the prophecy, perhaps, we can change what we will become? Who knows? Your cavalry arrives, lucky little queen. I must go. It was nice to meet you."

Nice to meet me?

Hope fills me even though I'm totally confused. If she goes I might be able to sit up, to smell something that isn't rotting skin and vanilla-bean intestines, to figure out what she's talking about, but then she leans in and whispers one last thing. "Do not let him out. No matter what they say, I want this end no more than you do."

"Wh-what?" My head swirls with confusion and she rushes off just as I manage to sit up. My eyes focus enough to see a large tiger, stripes standing out in relief against its pale fur, howl and race after her. The world shakes beneath their running feet. She roars.

I reach out to the tiger. "Gram . . ."

But Betty is already gone.

The woods become silent, quiet and waiting, as if disappointed that the action has moved on to a different part of the world. My heart clenches. My grandmother is chasing after that thing, and I'm in no position to follow. She could die. She could get hurt.

Flipping open my cell phone, I text Astley and then I promptly collapse back into the snow, letting the air chill me as my eyes close and I wait for rescue or death. I'm a target for any of Frank's or Isla's gang of pixies. I'm not quite sure which I would prefer—rescue or death—which sounds awful and suicidal. I'm normally not like that, but life right now seems overwhelming with no possibilities, no hope. What did she mean that I could stop it? Why was she testing me? What doesn't she want to end? The world?

The air smells cold and almost metallic. The freezing snow seeps through my clothes.

And what did she mean I'd end up in Valhalla or with her? Snow falls onto my face and evaporates just like my questions.

Two minutes later Astley appears, falling out of the sky and into the snow beside me. His foot flails out and hits me in the shin. That will be another bruise to add to my endless bruise collection of awesomeness.

"Sorry! I am tremendously sorry!" he apologizes, flustered as he scoots closer to me. He grabs my head in his hands, which makes me cringe and he apologizes again. "What happened?"

"A woman creature . . ." I shake my head. "She hit me from behind first. The blow must have made my vision blur."

"How are you now? How many fingers?" he asks, gathering me in closer to him with one arm while he raises the fingers in another.

I focus. "Two."

"How is your emotional state?" Astley asks.

His choice of words makes me laugh sometimes. "My emotional state is fine." I think for a second about what to say. "Betty's back and I think I may have some closure with the whole Nick thing."

He doesn't say anything. Astley is like that. Sometimes he'll wait to see if you'll add more. He gets the best information that way. He learned it, he says, from being a king, watching his dad rule. But since he's told me this before, I'm actually onto his little trick and I wait too.

He touches my cheek. "That is wonderful news about Betty—and Nick. I apologize for this morning. I was too quick to judge your actions. It was wrong of me."

I smile a little bit. "It was wrong of me to not tell you ahead of time, to get your input too."

"I want you to be happy, Zara, always happy."

"I know," I say. "That's what I want for you, for everyone."

"We shall fix this—all of this ghastliness. We shall make this right."

His teeth shine even in the dim light. His blond hair flops into his forehead as he gingerly touches the wound on the back of my head and he loses his smile, which is too bad, because his smiles are really nice. I breathe in the familiar smell of him and it gets rid of the decaying stench of that monster woman and the coppery smell of the cold. Almost against my will I lean my head against his chest, shut my eyes for a moment.

Honestly, I haven't felt safe in a very long time, and this time it doesn't last because the muscles in Astley's chest stiffen. Opening my eyes, I see what has made Astley tense. Just a few trees away is a beautiful, huge wolf. He sniffs the air. His ears are back and fangs bared as he growls his anger toward us. We're hugging in front of him, I realize, and he obviously doesn't like it.

"Nick." My hand reaches out to him, but he has already turned away and darted back into the trees, gone. Pain shudders through me.

Astley scoops me up into his arms. "We need to get you home."

"Yeah," I murmur.

"Are you hurting?" he asks, eyes staring into mine.

"Naw."

"You lie," he says, but he doesn't press it, which is really kind of him, I think. I let my side settle against his chest.

The sky is dark and cold. The snow keeps falling and the only thing that has any color in it right now is Astley's green sweater that's peeking out from beneath his navy blue pea-coat. Still, I breathe in. Still, I push the pain outside of me and solid up.

"I'll be okay," I protest. "We don't have to fly. You don't have to carry me. I promise I'll be okay."

"Of course you will, but right now I need to get you home and bandaged and let you have some rest." He eyes me. "You will tell me what happened as soon as you feel well enough. Deal?"

"Deal." I sigh as he lifts us into the cold air, brushing past the edges of pine tree branches and finally into clear unobstructed space just above the numerous treetops. "I feel well enough to talk now."

"Good," he says. "Tell me as we fly."

It doesn't take long for him to get us back to Betty's house. Unfortunately, Astley is not the best at landings and he tumbles in the snow. He twists his back to take most of the impact and his arms clench around me tightly, trying to brace me from any more bumps and pain.

"Sorry," he murmurs into my hair and then we stand up. I groan a little bit, but manage to stay upright. He insists on putting an arm around my waist and helping me inside my grandmother's house. The lights are on and the heat is going full blast, which feels so nice when we walk inside.

He sits me on the couch and I text some woozy messages to Devyn, Issie, and Cassidy about what just happened. I'd text Nick too, but since he is currently in wolf form and he saw me all beaten up and just ran off anyway, I figure I don't need to.

"I'm glad you were well enough to fly," I call out to Astley, since he's in the kitchen.

"Thanks to you and Cassidy."

"It was nothing," I lie, trying not to remember how it felt for every single cell to be drained of energy and life. I am going to repress that torture. That's just how I have to deal with it. It was worth it to get Astley strong and whole, I think as he strides back into the living room with a dishtowel wrapped around an ice pack.

He gently places it on the back of my head. "Your stomach and ribs?"

"They'll be okay," I say, but my teeth are gritted so it sounds more like "Theeebeeekayyy."

My phone starts beeping with new texts. Devyn and Cassidy are coming over. Issie can't because she's still under massive curfew.

Astley and I settle down on the couch, not touching or anything, but just waiting for everyone else to get here. The ice pack keeps slipping sideways and he insists on holding it on my head for me, which is so nice. He is always so nice. I shoot him a sideways glance. He looks calm and mellow. Not like me, I bet. I wish he didn't have to see me like this, even though I know he's seen me looking worse.

Someone scratches at the door.

"Betty," I say. "Be careful."

"I shall be fine," he says as he gets off the couch and heads to the door. He opens it like there's no danger at all from a were-tiger. Her huge white body enters and she blinks at him, gives a slight hiss, then storms to the couch. She pokes her nose right at the top of my head and sniffs at my injury there, and then at the bruises on my face. After a long, pondering second, she rubs her giant head against my shoulder and cheek, marking me, just like regular cats do. Then she pounds off into her bedroom.

Two minutes later she's back, changed and human.

"I lost it," she groans. Her long fingers lift up the washcloth and inspect my bump. She stares into my eyes. "Pupils are okay. No concussion, I don't think. Or you're already healing. Anyway, it was like the flipping thing just vanished in midair. I've been tracking it for days. She's been around, almost like she was stalking you. I can't believe she got to you."

"Why didn't you tell us?" I ask.

She sighs. Her bones crack as she stands up straight. "I was too busy being feral. And then this afternoon— Well, we didn't have a lot of time. I'm making some tea. You both are having some too. We all need something to calm us the hell down."

Devyn and Cassidy get to the house right after the teapot starts boiling. Devyn is all quick, intellectual energy. Snowflakes cling to his thick black hair as he squints his dark eyes at me, probably trying to get in as many details as he can. That's how he is. Cassidy strides in right behind him, long braids swinging from her knitted wool hat. She scratches at her neck and rushes inside and out of the cold. Nick trots in behind them and heads directly up the stairs in wolf form, dripping melting snow on the carpet as he goes. He doesn't say anything to anyone and anger rolls off of him.

"Nick is probably just changing," Cassidy says. She's attempting to make peace, but then she sees me and must lose that train of thought, because she pretty much flies over to the couch and reaches into her cool Tibetan-motif bag and starts taking out herbs and candles.

"It would be nice," she says sweetly, "if I didn't *always* have to heal you two."

Betty sets down some tea on the coffee table next to Cassidy's bag. "It's like we're their own private medics."

"I owe you a supply of candles," I say as Cassidy lights two big yellow pillars.

"I'll put it on your credit line," she jokes. "You currently owe me about $18,000.45 in candles. Matches? Those come free with the healings."

I start to smile at her but all the happy leaves the air as Nick comes back down the stairs, dressed in jeans and a maroon Henley. His dark hair is scruffy from the turning and there are fatigue lines by his eyes.

Devyn says, "Hey!"

Nick nods in acknowledgment and slumps into a chair, glaring at Astley. Astley smiles at him, which only deepens the glare.

Devyn clears his throat and opens up his laptop. "I promised Issie that we'd Skype her in."

Two seconds later he's got Issie's happy face on the screen. She's in her pajamas, wearing ear buds to listen to us.

"I have to be quiet or my mom will kill me," she whispers. She uses a finger to make a slicing motion across her neck. "I'm supposed to be in bed."

Cassidy's still murmuring some sort of elfish incantation and lighting an incense stick, and for a second I wonder how she even learned elfish—was it on the Web?—but I start talking anyway, trying really hard to ignore Nick, who is glowering in the corner. Guilt about the hug ripples through me even though I really shouldn't feel guilty at all.

I start off, "The attack came out of nowhere. It was a woman, sort of, she was half normal and half rotting flesh."

"Like a zombie?" Devyn interrupts, cruising through the Internet on his cell, probably because if he researched on his computer he wouldn't be able to see Issie.

"Yeah. Half zombie and incredibly tall," Betty says.

"Tell them what she said to you, Zara," Astley urges.

He reaches across the couch and touches my arm. I swear tension suddenly fills the entire room. I refuse to look at Nick as Astley quickly moves his hand away. My washcloth falls off, plopping into my lap. I fix it and tell them how the woman said that she didn't want to kill me, that she was testing me, that she wanted to see what I was made of.

"Oh, you're the chosen one!" Issie breathes out. "That's so cool."

"I am not any sort of chosen one," I argue. "That's a cliché anyway. 'The chosen one.'"

I spit out the phrase pretty disdainfully. Cassidy rests her hand against my shoulder and perches on the couch. She's so peaceful. It makes me feel a little better.

"She also said that I can't let him out," I add.

"Who?" asks Nick. It's the first word he's said.

I shrug, meet his eyes. "I don't know."

"Well, if it has to do with Ragnarok, it might mean Fenrir, the giant wolf you unleashed in Iceland, but that has already happened," Betty says.

Astley rubs the back of his hand across his eyes like he's either tired or trying to wipe the memory away. "Or it could mean Loki. The giant mentioned him too. He was—"

Cassidy interrupts. "I've been dreaming about him."

The conversation in the room stops. Cassidy pulls in a big breath and explains that she's been dreaming about a man tied up with serpent venom dripping into his mouth. His bindings are intestines that have turned to iron. He is pleading with her to help him get free.

Despite all my aches, I put an arm around Cassidy. "That's horrible."

She nods.

"That's probably it," Devyn agrees. "And look what I found. Is this the woman who attacked you?"

He passes his phone to me. There's a picture on the screen of a half-zombie/half-human woman. She's more skeleton than the one I saw and her flesh isn't two different colors.

"It's close," I say as Betty points out the differences. "Who is it?"

"Hel." Astley breathes out the word like it's a curse. Even Betty stops talking.

"Hell is a place," Nick says after a second of frozen silence.

Devyn directs all his professor-style attention at Nick. "In Norse mythology it is a place *and* a woman who rules that place. Hel is where people who die of old age and sickness go."

"As opposed to Valhalla?" I ask, dizzy. "Where you get to go when you die in quote-unquote glorious battle."

Cassidy blows out the match. "The Vikings thought that dying in battle was the way to go. It's what they aspired to, but Valhalla versus Hel isn't anything like heaven versus hell. It's not a good versus bad thing."

"Well, they weren't a society that promoted peace." Devyn walks across the room, shows the image on his phone to Nick, and says, "If you lived a long and peaceful life, you were destined to spend eternity with a zombie woman. If you killed people, then you were assigned to Valhalla, where you drank beer all day and trained with Valkyries."

"I think I'd rather go to Hel," Issie chirps from the computer screen.

"Me too," says Cassidy, all quippy. "I hate beer."

Astley looks at me and smiles super sweetly and I swear steam starts to come out of Nick's corner of the living room. It's frustrating, but I ignore his crankiness and try to get us all back on track by saying, "Then that is what we have to do."

Everyone looks at me with mouths hanging open, which usually means that:

1. I have had a massive jump in logical thought that nobody else is following.
2. I've had a ridiculously bad idea.

I've decided that it's the first option, so I shift my weight and explain.

"This Hel woman obviously knows what is going on." I start it out slowly, trying to rationalize it to myself as well as everyone else. "So we need to find her. To find her, we need to find Hel."

"Hel!" Issie whispers frantically. "We cannot go to Hel."

"It doesn't sound all that bad," I say as Betty harrumphs in the kitchen, where she's retreated to start making more tea.

"No . . . I just watched a History Channel special on hell," Issie insists, leaning closer to her computer screen, so close that I can see the pores in her nose. "And you do *not* want to go there. It's all tortured souls and screaming, nine layers of horrible horribleness."

"That's the Christian version," Cassidy says.

"And the Greek!" Issie says. "And the Roman."

"Issie, you're yelling," I tell her. "Your mom is going to hear you."

She gets terrified eyes and slaps her hand over her mouth. Then she lets go and whispers, "The special said there were gates kind of like in *Buffy*—hell mouths between here and the underworld."

"Like Dante," Devyn says, and then recites:

Through me you pass into the city of woe :
Through me you pass into eternal pain :
Through me among the people lost for aye.

The words echo in the room, creepy and silent, and Nick is the one who breaks it. "There is no way in hell, uh—"

"Excuse the pun," Cassidy interjects.

"—that I'm going to let you go to Hel, Zara. You've just been attacked by that monster woman, you've nearly died saving his life." He glares at Astley. "You just got back from Valhalla. No, just no," he finishes, standing up and glowing as if he's on fire.

A whole bunch of emotions rush through me simultaneously and I can't sort them out anywhere near quickly enough. He cares enough to be worried about me even though I'm a pixie. I'm grateful that he cares, but mad that he thinks he has power over me to "let me go."

I shake my head, and I'm about to say something when Betty speaks instead. "We don't even know how to get there. It's like Valhalla all over again."

"No," I say. "We're smarter now. Before, we didn't know if Valhalla was real. We don't even doubt this stuff anymore."

"Smarter now? Smarter?" Nick sputters. "You want to go to *Hel*, Zara. You want to chase after some zombie-beast-woman thing that just beat you up. She could have killed you."

"But she didn't," I argue, standing up. Astley grabs the facecloth as it topples off my head. I wobble a little bit but manage to stand okay.

"Right. She didn't. Because she was playing with you the way cats play with their prey, the way *pixies*"—Nick spits out the word—"play with their prey."

Astley drops the limp washcloth on the coffee table. "Do not insult us."

"Why?" Nick asks.

Astley's eyes twitch. Without a word, he stands up next to me and then takes a step toward Nick. Nobody else answers either. The room is just a chamber of tension and worry. I close my eyes.

"It's not up to you to decide if I go or not," I say, opening my eyes again and staring at Nick.

He meets my gaze. "Why? Because it's up to him?"

"No, because it's up to me," I say. "Or it's a group vote."

My head spins from the stress of it all and I sit back down. I try to figure out who would vote what way if we did have a group vote. I can't predict anyone's response except Nick's. How can he be so bossy? He ignores me and then *boom!* he's all protective again? Maybe this isn't even about me. Maybe this is about him losing his place as alpha, as pack leader and protector.

"People are so complicated," I groan into my hands.

"What?" Cassidy asks.

"Nothing," I say, pulling my head back up to look at everyone.

As usual, Devyn has been pretty much blowing off all of the tension and says in a totally level way, "A ton of people have already postured that the gate to hell—and I am saying hell with two *l*'s, not the Viking Hel with one *l*—has been in numerous places. Some believe it's in the Fengdu County in the Chongqing Municipality, some believe—"

"Where?" Betty asks.

"China," I say. One good thing about writing all those Urgent

Action letters for Amnesty International trying to protect people's human rights is that it makes me good with geography.

"Then there are people who think it's in Africa," Devyn continues, pressing the screen on his phone. "Specifically Erta Ale in the Afar Region of Ethiopia. It's a volcano. Locals call it 'the gateway to hell.'"

"That sounds promising," Astley says.

We all agree and Devyn tells us that some people think hell's entrance is in Clifton, New Jersey, where there are Satanic sacrifices and a thousand-pound ax allegedly blocking the doors to hell. Once you get through the doors you have to battle a glowing skull.

"But the best option is Iceland," Devyn finishes. "Iceland is where we've had activity before. They have an entire three-hundred-year period called the Viking Age in their history. There's a connection there that doesn't exist with Guatemala or Kansas."

"Damn it, but no." Betty puts her hand over her eyes and then recovers. She walks to the wood stove and opens the door, pokes the log into submission, and puts another one on top.

"Iceland," Astley repeats, looking at me. We both remember what's happened there, I bet. That's where my biological father died, eaten by a giant wolf that was meant to kill us. That's where Astley learned there was a traitor in our kingdom. We hadn't realized then that it was Isla, his own crazy-ass mother.

"It's a volcano again," Devyn begins.

"Of course," interrupts Nick. He throws up his hands like it's all too ridiculous and frustrating for words.

"A volcano by a resort—Namaskaro is the volcano. Lake

Myvatn is the resort. This is named after the lake, which is entropic," Devyn continues, but Issie interrupts him and demands he speak in English, understandable third-grade English. Basically, there is a volcano in a remote area of Iceland that has some interesting geographical aspects to it.

"And people think it's an entrance to Hel why?" I ask.

"Well, close by is a crater called 'Viti,' which means 'hell' in Icelandic." Devyn's eyes stay fixed to the screen as he paces back and forth in front of the fire.

"It does not seem definitive enough," Astley says.

"True." Devyn meets his eyes.

"It's more than we usually have," I say. "It's been called an entrance to Hel. It's got a Norse/Viking connection. We know there's activity in Iceland from the last time we were there."

Astley smiles at me, maybe because I'm being Optimistic Zara, I don't know, but it distracts me and I'm completely unprepared for Nick's freak-out.

"Don't smile at her!" he snaps.

Astley's eyebrows lift up toward his hairline. "What did you just say?"

"I said, 'Don't smile at her.'" Nick stands up again. "You keep smiling at her and touching her like she's your possession."

"Touching someone does not indicate ownership." Astley stands up too. "Your logic fails you."

The air ripples with male anger, all testosterone charged. Betty's hand rests on my shoulder as I announce, "I'm nobody's possession, Nick. People don't possess each other. They care about and support each other, but they don't—"

He stomps one step closer, finally making eye contact with me, and in those eyes is such pain and such anger that my heart breaks all the way down inside as he declares, "I want the pixie out of here."

Astley answers before I can. "You do not get to make that decision, friend."

"Don't call me 'friend.' You aren't my friend," Nick spits back.

Dropping her hand, Betty arches up and you can see the tiger in the way she shifts her eyes into something serious and wild and deadly calm. "Nick Colt. You are acting like a brat."

The clock on the wall chimes eleven. Cassidy breaks it with her singsong voice. Her braids sway, casting spells in the air. Her words soften the air just a bit. "You know, Nick, we are all working toward the same goal here. We all want the same thing."

"I know what he wants. He wants her." Nick points at me.

"This is ridiculous," Devyn says, finally acknowledging the situation. He looks so bird thin standing in between them. Either could knock him over with a punch. "We are all on the same team."

"Are we?" Nick huffs out as I close my eyes for a second, overwhelmed by the clichés and the tough-guy talk.

"I could ask the same," Astley says. His hands go to his hips in such a man pose as he talks. "Since you have returned you have spent more time glowering and undermining Zara's new power than you have supporting us in our efforts to eradicate Frank and determine what exactly the Ragnarok threat is."

"Nick just died," I start to explain. "He's had a lot to adjust to."

"Don't make excuses for him," Betty says.

Devyn gasps. On the computer screen Issie moans, "I can't see anything! Someone turn me around."

I reach over and pivot the laptop, although I don't know why Issie would even *want* to see this. The refrigerator makes a creaking noise that is so loud it echoes in here. It doesn't make them even pause.

"It's your mother and her brother who are the threat," Nick says, talking right over everyone else. "It's you who is the threat. I can't believe you're even in this house!"

"This is my house, Nick. He is allowed here. You need to calm yourself down." Betty stands up to her full height and looks at the door.

"Nick . . ." I start to walk over to him, to touch his shoulder and calm him down like I used to, but he jumps away. How can this be real? How can he act like this? "Nick."

But saying his name doesn't help. He brushes past me, slams outside. A second later the MINI starts up and headlights sweep down the driveway.

"Wolves have such tempers," Astley says, crossing his arms over his chest. It's not a kind thing to say at all.

"Don't," Devyn warns. "He's been through a lot."

Astley turns and looks at me. "We all have been through a lot. We all need to maintain our dignity and work together."

I tune them all out, go to the window and press my nose against the cold glass. My breath fogs it up, so I can't make out any shapes, any movement in the darkness, which is okay I guess because Nick is already gone. There is nothing to see.

Everyone leaves before midnight because it is a school night and their parents have rules. I trudge up the stairs, feeling physically better thanks to Cassidy but still kind of woozy. Even though it's not very green of me, I leave the porch light on and the one in the stairs. I don't want it to be dark when Nick comes back—if he comes back—and honestly, *I* don't want it to be completely dark either. It's just for tonight, I rationalize. Just one night I want to spend in the light. Betty says nothing about this. At the top of the stairs she hugs me and says, "You should take a bath. It'll help with the aches."

The house is quiet except for the humming of kitchen appliances and hot water pushing its way through pipes. The fire in the wood stove only makes occasional popping noises. Outside, the snow falls down and the wind eases into something sleepy.

Betty leans against the wall, and in her pajamas it's so obvious that she's lost weight in the time she was gone. The cotton fabric dangles from her bony shoulders. Deep, tired circles rest beneath her eyes.

"I'm not happy about this Iceland idea," she says.

I nod, holding up my towel. "I know, Gram."

"And I'm not happy about you being so important to whatever the hell is going on around here."

"The end of the world? The invasion of crazed-out pixies?"

"Yeah."

We stand there for a second and then I prod her, "But?"

"How'd you know there was a 'but'?" She almost cracks a smile.

"There's always a but or a butt." I make a movement with my free hand to mimic a big one.

She really smiles. "Damn, I've missed you."

"I missed you too," I say as the lightbulb in the overhead fixture flickers. "Are you going to tell me about your but?"

She wiggles her finger. "You watch it, young lady. Yes. But I don't want her death to be for nothing. I don't want the world, however messed up it is, to end. I don't want this town to be destroyed like this, and I don't want the poison of that Frank thing to spread beyond here. Do you understand?"

"I understand," I say quietly.

She moves toward me, kisses the top of my head. "Good. Now good night. And do *not* die in Iceland or I will kill you."

Laughing at her own silly logic, she sends me off to bed and I'm barely beneath the covers when a car rumbles into the driveway. The headlights flash through my window, illuminating the poster-strewn walls of my room, and flash out just as quickly, turning everything dark again. I can tell from the engine that it's Nick's MINI. A car door opens and shuts. I strain to hear his footsteps on the snow, then on the porch. The front door knob turns. A door opens. A door shuts. He sighs. And then he climbs the stairs, *one, two, three.* I want him to stop outside my room, open my door, and tell me he's sorry. I want him to come and . . . *four, five, six* . . . say my name and tell me how brave I was to save him, to thank me . . . *seven, eight* . . . He is at the top of the stairs, and for a second he actually hesitates, but it is just a second and then his feet move swiftly past my door. He goes into his bedroom, and another opportunity for real reconciliation—another hope for it all to go back to how it was—is gone.

It doesn't matter. We have a world to save, and if I have to go to Hel and back to save it, I damn sure will, no matter what the cost.

INTERVIEW WITH HOLIDAY INN ROOM #321 OCCUPANT
Investigator: So why are you visiting Bedford?
321: Sightseeing.
Investigator: In winter?
321: Yes.
INTERVIEW WITH HOLIDAY INN ROOM #322 OCCUPANT
Investigator: So why are you visiting Bedford?
322: Sightseeing.
Investigator: In winter?
322: Yes.

Having Betty back shifts something in all of us, gives us a sense of purpose, and yes, even a bit of hope. We are all a flurry of happy text messages and phone calls. In a meeting at the hotel's conference room, I manage to convince our pixies that having people fight with us is a good thing. Astley acts all proud of my leadership/speaking skills. Our pixies join in the training, showing all the humans how hard pixies are to fight in hand-to-hand combat, how weapons are pretty much necessary.

Austin looks over at Becca, who basically resembles a small cheerleader—the kind they toss around in the air. "This is our scary enemy?"

Amelie leaps in front of him. "Do not be an idiot, boy. Size does not matter."

Austin laughs like she's made a dirty joke. "What matters then?"

A light flickers in the high ceiling of the YMCA gym. "Fierceness." Amelie twitches almost imperceptibly—a signal to Becca, who leaps over Amelie's six-foot-tall frame, landing cat-like in between Amelie and Austin. Her hand grabs his neck. His eyes bulge.

"You are all very slow," she says. "Too slow for even a scary enemy like myself."

Becca has the best time doing this fighting stuff and she struts around like a vampire slayer or something, yelling out pointers and directions. Keith participates. So do Devyn's parents but mostly to check on Astley's health, I think.

Amelie groans as Callie tries to karate chop Sherman, a male pixie, in the knee. "What are you doing? What?"

"If you take out their knees, they fall," Callie explains.

"But you expose yourself, your neck, your back, and the movement is so slow." Amelie looks at me with a frantic, exasperated expression. "You must kick at the knee if anything. Go for the eyes. Blind us. Go for the head. Bash our skulls. This is child's play! Child's play!"

"We need better weapons," I say.

"We need a freaking army," Nick agrees. "This is pathetic."

"This is our army," I tell him. I cross my arms over my chest and look at everyone trying so hard.

"It is pathetic," he says again.

"The rifles will help," I say.

"Not everyone has a rifle." He states the obvious a lot, that Nick.

Later that day, Betty joins us for a pow-wow in the living room. We have a lot of new people here in the house—Becca, Amelie, Callie, Paul, Jay Dahlberg—along with the old stand-bys, and it's strange and sort of beautiful how Grandma Betty is letting pixies inside the house when not too long ago she refused to let Astley cross the threshold. And I like it—I like that most of us are trusting each other. I like that there are shifters and pixies and humans all in the same space. And it's during this meeting, with people in chairs and on the couch and even sitting on the floor, that we realize what the issues are.

1. We have to calm Frank's pixies the hell down so that they stop killing people. We need to round them up and get them out.
2. We have to stop the apocalypse.

SAFETY ANNOUNCEMENT ON FLIGHT 132

Flight Attendant: In the event of a water landing, your seat-bottom cushion may be used as a floatation device.

She demonstrates.

Flight Attendant: After exiting, slip your arms through the straps and hug to your chest as shown on the safety card in the pocket in front of you.

She pauses.

Flight Attendant: Have any of you heard about the strange news in Maine? All those disappearances. I bet you're glad to be getting out of there.

Awkward laughter.

For the flight to New York we are not seated next to each other. Amelie and Issie are in the middle and back of the plane, the plane-phobic Astley is sort of on the side, while I'm in 1F next to a thin man with shiny shoes and crisp suit pants, a bright pink shirt. He looks like he should discover the next social networking site and make billions. He helps everyone who comes on board.

You need to wait right outside the door to get your ticket claim for your carry-on.

You want to stow that up here.

He is nice and helpful, but I want to be next to Astley, who is five whole rows behind me, because something doesn't feel right. There's a heaviness, a watching, a creepy feeling that just seems to keep following me around.

As the stewardess glides down the aisle, the guy next to me watches way too intently, checking her out. I can feel his need for her. It hangs in the air. Pixie transformation byproduct I guess—feeling people's wants, emotions, but only when they are super-strong, super-intense. His eyes move to me and I shift closer to the window.

"Do you want water or anything?" she asks him.

"No, I'm good."

We drive by U.S. Air Force jets, dark gray and parked pointing at us, each has canvas green covering their engine parts.

"Excuse me." Astley stands over the man, then crouches to his level, whispers in his ear. The man unbuckles and vacates the seat, glancing at me.

"What did you say to him?" I ask.

"That you are gassy and that it would soon be quite obvious to him that he should switch seats with me."

I hit him in the arm, groaning. "Nice."

"I know." He buckles up. He's so pale, so afraid of flying in planes. The last time we were in a plane it was also to Iceland, and I had been the one who embarrassed him. I guess this is payback. Even so, he looks scared and nervous.

I grab his hand in mine and squeeze, trying to be reassuring. "I'm glad you're here."

He squeezes back. "So am I."

And since I know he doesn't mean "here in this plane," it has to mean that he's glad that he's here with me. I should be uncomfortable about that, but I'm not. I just keep holding on to his hand as the nose of the plane lifts up and takes us forward.

"Does it seem weird to you that we're going back to Iceland and searching for Hel?" I ask.

"Everything seems weird to me."

He settles into himself once the plane levels off at its cruising altitude. "Like you, I never imagined I would grow up without a father. I never dreamed that my mother would lose her mind or betray me this way." He drops his voice to a whisper. "I never thought that I would be the pixie king that would have to try to rein in others, that would have to stop Ragnarok, or that I would find you."

"Find me?"

"As my queen."

"Oh." As his queen. Is that because I'm so unqueenly? Or because he's worried about being stuck with me forever?

There's an awkward silence, which fortunately the flight attendant interrupts by offering us a drink. I pick juice. Astley picks water. Once she's moved the cart past us, I ask him, "Why do you think you have had to do this? You've said you're one of the youngest kings, which probably means you're one of the least experienced. And why aren't there any other kings helping you?"

"They have their own territories. This is mine."

"Yeah, but you'd think this would be a bit more important. It *is* the end of the world."

His eyes narrow. His fingers tighten around the little plastic cup that holds his water. "That is very true."

We're silent again. I think about how funny/crazy it is that Hel is a god but also the name of the place she rules, about how it's so different from the Christian version of hell, which is a fiery place bad people go to suffer. The mythology around Hel makes it sound like more of a cold place where everyone who didn't die fighting go to hang out. And Hel, even though she's half rotting, sounds nothing like Satan, the ruler of the other hell, because he's all nasty, all evil, and Hel doesn't seem like that—she seems powerful but not evil.

I pick a tiny piece of wolf fur off his sleeve. "Do you ever wonder if we're helping the good guys or the bad guys?"

He asks me what I mean and I try to explain. "Well, when Hel was beating me up, she said she was testing me. She said she wanted to make sure I was strong enough to stop it, and implied that she didn't want it to happen. From all our research, it seems that she wants to stop the apocalypse from happening."

"But her armies are part of what cause it."

"No. Her brother Loki escapes and that's what causes it. Then there are natural disasters and crazy monsters and then she brings the dead people from Hel to fight the warriors from Valhalla and that other city with warriors." And that's when I realize what bothers me. "I hate that none of the gods like Odin seem to care. It's such a fatalistic approach, like they have no control. Yet Hel is portrayed as the bad girl/evil one. She's in charge of the people who died of old age or sickness, not the ones who died killing. Why should killing deaths be better than dying peacefully?"

Astley doesn't answer. I place my hand on top of his forearm, feel the warm cloth beneath my fingers, and ask, "What is it?"

"I did not see my father there."

And I know he means in Valhalla. He didn't see his father there when he helped me rescue Nick.

"Oh." I try to think of something to say, but I can't. It would be so amazing to see our fathers again. I never even thought about the possibility, but Astley obviously has. His need for his dad and his sorrow seem to color the air a silent shade of blue, aching and haunted. I understand. I miss running with my father—technically my stepfather—the silly crinkles by his eyes, the way he'd let you hug him like he was a big tree, how he sang country songs with a fake twang that was half respect and half mockery. There are so many people gone, so many people I miss. The fact that we got Nick back is such a miracle. I want more miracles, I realize. I want everyone safe and I want Astley's sorrow to go away.

"This is so much bigger than us." Astley rubs his hand against his eyes and sighs. "Why would the gods want it all to end? If they do—that is a bit of an assumption."

I think about all the suffering and disease in the world, the war, the torture, the craziness, and I can think of a lot of reasons why you might want it to not exist, but for every bad thing is something beautiful, something awesome, like holding someone's hand, or having really good strudel, or having a dog wag his tail at you when you get home, or getting into your top college, or seeing a rainbow that doesn't explode. It doesn't make sense.

"Good question," I say, because, honestly, it is and then I shut my eyes for a second and wish I could just fall asleep. I am tired of good questions. I just want answers.

It's pretty soon after this that I smell him, the were-woods manly scent of him. Astley must smell him at the same time, because I swear, he actually bristles like a porcupine. We both stop reading and turn our heads to each other, simultaneously saying, "Nick."

A second later, he appears over Astley's shoulder, standing in the middle of the aisle. His smile is not happy. "You really thought I'd stay there and let you do this alone?"

No, but I hadn't actually thought about it. I was thinking about more important things like stopping the killing and saving the world, is what I want to say, but it seems kind of bitter. I put my book on Norse mythology in the seat back in front of me before I answer him. Astley raises an eyebrow and discreetly unbuckles his seat belt as I take all the time in the world.

"Nick." Why do I say his name? I have no idea. I just do. And then I do it again. "Nick. You are supposed to be helping people learn how to fight."

He moves up the aisle and turns so he's facing us. He apologizes to the man in the aisle seat next to Astley as he leans his hip against the seat. "Betty is doing that. She's more patient than I am at that sort of thing. And that Becca is there—"

Astley starts to say something, but Nick lifts his hand to signal that he isn't done talking yet. Astley stops, but I can sense that he's getting more than just a teeny bit annoyed at Nick.

Nick continues, "Plus, they'll never be good enough, Zara. You know that. We would need hundreds more people to make a difference."

"We could have a tweet up," I half kid, and then I explain to Astley that there's a social networking site where random strangers post short updates and links. Sometimes they agree to meet in massive groups to do strange things, like act out a zombie apocalypse. Both Nick and Astley snort at my idea. Astley's snort is shocked and Nick's is amused. For a second, it's like the old Nick is back—the one who thought I was funny and smart, stubborn but worth it; the one who believed I had a soul and that we had a future together that didn't just involve fighting off the evil kind of pixies.

"Is everything okay?" Amelie's voice comes from behind Astley. "The wolf snuck on somehow. I didn't smell him."

The woman in the senator suit, sitting on the aisle diagonally behind Astley, gives us a look. I can't even imagine what she's thinking.

"I have a few tricks," Nick says. He smiles like he's proud of it. I smile back. And he sees me do it and his smile leaves his face in a slow torturous movement of lips. He focuses all his attention on me. "No matter how I feel about your turning, I couldn't let you do something so dangerous alone."

"She is not alone," Astley barks, no longer masking his anger.

Nick looks him up and down and there's no mistaking the intent. It's all about sizing up another guy, seeing if he's worthy. The muscle in his cheek twitches and he says, "She *is* alone."

Astley flies out of his seat, pushing himself up until he's a mere inch away from Nick, who is taller and broader. They stand there for half a second and if they could breathe fire and ice at each other, I swear they would. Amelie whispers a curse and tries to move forward. The lady in the aisle seat gasps.

"You don't even know how to protect her," Nick growls.

"*She* doesn't need protecting," I burst in, referring to myself in the third person and trying to unbuckle my seat belt. My hands aren't behaving.

Astley talks as if I've said nothing. All his focus is on Nick. "I know how to love her. That is more than you."

Love? Something in my stomach seems to flip and fall. I finally unclick my seat belt and start to stand up.

Just then, almost on cue, the flight attendant scoots up to us and says, "We really can't be blocking the aisle. I'm going to have to ask you to return to your seats."

And miracle of miracles, they do.

Astley and I sit there for a second, both of us staring straight ahead at the seat backs in front of us.

Finally he goes, "Well, that was awkward."

"Yeah." I reach forward and trace the square of the monitor screen with my finger. It's shaking.

He swallows. His own hand lifts up like it's going to touch mine, but at the last second he pulls it back, rests it on his leg, and says, "I apologize."

"You don't need to."

His eyes close. He pushes his head into the seat. "Yes, yes I do. You are not some prize to fight over. You may be the queen to my king, but that does not mean that I should battle over you like some—like some—" He can't find the word, I guess, because he doesn't finish his sentence. "It is just infuriating sometimes to deal with all these emotions that I have for you when your heart does not belong to me. That is not your fault. I do not blame you, Zara. You must love whom you want to love, but it is a bit of a distraction at the moment, and I need to be in top form for what is to come, as do you, as do all of us."

I move my hand, brush a piece of his blondish hair out of his face. My fingertips graze his skin. He is so brave, tries so hard to be good, to let me make my own decisions. I lean toward his ear and whisper, "I am so lucky to be your queen."

His eyes flash bluer as he turns to look at me. I can't believe I almost lost him to that poison. I can't believe it's taken me so long to know how I really feel.

"Zara—" His voice breaks on my name.

Smiling at him, I nod. "I am. I am honored and lucky and so very glad."

I sit back in my seat, wrap my hands around his arm, and lean my head against it, letting my head and my heart rest.

"You are a magnificent pixie," he whispers into the hair on the top of my head. "I have never known a pixie quite like you."

LANDING ANNOUNCEMENT ON FLIGHT 132 TO
ICELAND
Flight Attendant: Weather at Reykjavik is zero degrees Celsius
with some broken clouds, which we are working to fix before
we land. As you disembark, please gather all your belong-
ings. This includes children and significant others.

We land in Iceland, land of super-short days and super-beautiful
people. We are going to spend the night in Reykjavik and then
journey to the volcano resort area tomorrow morning. Last time
we were here, Astley and I stayed at an adorable hotel that was
really modern, like IKEA times a hundred, but I fell out a window there. So this time we're staying at a Hilton that's about five
minutes away from the center of town.

Issie and I share a room of epic proportions. Two seconds
after we step inside she pretty much screams in delight and collapses on the gray covers of the king-sized bed while I open the
curtains to the huge window that covers an entire wall.

"You can see the ocean, I guess," I say, staring into the
darkness.

"All I see is dark and city lights." She sits up and then joins me peering out. She gives up trying and spins around, probably so she can have a better look at the rich wallpaper and the black modern-lined desk and chairs and headboard. "It's very swankified. I feel like a celebrity."

I nod. "I know. Astley's completely slumming it in Bedford. You should see his treehouse place in New York."

I let myself think about the other home he told me about on the Island of Skye and for a second imagine what it would be like to walk through that azalea garden with him, holding hands maybe, seals barking in the ocean, the sun beating down, no snow anywhere. I miss the sun, and flowers. If the Ragnarok happens, people will never enjoy that again.

We've already changed into our pajamas by the time Astley comes to the room to say good night. I'm wearing flannel bunny pajama bottoms and a T-shirt. He's still in his street clothes. His eyes are soft and kind and worried and strong all at the same time as he says hello. I wish they would just stay one color.

"You still wear your anklet," he says to me.

"Nick gave it to me."

"I know."

"You want me to not wear it?" My tone is uncomfortable.

Issie's been sitting at her desk Skyping with Devyn. She hops up and grabs her laptop, carrying it carefully as she scurries away. "I'm just going to talk to Devyn in the bathroom. Yeah. That's not weird or anything. We do it all the time."

As soon as the bathroom door shuts gently behind her, Astley strides across the room. He stops at the window, puts his forehead against the glass, tilting his head so his brow is the only thing that touches. I walk over there too, sigh, and wrap my arms around his back, rest my head against the softness of his shirt.

"You're hugging me," he whispers.

"I know."

He turns around so I'm no longer the big spoon and we're in a regular hug. His chin rests on my head. I breathe in the smell of him: soap and dinner. It feels so good to just rest against him. It feels so right.

"You are a very good hugger," I say.

"So are you." His words move against my hair. "I would never ask you to take off the piece of jewelry."

"Even though Nick gave it to me?"

"Especially since he gave it to you. I know what importance you place upon it. It represents things to you, things that mean a lot."

His heart beats beneath my ear, a slow, steady thump. That heart is so kind, so important. Shifting, I put my hand against his chest so I can feel it beat. One thump. Another. It sounds so strong, but it's just as vulnerable as mine.

"You are the nicest person ever," I say.

"Hardly." He kisses the top of my head and breaks away. "Good night, Zara. Thank you for helping me stop this, for being my queen, for accepting the pixie in me and in you. You make me so much stronger."

I shrug. "That's just 'cause of the pixie blood."

He opens the door to leave. The hallway is brightly lit behind him. It makes it hard for me to see his face, which is now in shadow, as he says, "Partly. And partly just because you believe in me."

Issie and I huddle together all night. Every once in a while, I touch the anklet Nick gave me. It reminds me that I was loved once. Why should I need that? I shouldn't. Still, I keep it on.

We drive out the next morning in a rented van that fits all of us. The landscape of Iceland in winter is all shades of white and gray with mountains of black occasionally thrown in. It's beautiful and austere and stunning. The sky is wide open above us.

"There it is," Astley says, pointing to a mountain sprouting out of land that's been deforested volcanic ash. Efforts to stop erosion are under way and I read that they've planted grass and are trying to fertilize the soil somehow, but the land is heaved by frost and battered by wind and it's a battle.

The white mountain reminds me of an upside-down boat.

"It's a series of craters," Amelie says. "Since the year 874 there have been at least twenty eruptions, which makes it the country's most active volcano, or at least one of them. It's 1,491 meters high, which translates to approximately 4,892 feet."

"Devyn replacement," Issie whispers.

I snort and keep staring at the mountain.

"It just looks like a mountain," Nick says, speaking my own thoughts, "not like a gateway to Hel."

"Immediately after the mountain's eruption in 1104, Cistercian monks told many stories claiming exactly that," Amelie says.

I remember something from my own research. "Benedict, this monk guy, said that Hekla was the prison of Judas."

"Judas?" Issie asks.

"From the Bible. Judas was one of Jesus's apostles. He was the one who betrayed him," I tell Issie, who is Jewish in descent, but the nearest synagogue is in Bangor, which is super-far away from Bedford, so they tend not to go. I have a logic jump, an aha kind of moment. "And if you think about it, that's weird because Loki is the god that betrayed the other gods in Norse mythology and he's trapped in Hel."

"Unless you free him," Nick says.

Amelie turns in the chair and stares him down. "The queen will not free him."

I smile to myself. I like how Astley's people are my people now too, and even though they know I have total goofball tendencies, they still have faith in me. Becca told me that when I risked my life for Astley, when I voluntarily gave him my energy, it sealed my place as queen.

We are going to stay at some hut in Landmannalaugar, and then snowcat to the mountain. Landmannalaugar is miles from the mountain, and the road is usually closed in winter, I guess, but Astley has paid people to get us in. We have supplies in the trunk of the car. Through the use of insane amounts of cash, he has managed to procure the snowcat and a cottage called Gil, which holds twenty-four people and is heated with gas ovens. We will sleep in sleeping bags.

When we arrive, the cottage looks cute and smallish. Inside, it is full of wood and utilitarian bunk beds with solid permanent wood ladders.

"It's adorable in a rustic-place-where-we're-going-to-die way," Issie says, plopping her sleeping bag down in the middle of a low bunk.

"Very."

There are other cottages nearby, but all look abandoned. The wind whistles through the area, making it even more foreboding. I shiver and meet Nick's eyes as he sets down a box of food on the little countertop in the kitchen area.

"You sure about this?" he asks. "Going to Hel voluntarily? We can still go home, Zara. Maybe start over. I feel like we're just forging ahead without really being sure what is going on."

I rub my hands together. "We need to figure out how to stop all this before it's too late."

But part of me knows that for some things it is too late. It's too late for Nick and me. I just don't want it to be too late for the world.

Amelie is her normal no-nonsense self as we gather together in the main area of the cabin. She reminds me of my mom when my mom does hospital business. It's all agenda and steps and forward motions. Amelie talks about provisions and strategies in finding the entrance to Hel given the fact that it is so snowy and icy and the terrain is so treacherous that there are warnings posted throughout the area. I zone out a bit. Through the large front windows the mountains of Iceland loom, volcanic, angry, ready to erupt. Surprisingly different colors peek through in places where the snow has blown off. Some mountains are pink. Some are blue. It's wild and wonderful and if I weren't already so worried about everything, I would be happy dancing over the beauty of it all. The nearby lake is probably gorgeous, but it's covered with ice. The Icelandic sunlight gives the entire land-scape a sort of hazy appearance.

"Devyn texted me right before we left the city," Issie says as she flops into a square, modern-looking orange chair. She grabs a white pillow and clutches it to her chest like it's a shield that will protect her from the world. "We have no reception here though."

I settle into a chair next to her and resist the urge to grab a pillow of my own. Instead, I cross my legs, fix the lace on my boot. Issie lets go of the pillow and starts trying to fix her own boots. She's no good at shoe tying. Sad fact, but true.

"Let me help you," I say, reaching down and taking over. I pause to check out the two people standing at the front door talking in Icelandic. They are tall and happy looking with blond-ish hair. The man has his arm around the woman's waist. Issie looks over at them and sighs.

"You miss Devyn?" I ask.

She nods and wiggles her foot. "But I'm glad I'm here."

"Yeah?"

"Very yeah." She laughs. "It's nice to not have to worry about you dying all the time without me. And I miss Devyn but you know . . . Guys or men or boys or whatever you want to call them are important but girl friends are just as or even more, you know?"

She smiles at me, revealing her tiny white teeth, and her eyes crinkle at the corners.

"I know," I say, smiling back. "We haven't had enough time together."

"Too busy killing off baddies, saving rotten boyfriends, and trying to stop the apocalypse," she quips. "It's hard to get in enough us time."

"So true." She kisses the side of my head as I say it and I can't help blurting, "You are the best friend ever, Issie."

"Ha! You are."

While we wait for Astley and Nick to finish talking to the Ice-landic couple who run the snowcat, I think about stuff.

There are certain things that have to happen in order for the world to end. This is according to Devyn, who has had the dreadful task of trying to collate and make sense of all the dif-ferent Norse mythology we've found in books and online. The problem with all the research is that it doesn't all correspond. Myths contradict each other. But there are a few things that he thinks are right.

1. Loki has to be free.
2. There will be three winters without a summer, which we totally haven't had, which is nice. Although Devyn thinks this might only be a metaphor. Devyn is a pessimist.
3. There will be huge battles around the globe, which is no abnormal thing. When have people ever not had huge battles? It makes me sad.
4. There will be natural disasters. This is always happening too, unfortunately.
5. A giant wolf, freed from his bonds, will swallow the sun and then his brother, the moon. I worry that this "sun" refers to my biological father, since Fenrir swallowed him. I mean, he *is* a son of someone.
6. This huge serpent, Jörmungandr, will break through land and the sea will collapse into the land.
7. A ship made of human nails will set sail.
8. The sky will break into two.

So all in all, it's almost positive. That's what I tell everyone now that the snowcat people are gone and we're grouped together again.

"I mean, none of that has happened except for Fenrir being free, but he's hardly eaten the moon," I say to Issie and Astley as we walk through the snow toward an equipment cottage where there's some cross-country skis for us to use. Amelie said it's impossible to get where we want without them. The snowcat people gave Astley directions to get them and they are going to come back tomorrow to bring us and our skis up the mountain because we've already used up so much daylight.

"It makes it all seem a little less dire, doesn't it?" Issie asks as we all trundle across the uneven earth toward the green equipment hut.

Astley ushers us to the door as Issie continues, "I mean, it would be if giants hadn't shown up, if that Hel woman hadn't told Zara she was being tested, if the prophecy didn't say that it was Zara who would stop or start it. I'd call that dire."

I resist the urge to say, "Way to think positive," and instead hold my breath as Astley says, "Actually in Old Norse, 'Ragnarok' is a compound of two different words. *Ragna* is the genitive plural of *regin*, which means 'gods' or 'ruling powers.'"

"Fascinating," I tease, but it actually kind of is.

Astley keeps going on. "The second part of the term, *rok*, has a multitude of meanings, including 'development, origin, cause, relation, fate, end.' This opens it up for interpretation, obviously."

Issie jumps up in the snow. "He sounds like a Vulcan."

We're all standing outside this big metal door that says something in Icelandic and then EQUIPMENT in English.

Astley keeps talking. "However, in the *Poetic Edda*, a different form twice appears, *ragnarök(k)r*. *Rök(k)r* means 'twilight.' This makes one wonder, especially since it means 'renewal of the divine powers.'"

I've been reaching for the door, but instead I stop and stare at him, trying to figure out the kernel of worry that's suddenly lodged inside of my chest. "That would explain it, wouldn't it?" I finally say, terribly slowly.

"Explain what?" Issie asks.

"Why some pixies want the end to happen," I start.

Issie finishes for me. "It's because they think it will make them more powerful, I bet. Or maybe they are sick of hiding who they are, living in a world full of iron."

"Exactly." Astley smiles at us all like he's proud that we have brain cells. Then his expression switches to something deadly serious. "And they obviously do not care who dies or what destruction occurs. Just that they achieve their goal."

"Sounds like typical pixie behavior to me," Issie says, and then catches my eye and adds, "You guys excluded, obviously."

"Obviously," Astley echoes, bitterness soaking his voice. He grabs the door and pushes it open. The hut is dark, but he steps into it. I follow right behind him. I'm barely inside when the door slams shut behind me, and Issie's clutching my arm as my pixie senses try to figure out what's going on.

"Zara," she whispers, "everything just got very dark and very creepy."

And then it gets worse.

FBI INTERNAL MEMO
Among the missing: fifteen male juveniles, eight female
juveniles. Local cattle have been mutilated. Evidence is
scarce. —AGENT WILLIS

Uttering an almost-swear, I flip around, grab the doorknob, and
try to yank it back open. The air reeks of pixie and anger.

"Issie!" I have to protect her. My hand rushes along the wall,
looking for a light switch. There must be a light switch. "Hold
on, Issie!"

"It's a trap," Astley, aka Captain Obvious, sputters into the
darkness.

As soon as he speaks, noises buzz through the air like arrows
zipping toward us.

I scream his name, trying to warn him and at the same time
trying to figure out what's happening, which is pretty much
impossible to do because it's so ridiculously dark. I reach for my
cell. If I can flip it open it'll give us a little light, but before I can
reach it, Astley slams his body over mine, covering it, protecting

it with his own. And that's when the arrows start hitting, one after another, after another. They slice through his parka and into his skin. I can hear the pain of it, feel it as he shudders from the impact. His body starts falling down, pulled by gravity onto the hard floor, which seems made of some kind of stone. Twisting around, I try to catch him, manage to wrap my arms around him a bit before the first arrow slams into my shoulder. Pain spirals out, but I'm so mad I can ignore it, so scared it seems like nothing. Then another hits, and another, and it's like I haven't slept in eight hundred years and I suddenly really, really need to sleep. They must have put something on the arrows, something to cause drowsiness. Just drowsiness, I hope, and not death. I don't know . . . I just know the darkness is getting darker and my hands can't find Astley . . . anymore . . . and I'm . . .

Gone.

It's the smell of my own burning flesh that wakes me. It's a nasty smell that can rouse you out of unconsciousness no matter how deep that unconsciousness is. My head is drooping and I'm staring at my feet, which are on a stone floor. There's some sort of fluorescent lighting coming from above me giving everything a yellowish ugly glow. Only one of my boots is still on. My left sock stretches red and woolly as I cautiously move my toes, trying to regain my orientation, trying to remember what happened. There's an arrow sticking out of my shoulder. There's another in my arm.

"She's waking up already, how quick," says someone with a high, bell-like voice. It sounds familiar. It sounds like Isla, Astley's mother. Lovely.

Lifting my head so I can actually see the room confirms it.

She's over by the sprawled-out form of Astley. She's yanking arrows out of him. He doesn't move. He's bloody, unconscious, but I can feel his breath as if it's my own, so I know that he's still alive, my king. Thank God. I try to calm my breath as I look at the metal door that slammed behind us.

Issie is over by the door, tied up, with duct tape over her mouth. Anger grows inside of me as I take in the rip in her coat sleeve, her big scared eyes, the dirt on her face. An arrow sticks out of the forearm of her puffy coat. It's my responsibility to keep her safe, and here I am freaking stuck to a wall, groggy and captured.

I don't like this.

Okay, that's an understatement.

I am really hating this.

The rest of the room holds cross-country skiing equipment, big and white hotel towels, bins full of toiletries. It's a supply building. They lured us into a supply building? Maybe the snow-cat people who told Astley about the skis in here were paid off, which is horrible. How can people do this sort of thing for money? And now that the lights are on, I can see that there are three male pixies all dressed in wool sweaters. They crowd around Isla, putting chains on Astley. One more, a brooding ugly giant of a man, is closer to me.

Nick will be trying to get in here once we've been gone too long. He'll try to bash down that door, but it looks pretty strong and who knows how long I've been out. He may have already given up. Amelie would think to go find a key. Maybe they'll be here soon . . . that is, if they're still alive. Swallowing hard, I promise myself that they have to still be alive if we are. It's obvious that Isla wanted us for some reason—I just don't know the reason yet.

Isla's tiny, golden-haired self yanks one more arrow out of Astley and then she nods to her pixie henchmen, who drag him even farther away from me and a tiny bit closer to Issie. He doesn't even grunt. His whole body is defenseless and still.

"You could at least put a towel under his head," I say, nodding toward the mountains of them. "There are enough."

She gives me her attention and melodramatically raises an eyebrow. "That's very sweet, Zara."

"What can I say?" I spunk back. "I'm a caregiver by nature."

The larger of the pixie men grabs a thick white towel and shoves it underneath Astley's head. The entire time he does this, Isla watches me. Occasionally her tongue darts out between her lips, which makes me think of a snake, or Jared Leto during a television interview. And while she watches me, I desperately try to come up with a plan. My cell phone is still in my pocket, which means nothing because there is no signal here. The only weapons I can see other than my own hands and feet are some cross-country skis and poles that hang from the walls. To get them, I'd have to get my wrists free in order to remove the ankle chains. Struggling against the binds, which are simple iron chains, sears my skin even more. Gasping from the pain, I try to think of another way. We should have taken extra anti-iron pills this morning. Our stupidity only makes me angrier and more desperate.

Why doesn't Astley move?

Why doesn't anyone come help us?

All sorts of horrible scenarios of what's going to happen to Issie and Astley twist around in my head, which only serves to freak me out when I need to be calm, need to find a way out of this.

Isla wipes her hands on a towel, which she delicately folds back into a perfect square before depositing it on the floor. All that time she took making it perfect was wasted. It crumples and lies there flat and discarded, close to Astley, who still doesn't move.

Move, I try to order him. *Move.*

His finger twitches, but that is all.

Issie shuffles an inch closer to him. She makes eyes at me.

Isla's voice shifts my attention to her, which is good because I don't want to give Issie away. "You expect me to kill you, don't you? You think I followed you out here where there would be fewer witnesses?"

She steps on another towel as she flits closer to me. It slips a bit on the floor but she doesn't lose her balance, just holds my gaze as I don't answer her.

"I do not need to kill you," she says, smiling.

Her breath smells of mint and basil. It is beautiful breath and she is a beautiful creature, but beauty doesn't equal good and it certainly doesn't equal sane.

"Did you hear what I said?" she asks. Her voice loses its lilt, so she's losing patience with me. "I said that I do not need to kill you. Are you listening to me? You don't seem to be paying attention."

"I heard." I swallow hard. My thoughts are scattering about like the towels.

"Well, would you like to know why?" she asks.

For a second I'm not sure if she's asking if I want to know why my thoughts are so scattered, but then I realize that she's asking whether I want to know why she won't need to kill me. I force my voice to sound noncommittal and say, "Not really."

Anger ripples off her, red and full of heat. I try to focus on

Astley, give him some of my power somehow, the way he did to me when I fought Frank, the way I did when he was poisoned. If I can make him stronger, then maybe he can move, attack them from behind—

She interrupts my thoughts again. "The point is not to kill you but to make my son weak and to torture him in the process. The poison was a good attempt. But you are too strong together. So the question becomes, how do I make him weak if poison did not accomplish that goal? I take away his queen. I've done it before." She smiles. "But that way was too easy . . . killing her like that. Instead, I have watched how his heart aches because he cannot attain you—not for real—because of your foolish pining for that wolf. Silly girl. It will be even harder for Astley's fragile little emotions if you are not his kind. He will lose you a little more. Love is his weakness."

Guilt pushes into my heart as she takes a fingernail and taps my chest. The tiny crescent of it hits just below my collarbone. She's right. I hurt Astley constantly because I hadn't loved him back the way he needed me to. And why? It's Astley's face I see now when I close my eyes. It's Astley I hope for right now, right at this scary moment. Not Issie, not Nick or Amelie on the other side of the door somewhere. It's Astley I worry about the most. Now that it's too late, my feelings are suddenly, completely clear. I love Astley.

"Don't you hurt him," I say like I'm in a position to demand anything, tied to a wall, wrists sizzling.

She lifts an eyebrow as if to say I am too silly for words. And I have to admit that it's nice she's stopped talking, but then she starts again. And the eyebrow lifting is a little overdone, anyway, and . . .

She says, "Do you know what I shall do?"

"Talk me to death?"

"Snippy. Nice. You always are spunky, so unlike my son." She spits out the word "son" as she trails her fingernail up to my chin and then grabs my face violently in her hand. "I shall make you human again."

I stutter, trying to turn my head out of her grasp, but I'm weak. The pain from my wrists, the iron in my system, has made me vulnerable. "Human?"

"You did not know I could do that, did you?" She flings my head to the side as she lets go of me. My ear pounds against the wall. Pain spirals through my head and it makes it hard to focus, but I manage to keep listening, and she, of course, keeps talking. "Let me inform you of something, Zara of the White, Zara of the stars. I collect clocks because that is where people of our race have always hid our secrets. We hide papers, spells, inside the mechanisms of time. It's fitting, I think, to hide the secrets of the past inside the machines that count us into the future. Tick-tock."

I slowly move my head back to look at her. She's smiling. Her lipstick has smeared just the tiniest bit and left a dot of pink on one of her front teeth.

"And I just thought it was because you were crazy," I sputter through the pain. "Maybe had some weird clock fetish."

"Never underestimate the people you think are crazy. They are the ones who see things you fail to see." She cocks her head and switches gears. "The point is that in one of those clocks I found out a secret. Any pixie can make a pixie if they kiss them with intent, but only queens can take a pixie and turn them back into a feeble nothing."

"Back?" I don't follow her.

"Back to human."

I must stare at her blankly for a second, because she smiles and taps my cheek gently. "You're in shock, dear. Close your mouth. You're gaping. It is unattractive."

"So . . ." I try to wrap my head around it. "You're going to unpixie me?"

She reaches up a long, delicate arm and pets me on the head. "Exactly."

I have a tiny and quick internal debate about whether or not I should ask her how this process happens, and as I do the wind rushes through a window that I hadn't noticed, blowing dust from the outside and pieces of dead grass across the floor. A mouse scuttles in the wall, probably looking for a safe place to hide from the cold or maybe to hide from us.

"Won't that keep me from starting the apocalypse?" I blurt.

She giggles. "So very stupid and so very wrong."

Issie scoots even closer to Astley. The pixie henchmen ignore her. She's human. She's obviously not a threat and Astley is unconscious, so even if she somehow manages to free him, what difference will that make? Still, I love her for trying. I just want her to be careful.

Isla's full focus is on me. A watch on her wrist ticks away seconds and then she asks, "Would you like to know what I have to do?"

I don't answer.

"A queen merely has to kiss with intention, just the same as before."

"You're going to kiss me?" I croak out the question. The thought is beyond revolting. Not because she's a girl, but because she's old and she's crazy-evil or maybe it's evil-crazy, one of the two.

She smiles. "I kiss you. You become human. Astley loses his power and the prophecy has no hope of becoming true."

Finally! She's finally said something important. "Prophecy?"

"You still don't know even that? But what can one expect from a group of heroes that can't even remember BiFrost is the bridge and not BiForst." She giggles. The mouse scuttles around some more. "So silly."

"It was both ways on the Internet," I spew back. "And the newspaper spelled it the BiForst way."

She arches an eyebrow. "The Internet? You base your defense against the apocalypse on information you've gathered from the Internet and a tiny local newspaper? Oh, that's so precious!"

She starts laughing for real this time, which really doesn't make me feel much better about myself, or the situation. If she's confident enough to laugh, then I really don't have a way out, do I? Issie's tied. Astley is passed out on the floor, bound up in iron, skin sizzling. There are two goons blocking the door that leads out of here, all massive muscle. There's been no sign of Nick and Amelie. And Isla is right in front of me, rubbing her hands together like she's about to get a brand-new clock or something.

"You just said that if I were human I could still start the apocalypse. But now you're saying that if I'm human the prophecy won't come true." Damn. She is so convoluted.

"The prophecy isn't about starting the apocalypse. It's about stopping it. If you are human you can no longer stop it." She backs up, away from me and closer to Astley, and pokes at him with her foot. Anger and despair flood into me as she says, "It's too bad he's unconscious. I'd like him to witness what I'm going to do to you. But at least the human will see. She'll be a witness to tell my son how horrible it was, how painful, how you screamed and begged for mercy. You will do that for me, won't you, Zara? You will scream? Or maybe just beg. I do have sensitive ears."

Swallowing hard, I wait as she approaches me. One step. Another step. Another. I look over at Astley and relief spreads into me. I don't want him to see this, I realize. I don't want any more hurt for him. He's endured so much. Just having a mother like this . . .

Her face hovers in front of me.

"Are you ready to be human?" she whispers.

The smell of lilacs engulfs me, overwhelming my senses. I don't answer, just close my eyes as her lips move closer. I turn my head, clench my own lips, though it won't matter. She snaps her fingers and the two goons stride away from the door and toward me. Large, strong hands move my head so I'm facing her again. She giggles and I can tell from the sound that she's just a couple inches from me. I try to think of some last-minute way to get away, some compelling argument to keep her from doing this, but sometimes you can't argue with crazy, sometimes you can't dissuade evil. Sometimes you just have to clench your lips, close your eyes, and pray. I focus on my power, the branches that Astley and I have twisted together. I try to take all the pixie energy in me and shape it into wings that take flight to Astley. I can almost imagine it, but then her lips touch mine.

Soft and minty smelling, they push against mine for a second before the sensation changes. Pain sizzles through my face and brain and then my body. Screaming, I jerk back against the cold wall, jerk sideways against the hands of the men, try to flee the kiss, but there's no escape, no escape at all. My hand yanks at the man closest to me, grabs fabric, rips at it, frantically trying to find something. I hear more scuttling of mice, the ticking of a clock, and Isla's giggle. A goon guy laughs. My heart slows. One beat. Another. I've failed. I've failed us all. Something wet touches my face. It's tears. My tears. I refuse to die like this. But no, it's not dying . . . I refuse to change like this.

My hand loses its hold on the fabric even as she keeps kissing me. Something skitters across the floor and hits my foot. Did Issie kick me a weapon? Blindly, I toe it up onto my boot and then kick whatever it is up into my hand, a maneuver I would never have been able to do as a human because I am not much of a soccer player. But for the moment I am still pixie and it works. Something cold and hard meets my fingers, which clutch at the metal of it. The back of my head knows what it is—a knife. It's a knife that must have been on the floor. Issie was going for that, not Astley. I clench it, solidify my grasp around it while the world spins. Opening my eyes, I see Isla's face, her beautiful, evil face that's kissing mine and that's when I do it—I plunge the knife into her chest. I plunge the knife and try to yell, but there's nothing left of me—no pixie left, maybe no human either.

And then my head implodes and I start to lose consciousness. The last thing I hear is Isla's scream, which far outlasts my own.

BEDFORD COUNTY SHERIFF'S DEPARTMENT
RELEASE
On 12–15 at approximately 1755 hours, RCC Dispatch
received a call from a woman in Trenton reporting a man
was whispering her name while she was in the parking lot at
the Bedford Marketplace.

When I wake up, I'm no longer hanging on the wall, but curled on the floor. Blood, probably my blood or Isla's, is splattered around me. Moaning, I try to sit up but fail. I must be human. I can't smell anything and I'm so terribly cold and alone feeling. It's like all my connections to the other pixies, to Astley, is just gone. Rolling onto my stomach, I do my best not to cry from the pain. Isla's men aren't here. Issie is still bound up by the door making "free me" noises and nodding her head toward the side of the room. That's when I realize that there's a blood trail leading to some stacked white towels. Isla's body is on the floor. She isn't moving.

From where he's still chained up on the floor, Astley stares at me with horrified eyes. I've killed his mother. I've orphaned him. I know she was evil, I know, but she was still his mom and I—I—

"I'm so sorry," my voice croaks out.

His lips shake. "I thought you had died, Zara. I thought . . ."

"Not yet," I say, staring at the iron around his wrists. The binds are so narrow, but so strong. It must be poisoning his system by now. That makes him the priority to free. "Let me get you loose."

But I can't walk. I have to crawl over there. It's not even really a crawl—more a drag punctuated by little moaning noises. Astley's eyes narrow as he watches me. I don't have to be a pixie to see how angry he is, how hard it is for him to witness how pathetic I am now. When I finally get close enough, Issie scooches over and I manage to free her hands. She rips the tape off her mouth but doesn't say anything, which makes me realize just how bad it is. When Issie is horrified she loses her voice.

She has lost her voice.

Even with Issie's help, it takes the last of my strength to get Astley free. The moment I do, he pulls me into his lap, pressing me against his chest, rocking me slightly. Issie huddles close too and grabs my hand, squeezing it tight.

"You killed her," Astley says.

"I'm so sorry."

"I wanted to kill her," he whispers desperately. "I wanted to kill her for what she did to you, for what she has done to all of us."

Isla lies there, unmoving, a beautiful, bloody shell of a woman. Her hair, as pale as a cloud, floats around her head, only the ends sullied by blood. And my own soul? My own body? It is full of webs and dusk, aches that seem to breathe too big for me to contain them any longer. How am I going to keep everyone safe if I'm human? How am I going to help Astley and our pixies? How can I do anything?

I've killed his mother.

I'm human.

I've killed his mother.

These facts just flap around and around in my head, one after the other, pushing everything else out. I should be wondering about Issie and Nick and the rest. I should be nursing Astley's emotions. I should be fixing things, doing things.

I'm human again.

I've killed Astley's mother.

"Can you change me back?" I whisper into his chest. My words cascade down into the air, waiting for an answer, afraid of an answer.

"Would you want that?" He rocks me in his arms, smooths back the hair from my forehead as I tilt my head up to look into his sad, tired face. "Would you want to be pixie again, be my queen? You know now what that means, truly know."

It means no matter how we felt about each other, we would be entwined forever. It means I would have to be responsible for all those other lives forever. It means that I would feel more, need more, sense more, and have to take a heck of a lot of anti-iron pills. I think about what it would mean for me to stay human. I can't fight well like this. I can't stop the apocalypse. I can't smell and hear as well, and Astley becomes weaker. But being a pixie means worrying about turning blue, worrying about hungers and needs and losing my humanity. "Does it matter what I want? It would be what's best, you know? I have a responsibility to you, to the pixies, to Issie and my friends."

A muscle twitches in Astley's cheek. His lips press hard against each other and tears spring to the corners of his eyes but don't leak out. "Yes, Zara. It does matter what you want. It matters very much."

Some sort of sob rattles around in my chest, but I refuse to let it out, refuse to let Astley see how much his words affect me.

Issie's hand squeezes mine and then she lets go, standing up and trying the door. She walks fine. I don't think they hurt her much. It's just her insides that are messed up. She's in shock, I bet. We're all in shock, and shock isn't going to do us much good. We need a plan. We need steps to take. We need to make this right, make me right.

"You have to change me back, Astley," I insist. My hand flutters up, touches the side of his face. It's so much effort just to move, just to touch him. I stare into his eyes and beg, "Do it now. Please."

His eyes soften. He moves his head so his lips brush against my forehead. It's the slightest of kisses, gentle and kind. He doesn't answer my request, just bundles me against him. Thanks to his pixie blood, the burns on his wrists are starting to heal already but the skin is pink and mottled. If he looks this bad, I must look so much worse. I can taste blood on my lips, see it on my hands. He moves across the concrete floor and up the three steps, bringing us to the door that goes outside. The air is dry and bitter. It's so cold. He pulls me in closer to his chest.

Issie isn't having any success with the door, which must be locked from the outside. She yanks her bobby pin out of her hair, the one that held her bangs back. Then she uses it to start working on the locking mechanism in the middle of the doorknob.

"What are we going to do?" I whisper at Astley like he'll have all the answers.

The hurt makes his green eyes deeper, more vivid. "We shall find a way, Zara. I promise you, we shall find a way."

But I am broken all the way down and for a second, only a second, I allow myself to think we won't, that we never will.

And just then, Issie manages to get the door open.

The cold and wind and sunlight stream into the room and she turns to us, smiling. "Got it!"

Her voice is so beautiful and still it doesn't give me hope.

ICELANDIC PRESS RELEASE
The National Police Commissioner will hold a news conference to discuss the increase of missing-persons cases in the
last few days.

It takes me two days to heal well enough to set out for Hel, which
we decide to do via vote. In some sort of weird twist, Astley is
against it and Nick is for it. Astley thinks that we should just
pack up, go home, and focus our efforts on keeping Bedford safe.
He wants to go to the Pixie Council and plead for help. Nick
rightly says that it hasn't done anything for us before. Nick thinks
that Isla's motivation for turning me human has more to do with
us being so close to Hel, so close to stopping the apocalypse.

"It's an act of desperation," he argues. "That means we have
to keep with the plan."

Amelie, Issie, and I agree.

"But why don't they just kill Astley then?" I ask.

"They must need him for something," says Nick. "Or they
are sentimental. Or they still hope to have him join their side."

"Oh yeah, changing his queen's a good way to do that."
Issie pulls her knees to her chest and rolls her eyes.

And then they argue about Issie and me staying here while
they search for Hel, but I refuse that option. So we wait an extra
day. I figure if I can walk, I can ski on the trail to the mountain,
which takes four hours to hike. Skiing is faster, even if I'm the
one who is doing it.

So I spend my first day as a human again on the bed with
Issie fluttering about. Astley flies off somewhere to get enough
of a signal to call home. Nick cooks. Amelie paces and patrols
outside, making sure there are no more threats.

The second day, I get up and stagger around, getting
stronger.

Being human again after being pixie is strange. It's like I've
lost another sense. I don't smell or see things as intensely. I
don't feel people's emotions as if I could grab them and hold
them in my hands.

But I don't miss the way I always felt right on the edge of
evil, that if my needs weren't controlled, then I would go feral
and violent, a crazy predator thing.

When the sun rises on the day we're going to ski and look for
Hel, I'm so stir-crazy I walk outside for a minute while everyone
gets ready.

The lake is no longer frozen. The heat from the nearby
volcano has warmed the water, broken the ice into massive sheets
that smash into each other. When the sides of one ice chunk
slides against another, it sounds like a roar. It makes me wish
Betty were here, that she wasn't still back in Maine battling and
training the others.

"We're leaving for Hel soon." Nick's voice startles me. He's snuck up behind me, and since I'm human I didn't hear.

My heart slows down so I turn and answer. "I know. I just wanted a second."

"Alone?"

"Yeah."

He's got a huge navy blue parka on with yellow insulation and a dark gray skull hat. Even his fingers are sheathed in puffy men's skiing-type gloves. His dark eyes crinkle at the corners as he smiles just the tiniest of smiles as he looks at me. "You aren't under his influence anymore."

"What do you mean by that?" I turn back to the lake, stare at the ice slowly moving on the surface of the water. Pieces of the solid fall into the liquid, but it's all just water no matter what its form.

"I mean his pixie power over you is gone." He squats and pulls at a broken branch that's been sticking up out of the snow. It reminds me once again of how Astley's and my branches were entwined. Nick holds it in his hand for a second, almost like he's balancing the weight of it, and then he chucks it toward the lake. The branch lands on an ice chunk and then skitters across it.

"He's still my friend, Nick."

"But that doesn't— It's not the same as him being your king."

That's true. Astley won't feel it when I need him anymore. I won't feel it when he needs me. We won't be able to read each other's emotions so easily. The world as a human is much thinner than as a pixie. It's like watching a movie on your phone versus seeing real-life events.

I miss being less vulnerable to cold and super-strong, stuff that went with being pixie. I miss it a lot.

It is nice to be able to touch iron, though. It is nice to not worry about randomly turning blue or feeling your emotions race so close to the surface all the time, ready to explode.

Ice cracks into ice. A bird squeals overhead.

We stand there for a minute, just watching the water slosh in tiny waves up onto the shore. It comes in and out, predictable because it always moves in those two directions, but unpredictable because you never know exactly how far into the beach the water will go. It crashes against some blackened algae-type stuff and slides back out to the lake.

Nick grabs my hand in his giant one. It's hard to feel his fingers through the glove, but I know the shape of them, their warmth and roughness. It's a good memory.

"You don't love me anymore, do you?" he asks. His voice breaks with emotion.

I close my eyes but don't let go of his hand. "When I needed you most, you weren't there for me, Nick."

Just saying it aloud makes it so much more real, and each word solids my heart just a bit more, making it seem less like something that beats and breathes and more like ice on the lake. He wasn't there when I needed him.

He moves closer, facing me. His free hand goes to my hair, brushes it away from my face. "What do you mean when you needed me the most? When was that? When you were shot? When Mrs. Nix died? I was in Valhalla, Zara. I couldn't be there and I am so sorry for that, baby."

My eyes meet his. His eyes are deep brown and beautiful, earnest and fierce. How can he have eyes like that and not understand?

"That's not what I mean." My lips dry out suddenly. They

are hard to move. "I mean when you learned I was pixie. I needed you to love me then. But you didn't. You were too busy with your hate."

His hand goes to my shoulder. "I did still love you then, Zara."

"No. You walked away. You left." My words break into crying things. "You told me I was soulless."

The waves keep breaking small against the shore. A car drives down the road toward the hotel, the radio is on so loudly that the bass beat thuds through closed windows.

"I left because I was jealous," he says. "Not because you were a pixie."

I think he's lying, but I'm not sure. If he is lying, he's probably lying to himself too.

"Whatever." I twist away from him, walk two steps, and realize I don't have the will to walk anymore, to move anywhere. I crouch down instead and this time I'm the one who grabs a piece of twisted driftwood. The water has stripped it of its bark, and insects or lake creatures or something have bored holes through it. I wonder what's happened to my branch now that I'm not a pixie. Did it separate? Is it all alone like this poor piece of broken tree? I don't know. I don't know if it matters. Nothing matters. My fingers trace the joint where a nub of a branch once was. That's not true. Things matter. Keeping people safe matters.

"We have more important things to do right now," I say. "And when that's done we can fix everything else."

"*If* we survive, Amnesty." He uses his old nickname for me. A splinter of driftwood sticks in my glove. "And what if we don't? We can't leave this unfinished."

"Yes, we can. Life isn't a television show, Nick. There aren't neat little bows to tie things up in the end. There isn't a soundtrack to cue the laughs and the murmurs of agreement. There's no way of always knowing what the right thing is. No clear endings." I stand up and yank out the splinter.

Refusal to believe me is written on his face. Then a slow smile moves across his features. His head moves slowly, and he kisses me on the cheek.

"You think so strangely," he says.

I think strangely? I ponder that for a second and then I step to the side, place my hand on his shoulder. "Everything inside me hurts."

"I know," he says. "I hurt too."

We go back to the hut where everyone else waits for us. Amelie's face is drawn and strained, which makes me wonder if Astley has chewed her out about the ambush or if it's because I've been alone with Nick. She's so protective of Astley. Either way, it's hard to look at her. Issie rushes across the room and hugs me, acting all happy rah-rah cheerleader, but the moment our bodies touch she whispers in my ear, "You okay? If you are not okay, I will kill these macho alpha boys for you. Got it?"

It makes me laugh the tiniest of bits to imagine her trying to kill either of them.

And Astley just looks at me, eyes full of sorrow and loss. I wonder if that's what my eyes look like too.

"We have the skis," he says, slugging on a backpack and handing one to Nick and one to me, "and provisions. It should take a couple hours depending on our pace."

I'm the one who will slow us down.

"And we're sure this is the way to Hel?" Nick asks.

Astley meets his eyes. "Are we ever sure of anything?"

I don't know if he's just talking about Hel or about whether or not he loves me anymore. Maybe he's like Nick. Maybe he can't love me if I change from fae back to human. Maybe everybody's like that. I don't know. All I know is that the inside of me hurts and that I have to ignore those feelings and just push on.

I've never been cross-country skiing before, but Nick and Issie are pros and have obviously mastered the fine art of simultaneously moving their arms and legs when they were toddlers or something. After a couple minutes, I get a handle on the whole thing and manage to adjust to the fact that my heel is free in the boot, which is totally unlike downhill skiing.

Astley uses a forward gliding motion with his skis, heading straight ahead, and Nick uses a V shape, which makes it almost seem like he's Rollerblading or ice-skating. It figures that they even ski differently. I try both ways and am equally bad at each, which also figures.

The sky here is such a brilliant blue, a crisp, amazing contrast to the snowy terrain and the glacial look of everything. Our bright parkas make us obvious dots on the landscape, and even though I know how fierce Amelie, Nick, and Astley can be, I still feel nervous. A good sniper hiding on the mountain face could pick us off, one by one. We don't talk much the entire time and occasionally take breaks for water and granola bars. My body aches and I'm not sure if it's from the cardio workout or just because I'm human again. I don't complain, though, because I'm not taking the chance that everyone will try to force me back. I'm not going back, even though it's so cold that Issie's lips are tinting kind of blue and I bet my lips look the same.

When we get to the base of the volcano, a sort of panicky feeling hits both Issie and me at the same time.

We stop and simultaneously say, "We should go back."

Our mouths drop open in shock.

Amelie cocks her head. "What?"

"I have a bad feeling." I try to explain while scanning the landscape, which is pretty barren and dead looking. "I mean, that's normal probably when you're standing at the bottom of an active volcano, but it's something different, something uh . . ."

"It's like how you feel right before a test for a class you've blown off all trimester," Issie explains. Her teeth chatter when she talks, so we have to pay really close attention.

"Or like a hand pushing on your chest, holding you back," I add.

Steam rises from the volcano. There are no birds in sight.

Nick cocks his head, looking around. "I'm not turning wolf. I'd turn if you were in danger."

"You didn't turn before the ambush," Astley says.

Nobody has an answer for that.

"Well, it's not perfect," Nick finally admits.

The feeling just increases.

"Maybe we should go. Maybe we should listen to their guts," Nick says.

Amelie shakes her head. "No. It's only affecting the humans, and humans are the least perceptive and the most easily influenced."

"What are you saying?" I bristle. I mean, I know what she's saying, but she could say it a little more nicely.

"I've heard that some very powerful fae—or gods, or whatever you'd like to call them—can bespell a place so humans do not come too near." She whips off her hat and cocks her head, listening, before she continues. I wonder what she hears, and miss my own pixie super-hearing. "They make you want to leave, make it feel dangerous, so humans don't accidentally walk into their homes or interrupt ceremonies or such."

"Can pixies do this?" Nick asks. He leans forward on his ski poles, using them to bear his weight.

"No," Astley answers while surveying the area. "It is a good clue though. It means that the entrance to Hel might truly be here. I have learned recently to doubt everything."

Even without my pixie powers of perception, I know that he's thinking about all the times his mother has tricked us, the people we've lost because we'd been so sure we were on the right path.

Astley focuses in on Issie. "Which way do you not want to go?"

She bites at the corner of her lip, thinking, and then points to the left. "There."

"You, Zara?" Astley's eyes meet mine.

"The same."

"Then that is where we should go," Nick announces, finishing Astley's reasoning. "We'll go where your gut tells us not to."

Issie gives me pleading eyes as Nick and Amelie rush forward and I try to stop them. "I'm not sure this is—"

But they've already moved ahead. Dread fills me as Issie grabs my arm. Her pole dangles from her wrist and bumps against my shin.

"I don't feel good about this," she says. Her voice is urgent and her eyes wide. Snow blows across our skis.

"It's either follow them or stay here," I say, trying to be rational despite the gnawing in my stomach. I try to have that same force of will, that same leadership gusto crap that I had when I was a pixie. "We can do this, Is."

She nods and we set off after the other three, putting our skis in the path they've created in the snow. The volcano steams. The air smells hot and cold all at once. The landscape wavers, full of snow and steam and fear. I keep checking to make sure Issie is right behind me.

The others have stopped and we stop too. The cold makes breathing hard, like icicles are puncturing my lungs with every breath, but I try to look calm despite my racing heart.

Issie's voice shrieks out behind me. "We really should go!"

Amelie lunges for her as Issie starts to turn around. She gets a hand on Issie's arm, a tight grip keeps her from running.

"We must be really close now," she says, her dreadlocks swinging. "The panic is worse."

"I am not panicking!" Issie announces in a completely panicked voice.

Astley starts mumbling some words in a language I don't know, but I think it's Norse again, Old Norse. Amelie keeps her eye on me like I might try to bolt too and says, "He has an incantation for removing glamours. We aren't sure it will work because this seems so strong."

"He never told me he could do that," I say.

"I bet he hasn't told you a lot of things," Nick says, and I can tell he's thinking about all the flack I gave him because he kept his parents' death a secret from me.

"He hasn't had time." Amelie glares at him and loosens her grip on Issie a bit. Just as she does the world starts to rumble like an earthquake, but not quite, because there's no accompanying noise like there is when you're in a house. There are no dishes to shake, no foundations that quiver, no wood straining to maintain its integrity.

And then—poof—the world is gone and we are dropping into some sort of darkness.

"Zara!" Issie's voice shrieks through the darkness, but I can't see her. I can't see anyone, feel anything. It is a void except for Issie's voice.

Just a second later, I land with a thud, back on the snow. Only it's not the same snow we were just on. There's no volcano looming. Instead there are frost-heavy trees everywhere. One tree that is larger than a skyscraper seems to hold up the dark purple sky with its frost-dripping limbs. This has to be Hel. I have only a second to think it before my attention flies to Nick, who has changed, snarling, into a wolf. He leaps in front of me. Issie and Amelie are trying to untangle themselves from each other. And Astley? Astley is behind me, looking the same direction that Nick is looking. Both of them are focused on some huge shapes that are rushing through the fast-falling snow.

"Heading toward us," Astley says.

Nick moves to stand next to him. Amelie moves up with them too and they look united, like they have a common purpose, and it would be nice if it weren't so dangerous. I squint, trying to see what's coming. Is grabs my hand just as I start to see forms to the shadow.

"Three wolves. Giants," Astley barks out. His posture straightens up even more. "And her—that must be her."

Issie actually mumbles a curse next to me and half faints as Hel comes into the view of our lesser human eyes. I let go of Issie's hand and grab her around the waist instead, trying to hold her up.

"She's half—" Issie mumbles. "She's rotten. She's half rotting."

I told them that.

Nick growls as the wolves pound closer to us. Their massive footfalls make the earth shake. Nick's ears flatten to his head and he bares his teeth, growling. The muscles in his flanks get ready to pounce.

"Wolf! No!" Astley commands, but Nick isn't his to command and he leaps away, pounding toward the wolves and Hel.

Amelie raises a bow.

"No!" Astley yells. "We come in peace. We come—"

As he's yelling, Hel raises her hand and his words break off midsentence. He doesn't move. His hand was reaching for something in his belt, but it's stopped. Nick, too, is frozen in mid run, his body stretched out like a photo image of a running wolf. And next to me, Issie doesn't do anything. Her eyes are wide open with fear, but they don't blink.

"Issie?" I shake her. "Issie?"

She topples over and doesn't make a noise. Whirling around, I realize the wolves, the wind, and Hel herself are all still moving. It's just us. We're the only ones frozen.

But I'm not. I can still move. The realization pushes me into action and I lunge forward, wrenching Amelie's bow from her hands. The wolves and Hel bound closer, closer . . . And I am shivering so much, but I manage to notch an arrow, sight the closest wolf right in the center of his auburn eyes, aim and. . . .

"Do *not* shoot my wolf!" Hel yells.

I don't move the arrow. "Unfreeze my friends."

She whistles and the wolf stops on cue. I keep the arrow trained on its head, but say it again. "Unfreeze my friends."

Somehow she is standing right next to me. The vanilla and rotting smell of her finally hits my human nose. She leans down and whispers in my ear. "We will not hurt them."

Her hand reaches out and grabs the crossbow. I let her take it. I don't know what else to do.

She tosses the bow out of reach and studies my face. "So, little human," she says. "I hear you were looking for me."

OFFICER SAFETY BOLO (BE ON THE LOOKOUT)
The attached bulletin from the RCMP-GRC contains information regarding Frank Belial, aka Bicknell, DOB: 10/12/1968, who is an escapee from federal custody.

On 12/1 at 1956 hours BICKNELL escaped from an escorted temporary absence while returning from Edmonton, AB, to Drumheller Institution. BICKNELL overpowered guards after he faked an illness. He is believed to have ties in New York and Maine. He is considered armed and dangerous and has made statements such as, "No cop will stop me," and "The apocalypse is imminent and I'm bringing it, baby."

The giant wolves romp in the snow, burying their great noses in it. They flip upside down and roll around, lupine legs flailing in the air. Then they start chasing each other with huge leaps, gallivanting around as if they are the happiest Hel hounds ever. Three small women, I think they are dwarves like in *The Hobbit* but I'm not sure, emerge from the woods, carrying swords. They are covered in green furs. They look happy too. Why are they happy in Hel? It doesn't seem like the right attitude.

Questions zing around in my head. I try to organize them into something practical, something that makes sense.

1. We are in Hel.
2. Some people/animals/dwarves are happy here.

3. However, my friends are frozen here. Frozen does not equal happy.
4. I am not frozen. Why didn't she freeze me? Or freeze me when I first saw her in Bedford? Instead she pummeled me.
5. It makes no sense.

I must look confused, because Hel explains, "I have more power in my own realm. Here I can freeze others into submission. They are not injured, just frozen. I can unfreeze them, and I shall, after we talk."

"They aren't hurt?" Staring at Amelie's strained face and Astley's awkward pose, it's hard to believe they aren't in pain somehow.

"No. And they are invulnerable to attack."

It is better than death, I guess, but it's not that encouraging having them frozen like this. I look around and try to take in where we are. We are in the woods, a forest really, and the trees are tall and covered with ice. It even encases their trunks with a shiny, see-through barrier and drips from the limbs in long, jagged points. There are no animal sounds, no wind. It's as if the world is waiting to see if it's worth it to move.

The land rolls gently here. There are no steep mountains, no obvious crevices to plunge into. The sky is a dark gray, as if there is a constant storm, and I wonder, logically, if there is a sun. The Norse said Hel was beneath the earth, so no sun should be able to come in, yet . . . how can trees grow then? How could there be any light at all?

I take a step backward and turn toward the root that must

be from Yggdrasil, which is the giant tree in Norse mythology that connects the nine worlds. One of the worlds is here, Niflheim, a land of harsh cold and fog. The branches on this side are actually the root system that holds up the mythological tree on the earth side. Although, you'd think that someone on earth would notice a magical, massive tree. Maybe it's glamoured. The branches on the Hel side snake through the forest, many feet above the ground. Extensions of it shoot off every so often. A stream runs on the ground directly under the branch, somehow not frozen like everything else, somehow moving. It makes no sense, but it's so real. Giant bite marks mar the tree.

Hel reaches up and gestures toward one of the marks with her hand. "A giant worm did that."

"Níðhöggr."

She smiles. "You have been studying."

"My friend Devyn does most of the research," I say. "Obviously not quite enough research or I might have known about the whole 'freezing us' thing."

"So you know about me then?" She twists her hands together and waits for me to answer. She's so huge and intimidating, much more so than the gods at Valhalla. Still, even though she's just frozen my friends, there's something I like about her, something more interesting than Odin and Thor and the others.

I pause for a second, trying to figure out what to say. I stomp around in place, trying to stay warm, and finally say, "Only what I have heard."

"Which is . . ." Her gaze widens.

I finish her sentence for her as the wind howls around us. "That you rule here. That you have huge mansions. You are the daughter of Loki and Angrboða; the wolf Fenrir and the serpent

Jörmungandr are your brothers. You serve a dish called 'Hunger,' sleep on a bed called 'Sick Bed,' and wield a knife called 'Famine.' Although that sounds kind of hokey to me . . . all that stuff. You are waiting for the world to end. So why?" I ask her. "Why do they want the world to end?"

"You don't think it's just because it has been prophesized?" Her eyes gleam.

"Nope." I cross my arms over my chest, shivering. I check out Astley and the others, frozen in midmotion. I wonder if they can hear us, see us. I wonder if they are cold too.

She snaps her fingers and dwarves run at me with giant furs; before I can move they've dropped them and wrapped them around me. "Thank you. But my friends."

"Are fine, I promise you." She smiles and it's both beautiful and grotesque, depending on which side of her mouth you're looking at. "You are the only one unprotected right now and if you die from cold, then you would end up with me forever. I don't think you'd like that. Not now. There is so much intention in you yet, so much you want to do, to save."

Staring at her, I try to figure out what she's getting at. She seems . . . sad? But who wouldn't be if they were banished down here? The whole act of being banished seems sadness inducing.

I attempt to calm my shivering and say, "I honestly don't think it would be that bad to be here, except for the cold."

She squats down in front of me. "Do you know why that is?"

I don't answer. She whistles. A carriage, deep red and pulled by giant frost-covered elephants, trundles toward us through the trees of ice. Icicles hang from the reins that connect the elephants to the sled.

"It is warm within the mansions of Hel." She reaches out

her hand for me to take. And she must see my hesitation because she chuckles. "Do not worry. It is not the flaming hellfire your culture speaks of. You will see."

I take her hand even though it's the decaying one and try not to vomit from the way her naked bone feels beneath my fingers. Instead, I focus on the side of her face that is whole.

"See?" she says as she helps me into the sled. "This is why you are chosen. Not because of who your father is, not because you turned pixie queen. It is because you choose to look beyond the ugly. You choose to see the good even in monsters, Zara White. That is why you are different. That is why you are important."

She puts more blankets over my legs and tucks them in beneath me before stepping in. "Bring us to Hel," she tells the driver, a woman with black, frost-covered hair. The elephants snort and then move forward through the snow and ice. Hel turns to me, brings my face close, and breathes upon my skin to warm it up, the way a mother would.

"Sometimes the monsters are not monsters," she says.

"I know." I nod. "And sometimes the monsters are within us all, even in those we think are the most good."

"You are shivering too much. Do not talk until we get to Hel and you are warmed."

And so I don't. We rush through the fog. It slaps at my cheeks like tiny pellets of ice, stinging the skin. I don't see any animals other than the elephants. I don't see any life, including any sign of giant worms. Thinking about Astley and the others, I say a tiny, silent prayer that Hel was not lying and that they are indeed safe.

She touches my arm through the blankets. "What is wrong?"

"My friends."

She doesn't say anything for a moment and we crest a hill, revealing huge, amazing mansions that gleam almost golden, dotting the landscape, shining with the suggestion of warmth. They remind me of French chateaus that kings used to visit, bringing their entire retinue.

"Hel is beautiful," I gasp.

She smiles, revealing gums and teeth. "I will send for your friends, Zara. But if they become threats to my people, I will freeze them again. Understand?"

My heart beats a bit warmer even though the temperature hasn't changed. "I understand."

Hel has many mansions, each beautiful and elaborate and full of beings, but not so full that they are crowded. Tigers and bears stroll alongside each other, apparently peaceful. Old men lounge by fireplaces reading. Young women smoke cigars by the stairs. People wear modern clothes, ancient clothes. Some are missing flesh, like they were bitten by something. Some have marks from their illnesses upon their cheeks. But their eyes are lively and they seem content. I could stare and stare at them, I think.

"Not what you were expecting?" Hel ushers me through the front hall and into a long room full of mirrors. Gold trim glistens along the edges of the ceiling. A fire roars in a white marble hearth.

As I settle into a leather chair I say, "Not at all."

The flames in the fireplace flare and give off the most beautiful heat in the entire universe. For a second, I let myself close my eyes and just breathe in the warmth.

"So, why did you come to Hel, Zara White?" Her question

and voice are suddenly formal. When I open my eyes, I can tell that her posture is more rigid as well. She stands by the fire, waiting.

"We wanted— We wanted to know how to stop the apocalypse." It sounds stupid when I say it like that.

"And you thought I would just tell you?"

I smile. "Um . . . yeah. We were hoping."

She laughs. A slow-walking woman with hair like straw shuffles into the room carrying a tray of what looks like hot cider. I take one and thank her. One sip and I'm instantly warmed. Standing up, I investigate the room. We're alone, but the mirrors show dozens of us. My hair is dripping onto my coat. It must have been frozen and it's thawing now.

"I shall give you a choice," Hel says, placing her own porcelain cup onto a silver tray.

I wait.

"You may either know how to stop the end or you may see your father again."

My heart stops.

"My father or my stepfather?" I clarify because I have a biological father who died in the jaws of Fenrir, and I have a real father—the one who raised me. He died of a heart attack on our kitchen floor.

"Your stepfather."

In the mirrors my face has paled. My eyes widen with shock and want. I want to yell that's not a fair choice, stomp my feet, and demand both, but instead I say, "That is cruel."

"I can only give one. I want you to have the choice."

"Another test?" I ask.

She shrugs slightly. That's all the answer she'll give me, I know.

"Pick one. Your father or the world."

There are little gold figurines on a side table. They shine in the light and I can't resist the urge to pick one up. It's the form of a deer lying down, legs tucked under her body. The weight of it in my hand is soothing and I stare at it so I don't have to look at a mirror, don't have to look at Hel.

In the past year, I've lost two people that I've loved so totally. The first was my dad. The second was Nick. And when you lose someone like that, it's hard to describe, but it's like something gets ripped out of your chest and you'd do anything—even turn pixie—to fix that hole in the center of you, to get them back, to see them, to talk to them. Before all this happened, I believed in God in the Judeo-Christian or Muslim sense but I still felt that incredible loss when they both died, and Mrs. Nix too. And there was doubt. There was this big doubt inside of me even though I believed in God. I was worried that they had just stopped existing. Not so much with Nick because I saw the Valkyrie take him away, but with my dad and Mrs. Nix nobody came. They were just gone, forever gone, and now—now I have the chance to speak to my dad, to see him again because he's here, right here.

"I thought he'd be in heaven," I mutter, examining the underside of the deer like it has all the answers. "Is there even a heaven? Or are you gods it? The ultimate?"

Hel gently takes the deer from my hand and places it back on the table. She sighs and her hands move to the sides of my face. "We are not all there is. Even Odin, who knows more than the rest of us, does not know everything, despite all the myths that say he does. There is power above us, yes."

I cock my head a little, moving my cheek closer to her rotten hand. "Promise?"

She smiles, and even though there is jaw bone and teeth revealed in half that smile, it's still beautiful. "I promise."

A moment passes and then she drops her hands from my face and she turns away, giving me room.

I love my dad. He was the one who taught me to think, to write about human-rights violations, to care about people's feelings, to memorize Booker T. Washington quotes. There would be nothing better than seeing him, hugging him one more time, smelling his dad smell and feeling his bristly skin where his beard grows in too fast.

But he wouldn't want me to do this.

Not if it meant the world could end, although let's face it, the world has issues. Big issues like sex slaves and genocide, racism, poverty, homophobia and wars, religious conflicts and environmental disasters—but the world is also worth saving because it has writers like Foucault and people like Issie and Grandma Betty. I know it's not all cuddly puppies and rainbows and ice-cream sundaes, but it needs a chance, as many chances as it can get to survive.

"Tell me what I need to do," I say.

The moment the words leave my mouth, the loss of not seeing my dad again hiccups through my chest, knives my heart into two. I bend forward from the pain of it.

Hel's hand touches my shoulder. "Are you sure?"

I nod because I can't trust my voice not to break. It's hard for the words to come out of my throat. It's like they have to push past something big and solid to make themselves heard. "I want to know how to stop the end."

That's what he'd want me to do, because it's the right thing to do. Still, it feels so wrong. My legs crumple beneath me, and I sit down on the ornate couch without really realizing it. Hel reaches out a hand and gently touches my arm, and that's when I realize that gods don't work like people do. They barely speak our language. And they rarely make decisions out of empathy. Instead, they force choices upon us, always testing our character, always seeing what we are made of. Gods know that you can't stop hurt. Gods know that you can't stop endings and choices and pain, but people keep trying to do exactly those things.

I hide my face in my hands so she won't be able to look into my eyes, won't be able to see how much this decision hurts me, but I am sure she already knows.

She seems to understand and becomes brusque, no-nonsense, as if intuiting that any extra kindness will break my will, change my mind.

"I am sorry," she says, and in those three words I can tell that maybe she doesn't have a choice either. Maybe the rules are older than either of us, and stronger than I can ever imagine. Or maybe not, but I don't think she can change the rules she must play by.

I grab her hand, the rotting one, and squeeze a little bit. "Tell me what I need to know, please."

I tack on the "please" because I figure it's best to be polite to Viking gods. My dad taught me to be polite to everyone. Have I forgotten that? My dad . . .

"Are you sure you are ready?" she asks.

"Yes." The word just slips out.

She walks over to a mirror, not let going of my hand, and all I can think of is the mirror in the Harry Potter books where you get to see whatever you desire. But when we stand in front of it, the mirror doesn't show us a vision of me saving the world. It just shows us, standing together.

"You are amazingly tall," I mutter, and my voice sounds astonished, even to me. "You must be seven feet."

She smiles but doesn't say anything. She waves her free hand at the mirror and it opens on a hinge like a door. The air behind it smells of fire, rotten eggs, death. But the light isn't red like you'd expect. It's an icy blue like the inside of an iceberg.

"Step forward and look," she says. "But do not let go of my hand."

Her fingers tighten around mine and her arm extends to give me enough room to really see. The moment I step away from her, I can feel the tug of it—a gigantic pull, like gravity times a hundred. It's a pit, an icy blue pit, that belches out a heat like an oven but worse, much worse. The pit or hole or whatever seems to go down forever and ever.

"What is this?"

She hauls me back to her. "The mouth of Hel."

"Your mouth?"

"The Hel of this place, this land."

I try to digest that. Issie had said there was a hell mouth in *Buffy* shows. I should have paid more attention. Why do I never pay attention to pop-culture references? Probably because that one involved Issie going on and on about cute British vampires.

"This is what will swallow up the world," Hel's voice breaks into my thoughts, "if you fail."

"And I succeed by not doing what exactly . . . ?" I try to get her to just come out with it.

"There is a prophecy that not many are aware of. It says that the fall of one who is half of the stars, half of the White, half of the fae, half of the willow, can stop this."

"And you and Frank and Isla believe this is me?" I say. "But not anymore. I am not a pixie anymore. Not any of me." The hopelessness of it gets to me. "I can't stop this. It's already too late. Isla turned me back—I wish she'd just killed me! Why didn't she just kill me?"

"That I do not know, but you still have power, Zara of the White. And some might want that power."

"I am human." I sputter it out almost like being human is a fate worse than death.

"Do not devalue humans."

"I'm not! It's just that the prophecy says 'half fae.' I'm not even that anymore. I'm all human now. So, honestly, how can I do this? Astley says I could die if I turn pixie again. I can't save anyone if I'm dead." I let go of her hand as the mirror door slams shut. "And you haven't told me how I fall. Do I fall in the pit? Do I fall down on the ice? Why must prophecies be so freaking obscure? Why can't they just state things nice and easy, like, 'Zara White must be in full pixie form and fall down outside her high school at precisely two a.m. on December 23 for the apocalypse to be averted.' Why can't it be like that?"

She sort of chuckles. There is nothing worse than gods chuckling.

"It's not funny!"

"Are you speaking back to me?" she asks, laughing even harder.

I cross my arms over my chest. "I guess."

"Only gods do that."

I apologize.

"I found your ranting amusing," she says, composing her face into something slightly more serious. It looks like it takes her some effort, because her eyes are still twinkling.

I make a harrumphing noise, which I figure is a nice cross between politeness and showing my disapproval. "I just wish I knew exactly what to do."

She places both her hands on my shoulders and I tilt my head up so that I can meet her eyes. Her voice is serious again as she says, "Let me give you a warning."

I wait.

"Zara, others may still try to trap you, even turn you back into a pixie, to make your power their own," she says.

I feel like that little glittering deer figurine, unable to move by myself, trapped by everybody else's wishes and needs, trapped by destiny.

"You mean Frank?" I spit out his name, then realize she might not recognize him by that one. "Belial?"

Nodding, she drops her hands from my shoulders, moves back to the wall of mirrors, and rests her forehead against one. "When you are turned, your king's needs become your own. His darkness or his light begin to infect your soul. With the star king, it was light. His goodness and your goodness combined to make you and all your pixies stronger. Even though you are no longer a pixie, you still have that goodness and you are still the key to stopping the apocalypse. However, that also means you may still be the key to starting it."

"So even though I'm not a pixie, they need me to start it all."

"No matter what your enemies might think, *starting* the apocalypse has nothing to do with being pixie. It has everything to do with being human. However"—she pauses—"the pixies who want to end all things human believe that if they kill you immediately after the apocalypse begins, there will be no entity capable of stopping it."

"Oh," I say.

"Yes," she echoes me. "Oh."

FROM AGENT WILLIS'S PERSONAL LOG
I think I'm going to have to request more manpower in this case. I honestly feel like I'm in a sci-fi episode playing the clueless federal agent, but I have never seen such a lack of evidence or pieces that just do not go together. Sometimes I think we are dealing with one killer. Sometimes I think we are dealing with dozens. Possibly a Satanic cult? The town is on the edge of all-out panic. People are leaving on extended vacations, and those who have stayed behind have a look of intense anxiety. I am failing these people. I know it.

Hel gives me a second to compose myself, which is kind of her. She moves out of the room and issues orders in a language I don't understand. The air trembles with the first sounds of a flute. It trills into a beautiful song that lilts with the promise of spring and kittens and flowers poking from the earth. There is music in Hel. Who knew?

The chandeliers jingle lightly, almost as if they are reacting to the flute song. I walk past the mirrors and giant windows that look out upon the snowy landscape. I move past the gilded moldings and the seven-foot gold candelabras that burn with crystal flames. Each step on the marble floor pushes a little more strength into me. Each step convinces me that I've done the right thing. Each step makes me harden up a little more, because if I don't make myself harder, I will just fall down and cry over losing the chance to see my dad.

Hel waits for me at the end of the hall. She envelops my hand with hers and ushers me onto an interior balcony that wraps around a large courtyard-type room full of people who are both lounging and busy. The flute music comes from a little girl who sits on top of a gilded piano in the center of the room.

"She's so young," I whisper.

"Many of us are young when we die." Hel states this like it is nothing, and maybe to her it *is* nothing, but to me? It's a whole lot of something.

As we walk, I get a better angle at the room below us. There are about two hundred statues, spouting water. They are bronze and gold and crystal, and most seem to have something to do with Norse mythology. Giant wolves snap at the moon. Horses paw at the air. Giant tree sculptures reach up to the ceiling and embrace it.

"So," I say again, hoping for more information, "how do we stop this Ragnarok thing?"

"You can't wait for it to happen. You have to go to it. What is the word you use in your country, in your time? You have to be proactive, not reactive?" Her hand flutters up into the air like she's trying to find the right way to tell me.

"Strike first?" I can't believe a god is telling me to be proactive.

"In a way."

"Everything we've read says that freeing Loki is the big signal that starts the apocalypse rolling. It's in all the books, the ancient texts, the Internet sites. Because I can refuse to do that.

I will never do that." My voice comes out so hard and so tough that it surprises me.

She stops and leans on the marble railing. Her hands look so different from each other. I stare at them as she says, "You cannot say what you will never do, Zara. Loki is trapped unfairly. Though I am partial because he is my relation. But it is better for him to stay trapped than to kill all in your world. Still, there will be circumstances that may sway you."

I ask, "Can you see what happens like Cassidy does?"

"The girl with elf blood? Like her, I see only glimpses." She sighs, uses her ghoulish hand to pick a speck of dust off of the railing. She holds it in the air and lets the current of wind whisk it away. It catches the light and then I can see it no longer. "Let me tell you what I can: you need an army that has nothing to lose."

Her voice matches my insides like they are made of the same sad emotion. Where do I find an army that has nothing to lose? I think about all the kids we're training. They all have so much to lose. Still, we *are* fighting against an apocalypse, so we sort of have nothing to lose. I start to explain this and ask her if I'm right. She gives a slight shrug, the kind of shrug that makes me think I am probably wrong.

"Can you tell me anything else?" I ask.

"Only magic will stop them."

"A magic thing?"

"The kind of magic that comes from inside."

Something beneath us has caught her attention. I figure out where she's looking. It's past the galloping horses fountain, past a lovely old couple in tweed, over to the left a bit and—

"There's something going on down there," I say.

"There is," she agrees.

"Should we check it out, maybe? Is everything okay?" I'm worried by her lack of concern.

The air in the room seems to empty out. The flute stops. I see him.

My voice fills the void with a rushed whisper. "That's my dad, isn't it?"

"Yes. Yes, it is."

He's leaning against a wall, talking. His legs are crossed casually at the ankle. He stops in midsentence and his head slowly moves up so that his gaze meets mine. His lips part just the tiniest bit like they always do when he's surprised.

"Daddy!" It's a little-girl word, but I don't care. That's what he is. That's who he is to me.

I fly down the stairs, head spinning, any resolve I had before about not seeing him no longer mattering. My father—here. He is truly here. I hadn't quite believed it. And so close. And he is running too, racing across the marble floor. People part for him, stepping out of the way so we can get to each other more quickly.

"You're here! I mean, I knew you were here, but I'm not supposed to see you. I chose . . ." My words have rushed out of me before I even know what I'm saying, and I break them off as he scoops me up into what we used to call the Daddy Bear Hug. He squeezes and squeezes and I clutch on to him. Nothing has ever felt so good. Not ever. I hold on and hold on. I will never let go.

My feet come back to the ground, but we still hug.

"You died?" he whispers. "So soon?"

"No! No! I'm still alive, just trying to save the world." I rush out the briefest explanation I can and since he's my dad and ridiculously smart he understands all of it pretty much instantly.

"I'm so sorry I left you like that, Zara," he starts. His voice breaks and he tries again. "I-I've been so worried about you and your mother. I'm so sorry. So sorry I'm not there for you, to help you, to take care of you."

"Daddy, you can't apologize for that." My fingers flutter up, go to each side of his beautiful dad face. He is scruffy. "You didn't choose to die. It's not your fault at all."

He swallows so hard that his Adam's apple visibly rides up and down in his throat. An icicle of light shines in his brown eyes.

"I saw him at the window and I was so shocked. My heart froze in my chest. That's what it felt like . . ."

"Saw who, Daddy?"

He eyes me. "Your biological father."

The air whooshes out of me. All this time, that's what I'd thought had happened, but knowing it still shocks me. My biological father frightened my dad to death. The horribleness of it makes my stomach clench.

My dad's hand moves across the hair on the top of my head. "I am so proud of you. We never told you so much about who you are, our history, and you—you are so strong and beautiful, Zara. You're so strong."

I shake my head and laugh the kind of laugh that means you think someone is being silly. "I wish, Daddy. I wish I was. I wish you were still with us. I'm so glad to see you, but we miss you. We miss you so much."

"I miss you and your mom and Betty, too, honey. So much."

"Daddy? Why the books? Why did you hide pixie notes in

books? Why not just write them straight out in a notebook or something?"

He smiles. "I thought people might find them and think I was crazy. If I wrote them in margins of books, people might think I was writing my own. I was young, Zara."

"I wish you'd just told me. You and mom."

"We wanted you to be safe. We wanted you to grow up free of fear."

People around us murmur. Have they all been listening? I forgot they were here.

"Zara, we don't have much time."

"What do you mean?" Throughout all of this, I've pretty much refused to blink because I don't want to miss one second of seeing him. Trying to memorize his face all over again, I watch his lips move as he talks.

"When we are done with what we are meant to do here, we move on to another place."

The room goes silent. There are no murmurs.

I speak into that silence. "What other place?"

"Nobody knows."

I whirl around to look at Hel because she must certainly know.

"What place?" I demand.

My dad's finger touches the point of my chin and gently turns me back to face him. "Not even she knows. But it's good. We know it's good and I can feel it happening. It's happening now, honey."

"How can she not know? How can you know it's good? Daddy, explain this to me."

Even as I speak, he seems to change, to glow. He unclicks

the big silver diver's watch from his wrist. It has a blue face and lots of dials. I used to love it when I was little. We buried him in it.

"Take this," he says, and slips it over my hand, onto my wrist. It's far too big for me and hangs off my wrist bones. "Know that I love you, that I always will love you no matter what choices you make, what paths you have chosen, and what paths you choose in the future. I will always, always love you, baby girl."

I can feel my face squish into itself, the way it does when I try not to cry but the tears just want so badly to come. My dad smiles a sad, sweet, tender smile.

"You can't take something from Hel without giving something up in return," he says. "I'm so sorry, Zara. It has to be something that matters to you."

"But I just have my clothes and they are just *clothes* . . ." Then I realize I'm wearing Nick's anklet still. It's the only thing on me that matters even the tiniest bit. It's the one last thing I have from when we were happy together, and even though it's dorky I don't want to be without it, but still I squat and reach into my boot to unclasp it. A dolphin and a star dangle from it. The color changed again. Every time I change species, it changes. I have no idea why. In that short amount of time that I've been fiddling with it, my father has changed too. He's turned completely gold. He's shimmering with it, shimmering and beautiful. I hand him the thin chain. "Here."

He takes it and tucks it into his shirt. "Thank you. Tell your mother I love her, and know, Zara—please, please know—how I love you."

"I love you too," I whisper.

He taps the watch face on my wrist with his big, solid finger. "I am always with you. Always."

He steps back.

"Daddy!"

And then he smiles, one final, slow smile that reaches his eyes. He tilts his head and mouths the words "I love you" just before the light coming out of him becomes too intense to witness. I close my eyes for the briefest of seconds and feel it—the rush of him leaving, the good soul of him hanging in the air like the sweet smell of magnolias in Charleston.

"He's gone." I gasp as people around me start to applaud.

As I struggle to take it all in, Hel's arm wraps around my shoulder. "This is a halfway place, a step toward somewhere else."

"What somewhere else?"

"Your father spoke the truth. I do not know." She squeezes a little and then drops her arm. "However, I am positive that it is somewhere good for him. Do you not feel it?"

The gold of the air still shimmers around me. "I feel it."

"It is not always so," her voice warns and then lightens again. "Your companions await. You must go."

My fingers reach out to touch the watch that dangles on my left wrist. It is there, solid, functional, and completely my dad. Still, it feels right and I am so glad it is there.

"You let me see him. You said it was an either-or situation. Either I see him or you tell me how to stop the end, but I got both."

She doesn't answer my question, but instead leads me back toward the marble stairs. "Come with me."

I follow, wiping at the tears streaming down my face. People stare at us as we walk up, make way for us as they come down the stairs. The balcony is empty when we get there. She leads me to an overlook. The courtyard below us has filled with people—all sorts of people of different races and genders and ages—and there are animals that I assume are weres, and there are tiny Tinker Bell–type people, flitting about the water fountains and resting on full-sized people's shoulders. There are a couple people who might actually be giants, and there are pixies, blue in skin. Then, as I'm staring the room doubles and then triples in size and instead of looking down at hundreds of people, I'm looking down at thousands.

"What?" I start to say, but Hel speaks over me.

"Earn your army."

"What?" I say again. "What do you mean?"

"They have nothing to lose, Zara. Make them fight for you when the time comes."

"But I'm not even a pixie anymore."

I swear she rolls her eyes the same way Betty does when she's completely exasperated with me.

"It does not matter," she says, looking down at the thousands below us. "It is your character that makes the difference, not your species. Now begin."

Begin? How do I begin? They stare up at me, thousands of eyes and heads, thousands of souls, waiting to listen to me, Zara White, former pixie queen, current human being. I remember failing so miserably when I had to first talk to our pixies. I'd been so immature. And now? Now the fate of our world might depend on this speech. I breathe in as deeply as I can and grab the railing. The marble is cold beneath my fingers. I want to make my dad proud of me. Actually, I want to make me proud of me.

"My name is Zara White," I begin, "and I am asking for your help."

I don't imagine everyone in their underwear or anything because some of them are pretty gross already and they need all the clothes they have to cover up wounds and sores and burns. It's never good to vomit in the middle of a speech. Plus, it just seems kind of pervy to imagine everyone half naked. Instead, I take a couple big breaths to calm myself down.

"My name is Zara White," I repeat. "I stand before you to swear that this will not be the end of the world, but a beginning. I stand before you to beg for your help."

There's a murmur among them. Hoping it's not a disgruntled murmur, I continue. "Centuries ago there was a description of a great apocalypse that would befall the world, the Ragnarok. All but two humans would die. It is my responsibility to stop that fate, and I need your help."

There is another murmur. I scan the crowd for Astley, Nick, Issie, and Amelie, but I don't see them there, can't find them among all the heads.

"I don't know what century you all are from, but the world is still full of goodness and badness. It is still full of love and pain. And each person in it holds the power to determine his or her own fate. Each person has a chance to live his or her own life to its absolute fullest, to choose to live kindly or not, to love or not . . ."

I spot Astley in the crowd. He nods at me and smiles. My heart warms from seeing him moving, looking alive, looking at me.

"But the side of evil, of unchecked needs and lust for power, is strong now, too strong, and it wants the world to end—the world that you all probably loved so much, the world that I love so much despite all its problems."

Nick stands by Astley, just behind him and to his right. Despite the massive crowd around them, I can see his face. It looks like he's holding his breath. My ankle feels empty without the chain there, but it will be okay. We all have to feel empty sometimes.

"I'm just a human, but I know that I can't dare to forget, today or any day, that I have a responsibility to my friends, to my town, to my world. And I know that you were once of that world, too, and I know that you have left that world behind and that this place—this place—"

I remember my dad glowing so beautifully, so full of love.

"—is just one step in your journey, in all of our journeys, toward something bigger and more beautiful and more glorious. But that doesn't mean that we don't have a responsibility to others, to let them have the lives they need to have, to let them have lives free of terror, to let them have lives where they can be the best people they can be.

"I beg of you to help me when the time comes, to choose to fight for those you've left behind, for the world you've left behind. It is not perfect, but it is your legacy. It is not perfect, but it is a testament to years of human courage, of hardship, of joy. No, it's not perfect, but none of us are. Our lack of perfection doesn't mean that we should not be brave, love, and do perfect deeds. I know that when I think about the people I love that I dare not forget where it is I have come from. Do you? You leave behind you the heirs of humanity, and it is our duty—our absolute duty—to keep them safe. You have one more chance to do one more selfless thing. You have one more chance to save our world. Please join me when the time comes. Please show the world that evil does not always triumph, that good can overcome. Thank you."

They are silent. Did I blow it? I think maybe I've blown it.

One small baby girl, maybe about five years old, yells, "Hooray!" and then there is applause—huge, thunderous applause. The balcony echoes with it and it sounds like horses stampeding to the rescue, like hope, really. Yes, like hope. My heart beats again. My eyes close.

"You have your army," Hel whispers in my ear, and somehow I can hear it despite the noise of the dead clapping. The smell of vanilla and death is overwhelming again.

I argue. "But I'm not magic. You said that magic stops—"

"Sound the alarm. They will come." Hel smiles at me. "Trust in yourself, Zara White. Have faith."

And then she claps a rotting hand on my shoulder and says, "I hope when your time comes to pass, that you will stop here and not Valhalla."

"Me too," I say. "Me too."

COUNTY SHERIFF 911 TRANSCRIPT

Boy: I can hear my name. Someone's in the woods by the road saying my name.

911 Operator: What's your location?

Boy: Can you hear that?

911 Operator: Sweetie, I need to know where you are so we can send help.

Boy: The Shore Road by Water Street. I'm walking. Oh . . . I can hear . . .

911 Operator: Hello? Hello?

It's hard to find my friends again because of the milling crowd below and then I spot people moving aside, as if others are trying to get through to me. Nick is pushing his way through the dead, the others trailing behind him.

Issie's thin voice yells, "Sorry! So sorry! Excuse us."

It makes me smile. And then Astley must give up, because he soars up through the crowd and lands on the balcony next to Hel and me. He manages to land on one foot and wobbles a bit, but doesn't fall down.

Once he's steady, he looks to Hel and they exchange greetings that are formal and boring and then he sputters out, "Freezing us was decidedly uncalled for!"

She raises an eyebrow. "I needed to talk to Zara alone. Do

you dare confront me in my own realm, Star King, and tell me my procedure is unwarranted?"

"Yes. No. It's just—"

"You can see that your queen is unharmed and you have been unfrozen. Do not make me regret my hospitality," she says with a warning tone, and then she retreats a few steps back and calls to a man to come attend her. The moment she is gone, Astley swoops me into a hug and lifts me up, spinning me around.

"You were brilliant!" he gushes. "So brilliant and queenly."

"No bunny pajamas this time," I kid.

"I was so proud of you, I almost forgot to be angry at her," he says, kissing the side of my head and letting me back down.

As Nick, Issie, and Amelie get closer I grab his arm and whisper, "I saw my father."

His eyes widen. "Which one?"

I explain it was my stepfather, the one who raised me, and his smile grows so big that his face can hardly contain it. "That is so wonderful!"

He spins me around again in his joy and I laugh with him, letting happiness fill me before everyone else comes. They rush up the stairs, and then for a second we all just stand awkwardly around. My feet plant on the floor. Issie glows with happiness despite the fact that she was frozen a little bit ago. Nick looks part angry and part confused.

"You know," Nick says, breaking the silence as he surveys the scene around him. "This isn't at all what I imagined Hel would look like."

"Me neither!" Issie chirps. "I imagined it a lot less frozen outside, with demons and pitchforks and hellfire flames everywhere. This is totally better."

Amelie raises an eyebrow.

Hel's voice rings over us, much more commanding than it was before. It seems to have layers of depth to it. "I hope it is a pleasant surprise."

Issie's mouth drops open. I guess seeing a half-zombie, giant-sized woman from a distance isn't as traumatizing as it is being up close and personal with one. Issie stutters, but stretches out a hand. "You must be Hel. It-it's good to meet you. I'm Issie."

"I am delighted to meet you, Isabelle." Hel shakes Issie's hand and smiles. To her credit, Issie's shudder of revulsion is really barely noticeable. Hel greets the others as well and then turns to me. "It is time for you all to go back."

I nod. Something inside me twinges. Strangely enough, it feels so safe here. And I think I'm going to actually miss her.

"If you would not mind giving us provisions," Astley says, "we would greatly appreciate it. Your land is cold and we have humans."

Hel smiles and motions for us to follow her. She leads us back into the long room of mirrors and windows and gathers us all around a stained-glass window that depicts her reaching up beyond a frozen land and into the warm earth above it.

"Hold one another's hands," she commands.

I grab one of Astley's and one of Nick's because they are on either side of me and for a second I feel awkward and strange. But it passes because the world shimmers and shakes and then it's as if all of my atoms have exploded and then slammed back into each other again.

Nick swears. Astley holds on tighter. Everything is white, terrifically blinding white light. And then it flashes out. I resist the urge to rub at my eyes and keep holding on to their hands as the world comes into focus again.

Nick curses under his breath and lets go of my hand and Issie's. He twists around looking for threats.

"Wait. We're uh . . . ," Issie starts.

We're back in Iceland, right by our cottage. The air freezes against us and I am suddenly very tired and confused and energized by what just happened.

"We teleported," Issie finishes. "Like in *Star Trek* or *Harry Potter*, sort of. No! Like in *Dr. Who* in that episode with the Sontarans and the brilliant human boy, or really any *Dr. Who* ever if you think of the Tardis! Holy canola! That is just the coolest thing ever! Wowie, wow, wow!"

She starts jumping in place, excited beyond belief, I think. I laugh at her and she rushes to me and hugs me and says again, "This is the coolest thing ever!"

Nick smiles because he's obviously no longer on high alert. "The world may end, but at least Issie got to teleport."

"Wait till I tell Devyn! He's going to be super-jealous! Then he'll start explaining how the laws of physics work and blah, blah, blah, make teleportation absolutely impossible, but he'll still be soooo super-jealous," she says, letting go of me and still smiling. "I wish he got to do it too."

"He does get to fly, Is," I say. "And shape shift. You know those are pretty impossible things."

"True. True. I'll tell him that the next time he goes into his 'time travel is impossible' lecture mode."

I adjust her hat, which has gone all lopsided, and announce to everyone, "Let's get back to the airport. It's time to go home."

On the ride to the airport, I tell them all what happened with Hel, how she said magic and the army were important, how she said we had to be proactive and not reactive with Frank's pixies, which means that we have to attack first.

"But how do we do that?" Issie asks.

"We could use bait," I explain. "We get them to gather in one place because they think they'll get something they want, something unprotected. Then we attack them."

"What if that is what they want us to do?" Astley asks. He shifts around in the seat, lifts the seat belt away from his chest, reaches into his back pocket for a cell phone, and then settles back in.

"Well . . ." I obviously haven't thought this completely through and I'm okay with that. "If we have a battle, we can eliminate Frank's pixies, get Bedford safe once and for all, and then focus more on this whole end-of-the-world thing."

Nick snorts. "And what is the bait?"

"Me."

"Hell no!" he says. "Hell no."

Astley says more calmly, "I do not believe that is a good idea."

"How are you even bait anymore?" Amelie asks. "You are human now."

I explain that Frank will still want me. He will try to turn me again, make me his queen instead of Astley's. He won't care if I die in the process. He just wants to try.

We argue and argue about it for the entire ride back to the airport. The sky is dark against the car but it's warm inside from all our body heat and words. After a while I lean back and close my eyes and let the rest of them hash it out. I know my plan is right. I know my plan is dangerous, too, but it doesn't matter. I move the sleeve of my parka enough so I can touch my father's watch. It gives me hope and strength, and when I look around the car, I see my friends. I listen to them argue, and even though it's cheesy I feel all full of love for them. No matter what happens, it's worth it. It's worth it to save them. I know it beyond a doubt.

The moment we drive into an area that has cell reception again, I call Betty.

"For crap's sake," she swears above the sound of the ambulance siren. She must be on an ambulance call. "Where the hell have you been? What's happening?"

I breathe out and breathe in, snuggle my shoulder closer to Issie's. "Well, to start with, I'm human again."

"Very, very human," Issie says, planting a kiss on my cheek, but sort of missing and getting my hair.

I repeat it. "Very, very human."

And then I tell her the rest of the story. When I finally finish, we're halfway back to the city and Betty says in a quiet, steady way, "So, we attack them first."

"Yes." I look around the car at my friends. They already look tired, their faces are lined and battle weary, stress has thinned out Issie's cheeks, hardened Nick's mouth, made circles beneath Astley's eyes, and caused Amelie to start pulling on her dreads.

"Well," Betty says. "I guess we'll really have to give the teenagers some more weapons."

After we hang up, we all settle into a nice sort of silence. One of Astley's men has been driving the whole time and he seems competent despite his suit and porn mustache. There's a tattoo across the back of his neck. It's some language I don't know.

I stare across the seats at Nick and Astley. Nick is sitting in front with the driver and Astley is positioned directly behind him, sitting with Amelie. Issie and I are in the last row of seats and Issie's fallen asleep, her hand clutching her cell phone. My gaze returns to Astley. I could reach out and touch him if I wanted, tug on the fabric of his winter hat, get his attention, ask him what he thinks about me now that I am human again, what he thinks about our chances of surviving all this.

It's now or never really. The clock is running out, and there's no way I can turn around and head back to the old Zara life—a life without snow or death or imminent world destruction, a life without pixies and shape-shifting humans and gods. Somehow, I have to stop the end of everything. I will.

I tuck my hair behind my ears, fix my own wool hat, and sort of sigh. The landscape is open out here, and we've been going through it for a while. Stretching my fingers out wide, I look at my human skin. It's pale. It's weak. How can I stop the end if I have no magic? The thought unsettles me. Doubt creeps into my stomach, making a pit. Just then, Astley turns around.

"You okay?" he whispers.

I shrug, which is the best non-answer I can think of at the moment. Astley rubs at the bottom of his stubbly jawline, and his eyes shift away from me, out the back window.

"We are being followed."

I turn to look.

"Do not turn!" he says urgently, but it's too late. I already have. He leans forward and tells the driver, but there's nothing we can do. We're on a long stretch of road through plains. There are no exits. Nowhere to turn off.

"They might not be following us," I offer. "That's sort of a worst-case scenario. I mean, why would they even need to follow us?"

"Intimidation," Amelie says through gritted teeth. She opens her mouth a bit more to keep talking. "Or perhaps they know that we went to Hel, that we have more information on how to stop them."

"Hardly enough," says Nick, waking up thanks to Astley's shoulder-shaking efforts. He growls a little bit beneath his breath. "Hardly enough information."

"Or he wishes to turn you back," Astley says, eyes narrowing, "now, while we are weaker, away from our comrades."

"Where are we?" I ask as the driver tenses his eyes in the rearview mirror.

"They are speeding up," he tells us.

We speed up too.

"They are maintaining distance," he says.

We speed up more.

"Still maintaining distance," he says.

Astley pulls out his phone. He punches in numbers.

"Who are you calling?" Amelie asks.

"The law-enforcement authorities. I shall report an erratic driver. Hopefully, they will respond," he says, and I'm assuming this is what he does, because he stops speaking English. After a minute he clicks off the phone. "They will respond."

"Soon?" Amelie asks. She's holding up a mirror and angling it to see the dark car behind us. It's an SUV and pretty solid looking. "Because they are—"

The car jolts forward and swerves. My seat belt presses hard against me. People swear. Issie wakes up, mumbling and confused. I try to calm her down and tell her what's going on, but before I can, the car jerks forward again and zigzags as the driver tries to maintain control.

"I hate freaking pixies, and I hate the freaking apocalypse, and I hate freaking Iceland," Nick growls, pivoting. "Does anyone have a gun?"

Nobody does.

"How can nobody have a gun?" he asks, his voice getting hysterical. "We're on a mission to save the world and nobody has a gun."

His voice takes on a new edge.

"He's changing!" I warn. "Crud. Crud. Crud!"

The car slams into us again. The back end is now much, much closer to where Issie and I are sitting. The glass in the window is shattering. I unbuckle Issie's seat belt, urging her to move to the next row of seats.

She clicks into place. A wolf snarls in the passenger's seat. He pivots and glares at Amelie and Astley.

"Not them!" I scream. "Not them. Good guys, Nick. Good guys!"

His growl deepens and he swings his head to look at the driver. The driver's pulling over? He's pulling over and smiling and I suddenly understand that he's a part of it, a plant or something.

"Get him!" I shout. "Get him! The bad one is right there! Get him!"

SCANNER TRAFFIC, BEDFORD POLICE
DEPARTMENT
Control to 14: We have a report of a blue man running down
Water Street with a disembodied head in his hands. Again.
We have a report of a blue-skinned man with a head in hands
on Water Street. 10-3.
14: En route.

Nick lunges after the driver, knocking him out of the car. They
both tumble onto the road, a twisting mass of teeth and claws.
It barely has time to register but Amelie's already bolted out
after them, diving over into the driver's seat and out the now
busted open door. She slams it behind her.

Astley takes the time to say, "Stay here," before he's out his
door too, and I suppose I should appreciate that, but instead,
I'm mad. There is no way that I'm staying in here when they are
outside fighting. They could get hurt. They could—

I've got my hand on the door handle when Issie pulls me
back. "Zara!"

"What?"

"You can't go."

"What do you mean?"

"You have no weapons. You're human." Her voice is both urgent and apologetic.

And for a second, I think she's right, that I can't go, that being human makes me weak, and it does compared to being pixie, but what really makes me weak is not being brave. Sure, I don't have a weapon, but I can still do something, somehow, right? I shrug Issie off. "I can't *not* help."

"Sometimes not helping *is* helping," she pleads.

"Not this time." I'm out the door before she can make me doubt myself anymore. It's freezing. The wind makes part of the car's back bumper rattle against the ground and whips up snow. Close to me, Amelie is fighting off two pixies. Nick has taken another one down. I look away from that because it's gross and violent and bloody, and even with all the fighting I've done, I still don't like it. Farther down the road, close to the back of the second car, Astley's battling two more. He's doing a good job too. His fist connects to a stomach. He back-kicks the other behind the knee, dropping him.

The one still standing sees me and yells, "She's out of the car."

Oops. Maybe I *was* the target.

My knees bend and I grab at the bumper. It's not too hard to rip off because it's already damaged. One of the pixies leaps at me, springing like a cat, claws outstretched. Wielding the bumper like a baseball bat, I smash it across his head. Flesh burns.

"Nasty," I mumble. He twitches and stays still, sprawled out, eyes closed. I adjust my hold on the bumper, plant my feet. "Who is next? Huh?"

One that Amelie had been fighting raises his eyebrows and takes a step forward. My heart beats faster.

"I said, 'Who is next?' If there's no takers then y'all need to leave," I announce, and I have to admit I'm pretty proud of how brave my voice sounds. You can even hear it over the sound of fighting wolf and cursing Amelie.

The pixie that Astley had dropped starts to get back up. I rush toward him, bumper ready, but something knocks me down from behind. My face smashes into snow. I turn it sideways just in time to keep from breaking my nose. Claws wrap around my head.

"Damn it, queen!" Amelie roars, yanking the pixie off of me.

"I'm not a queen anymore." I hustle back up and belt the pixie over the head with the bumper as Astley dispatches another one. Nick's taken care of Amelie's second enemy. For a second all is calm, and groaning or dead pixies lie around us. It's horrible and disgusting, all this loss of life. Something sobs inside of me.

Astley notices.

"Come on. Let's get home." He drapes an arm around my shoulders, and even though he's gross and bloody, it feels good.

"It looks as if someone doesn't want us to get back," Amelie says as she gets in the driver's seat. We all have rushed back into the car, which seems safer than outside.

"Or wants us dead. Or just wants us." I grab a bag, throw Nick some clothes, and then dig into my own bag for the first-aid kit we brought with us. I start working on everyone's wounds, crawling over everyone because it is awkward and crowded.

While I'm cleaning a cut on Astley's hairline, he touches the inside of my wrist gently. His eyes meet mine, and I feel almost as connected to him as I did when I was his queen. He pulls his lips in like he's wetting them and then whispers, "You did well with that bumper."

"Assorted car parts. Weapons of choice," I quip, taping a gauze pad down.

Before he can answer, I move toward the back of the car and the now-dressed Nick, checking for any wounds that his were blood hasn't already healed. He shakes his head, telling me he's okay, and I start toward Amelie.

"Driving!" she says. "No patching up while I am driving."

I sit next to Issie and grab her hand. She squeezes. We move on toward the airport, silent.

PROBABLY NOT SANE BLOG
Latest Post:
Dude. They are outing themselves—these crazy-ass blue things with shark teeth. I freaking swear. Some are good. Some are evil. It's très confusing, but they say there's some sort of apocalypse coming and the only way to stop it is to fight it. Pixies. Human sized. Ka-bing. Some are hot too. I don't know. I don't know. But they don't want us to blab about it, which is why I am, you know, blabbing about it. Color me a rebel.

For the next two days, we don't stop moving. We use locked groups on social-networking sites, plan on chat rooms, do everything we can to get everyone in Bedford on the same page. Issie and I are in charge of this part of the effort. At first, older people don't quite believe, but Betty handles those. Because of all the lives she's saved, and legs she's splinted, and spaghetti suppers she's volunteered at, she's respected by the people of Bedford. Plus, she doesn't give the impression of being crazy. And for those who still doubt, we have Amelie or Becca change in front of them. When people see attractive women morph into blue-skinned, razor-toothed pixies, it tends to convince them.

We worry about it going viral, about someone telling the rest of the world, but the stakes are too high to get obsessed over it, and the one guy who narks on all of us via his blog is quickly berated by the rest of the blog-i-verse, or the equivalent, which is like thirteen anonymous users.

Nick finds it amusing. At night he reads the blog comments to Betty and me before Betty falls asleep in the armchair. We're hanging on the couch in a very happy and very non-boyfriend/ girlfriend way. He's got a laptop perched on his knees. Betty's snoring and I've thrown a blanket over her. She snarls and snaps at you if you try to wake her up and get her to go to bed. Believe me, I know. So we leave her there.

"Listen to this one." Nick laughs and then puts on this fake surfer voice. "'Dude, if they are hot and the end is coming just bang one.'"

I roll my eyes and he laughs some more. I swear, it's nice being friends with him again. Then he turns and looks at me, closing the laptop.

"We can do this, Zara," he says. "Try not to worry too much."

I swallow hard. "People will die, Nick."

I want to say, *like you did.* But I don't.

He nods, puts the laptop on the coffee table, and says, "It will not be your fault if they do."

"It feels like it is."

"It isn't. You didn't start this, Zara. Astley's cracked-out relatives did. You didn't make Hel or Loki or any of that real."

"But I made the decision for us to be proactive."

"We all did. We have to do it this way and you know it, or else we're just sitting ducks wondering when they'll attack. Amelie's recon shows another hundred pixies have arrived. We have no time left, Zara. People are *dying*. You're such a martyr sometimes. I swear that—" He starts to say something else but there's a knock on the door. "Astley."

He gets up and opens it. Astley's on the porch with his retinue. They look serious and snowy but well dressed. Everyone except Astley wears parkas like they are about to spend time on some Aspen ski vacation. Astley wears his old leather jacket, no hat, no gloves. His eyes meet mine and my heart beats a little faster as he says, "May I come in?"

His voice is mellow and calm.

"Of course." Nick opens the door wider. It's a big step for the two of them to be talking and civilized. If they can work together it gives me hope—and hope is kind of rare right now.

I can't help smiling as Astley steps inside and Nick closes the door, blocking out the cold. Astley smiles too. The others stay out on the porch. Frank and his minions are stalking Astley and me constantly. He can't go anywhere without Becca and Amelie and three other bodyguard pixies, and it makes it hard to talk to him, hard to tell him what I'm feeling.

"I'm going to head upstairs," Nick says, grabbing his laptop.

Astley waits until Nick's retreated up the stairs and then he nods at Betty. "Is she—?"

She snores.

"Can't you tell?"

His smile doesn't show teeth, just pressed lips together. I bring him into the kitchen so we won't wake her up. He leans against the counter, right by the fridge. I lean against the island, opposite him. There's a tiny bit of gold dust on the floor. For a second we just look at each other.

"I miss being connected," he says.

"Me too."

Carrie Jones

An awkward silence descends upon us. He runs a hand through his hair. "I cannot change you back, Zara. The Council believes it will kill you. I cannot take that risk."

I know it's all melodramatic, but I close my eyes. I can't stand looking at him right now—looking and not being able to tell what he's feeling. I turn toward the island, put my elbows on the wood top of it, and hold my head. He comes up behind me and after a moment, puts his hands on my shoulders.

"Zara—" His voice is a hoarse whisper full of emotion.

"I just need a second. Sorry." I swallow hard and stand up. He spins me around so we stand facing each other and my eyes are open again, open and staring up at him.

"Our branches are still entwined," he says.

"You saw them?" I ask the simplest question instead of the hardest. I can't believe he even risked going to them. If Frank followed him—

"No. I had their guardian check." His hands move from my shoulders and down my arms, almost to my elbows and then back again. I am glad that he doesn't turn me blue anymore. He used to before I changed. It was some sort of weird reaction of my half-pixie blood and it happened whenever he was near. He may not do that, but he does still make me woozy—lightheaded almost, when he touches me.

I ask the hard question. "What does it mean? That they are still entwined?"

He tilts his head just the tiniest of bits. "That we are still entwined? That our souls are connected or our fates? I do not know."

My head moves forward so the top of it touches his chest. "Do you think we're still connected?"

206

He inches away. His fingers graze my chin and make me lift my head back up so our eyes can meet. His are blue today. The pupils are large and dark. His voice is deep. "I do think so."

I nod. His fingers move from my chin to my neck, just gently placed against my skin, and I say, "I can never thank you for all you've done for me. For getting Nick back. For helping us. For just—for being here."

He blinks. I don't know what he's about to say or do. When I was pixie I could tell, but not anymore. Now I'm just human. I try to will him to kiss me, say it in my head, *Kiss me. . . . Kiss me . . .*

My psychic powers obviously suck, because he says, "And I thank you."

"For what?" For not kissing him? For not making this more awkward? For staring at his lips like they are this really important book I need to read for AP Language and Comp?

He barely moves except for those lips. The clock on the microwave clicks ahead another minute, but we stand still here in the kitchen. Nick still stays upstairs, hopefully not listening with his wolf ears. Betty is still sleeping. Everything is that one word—still. We are still.

"Thank you," he says, "for being brave after being thrust into a leadership role. For trying so hard to do the right thing for my people and for yours."

"And for loving you?" I ask.

That was awkward.

His breath pulls in. "You love me?"

I can't say it again, but I can nod. His fingers spread out, press against my hair and skin. He closes his eyes for one full second.

"You don't have to say it back," I whisper.

But he does.

"I love you, Zara. I love you and I cannot bear to lose you to this—this—" He searches for a word. "This war. You are human now and so vulnerable."

"So are you," I interrupt.

"I am a pixie king."

"And you can die. We are—"

His head moves even closer to mine. "Do you remember kissing me?"

"When you turned me? Of course." I shudder.

"No, in the parking lot of that grocery store—Hannaford's?" He whispers these words into my ear and I remember. I remember feeling guilty about Nick. I remember feeling that it was right. I remember pushing all those feelings away. But now . . . now I wrap my fingers around his waist, touching the leather band of his jacket, the edge of it, and pull him closer. He lifts me up onto the counter. My feet dangle free.

I whisper back, "I remember."

And then I kiss him, because sometimes you have to take a risk, because sometimes you just can't wait anymore. Our lips meet and call out, pushing toward each other. The world turns silver like his real eyes. My body seems pointless. It is just souls meeting, gesturing against each other, needing and hoping.

"You won't turn me?" I ask, pulling away.

"We cannot risk losing you." His words whisper against the skin near my lips, heating it. "I cannot risk losing you."

My hands find his hair. My fingers sink into the softness of it and then our mouths meet again. In the back of my head, I hear something. A door?

Astley pulls away, turns his head to look. Issie, Devyn, and Cassidy all stand in the living room. Betty still sleeps behind them. Cassidy's mouth is open in a big O shape, but Issie's the one who speaks.

She punches Devyn in the arm. "We never kiss like that."

"Sure we do," he says, all defensive, rubbing his arm.

"We kiss like old people," Issie retorts, crossing her arms over her jacket. "Like old people on TV, actually."

Cassidy laughs as Devyn starts making excuses.

I decide to save him, so I wink at Astley, jump off the counter, and say, "Time to plan more?"

Astley nods. "Time to plan."

FBI INTERNAL MEMO EXCERPT
A local fund-raiser tonight should corral the population into one small area for many hours. Due to the high probability of an event occurring when people are returning to their motor vehicles, I have placed both my people and the Bedford Police Department on high alert. Curfews are in place, but I don't feel that's a sufficient measure to keep the town citizens safe.

Originally, they were going to cancel the Winter Showcase, which is a fund-raiser for show choir and jazz band, but Betty convinced the acting principal, Mrs. Fuze, to let it go on. Our last principal is missing. A lot of people are missing. Mrs. Fuze understands this. When Issie and I head down the maroon-painted aisle to take our seats in the front row of the theater, Mrs. Fuze gives us the tiniest of nods. Her hands twitch at her sides. She's a wreck.

People have packed the Grand Auditorium. The showcase is always here. It's a tradition. The smallish theater holds maybe five hundred people in between its art deco walls. The columns are painted with maroon and fake-gold triangles. Issie tells me that it makes her think of Klimt, this artist she was into her freshman year. I am proud of her for even trying to make conversation. I'm so nervous, I can barely think. So many things could go wrong. I grab Issie's hand. "Tell me how Buffy averts the apocalypse."

"Which time?"

"You pick."

She looks up at the curtains as if they will give her inspiration. "There's so many choices."

There were theater curtains in Cassidy's vision of me dying. That vision also included burning and violence and me in Astley's arms. It's doesn't have to come true. That's what Cassidy says. With destiny there are always too many variables involved.

Betty strides down the aisle and folds herself into the chair next to me. She pats my hand. "We will kick their asses. You'll see."

Her voice is almost a hiss. She wants so badly to shift. I think she can barely hold it in.

Issie leans over me to talk to her. "Where's Devyn?"

"Backstage," Betty says, voice low. "With Cassidy and Nick and Astley and the rest of the musicians and a good amount of the pixies."

Part of the plan is to lull Frank's minions into a false sense of security, to make it easy for them to strike. The only known shifter in the audience is Betty. The only known pixies of Astley's are Becca and Amelie. The rest of them wait backstage in the greenroom and just down the street. Some are hiding in the tiny two-stall bathrooms.

The audience itself is full of armed humans and Frank's pixies. It's a standing-room-only event, thanks to us. The weirdest part about it, if anyone was noticing, is that there isn't one kid under fourteen. There are no toddlers here to watch their big sisters. There are no fussing babies. There are hardly any old people either. But it's still packed. The show choir members, if they survive, will have a bunch of money to help get them to nationals at Disney World. That's assuming the world doesn't end, of course.

Betty's face hovers in front of mine. She snaps her fingers. "What are you thinking about?"

"Nothing. Uh . . . I don't know."

With my right hand I check for my weapons. A special knife that Devyn's parents coated with a fast-acting pixie poison, and some mace that's not really mace, but something they've devised working off our blood. Hours ago, Keith and Cassidy and Jay and some others stashed crossbows and swords under the chairs. Hopefully, none of Frank's pixies will realize they are there.

It doesn't feel good enough.

"I just want everything to go right," I say.

Betty raises an eyebrow and I'm not sure if it's because she's annoyed that I'm doubting myself or the fact that I'm so grammatically incorrect.

"I'm glad Mom's not here," I say.

She grabs my hand. "Me too."

The lights flicker and Mrs. Wilson comes out on stage. She's got two cans of mace tucked underneath her red holiday sweater and one of the pins holding up her thick black hair is coated with pixie poison. I know, because I put it there. She smiles at the audience and opens up her arms in a super-dramatic-theater-person way and says with her strong, soprano voice, "Welcome to the Grand Auditorium and Bedford High School's award-winning show choir and jazz band's Winter Showcase."

She nods at us, encouraging the audience to clap. We do.

Issie leans over and says in my ear, "She's such a pro. She doesn't even look nervous."

"Theater people," I say.

Issie makes big eyes.

"No. Really. They are so good. They can even act in real life-or-death situations," I say as Mrs. Wilson does a dramatic bow and exits stage left. The maroon drapes made of heavy velvet open to reveal a set of white Christmas trees and menorahs. Glittery snowflakes dangle from the ceiling. They look like the same ones from the dance.

"It's pretty," I murmur. "They make winter look nice."

Betty snorts.

"They do!" I object. "You're just cranky because you don't like show tunes."

"It's like being stuck in an episode of *Glee*," she retorts as Cassidy takes the stage. The banter is nice but I know we're just pretending to be calm.

My fists clench as I watch Cass. I'm nervous for her. I'm nervous for us. I have stage-fright empathy and prebattle jitters. Cassidy's braids are all pulled back into one big ponytail that we wrapped up. She's wearing a dark black hippie kind of dress. There's a knife strapped to her thigh. You can't tell it's there. She sings a song from *Les Misérables* about dreaming a dream and then some guy taking away your virginity, leaving you pregnant, and your dreams all dying. Happy stuff. She's good though, really good. I never knew that she could sing. I take a quick look around the auditorium and see all the people who are being so brave, risking everything. There's so much I don't know about each of them. I don't know if they dream of being social-networking moguls or rock stars. I only know that they are being brave, so incredibly brave tonight.

My phone vibrates. I pull it out and read the screen. It's Nick: Still alive.

Stay that way, I text back while the foreign-exchange students sing "Silent Night" in all their primary languages. The three of them look pretty in their white dresses. I wish they'd gone back home. It would have been safer for them. Instead, they have mace and knives, swords hiding backstage.

"This is so wrong," I whisper to Betty.

"The skinny one is off-key, but it's not that bad," she retorts.

I elbow her. "You know what I mean."

"We can't call it off now."

"I know. I know."

We sit through a sexified version of "Winter Wonderland," Adam Sandler's "The Chanukah Song," and a modern dance version of Lady Gaga's "Paparazzi," which involves a lot of reaching over the head and flopping on the floor. Normally I'd be enjoying this, but not tonight.

My phone buzzes with another text.

We shall overcome this.

It's from Astley. Nobody else would use the word "shall." I think about what he texted: *We shall overcome this.* What? Me being human? The potential apocalypse? The talent show? All of the above?

I text back: I believe in us.

Betty totally snoops over my shoulder and raises an eyebrow. I roll my eyes at her. It was a good response. People applaud the ending of the modern dance. Issie taps the program. Nick and Astley are up next.

Astley's got a guitar strapped over his shoulder, which until recently I never knew he played. Taped to the back of it is a long, thin, saber-type weapon. Nick is weaponless and without an instrument. They take the stage and Astley smiles almost shyly, nods his head to the crowd. Nick fixes us with a much more confident gaze.

"He's always a showboat," Issie says. "The apocalypse obviously doesn't tone down Mr. Charisma."

"It's cute," I offer.

She nods but her hands twist together, nervous, on her lap. "It is."

"He doesn't suck, does he?" I ask.

"Oh, you'll see." She gives me a knowing smile. I love Issie, but I hate knowing smiles unless I'm the one doing the knowing.

Nick adjusts the microphone as Astley perches on a stool. Another microphone is in front of him. He doesn't move it. He scans the crowd and looks at me. His mouth twitches a bit and then he gives me a thumbs-up sign as Nick starts talking.

"So, hey? You all ready to rock the house down?"

Oh my gosh. It's so corny, but he's so charismatic that people actually yell, "Yeah!" and stomp on the floor.

"I said, 'Are you ready to rock the house down?'" he asks again, and this time Betty howls and even Issie whistles. The noise is deafening.

"Good!" He lets go of the microphone. "Good! Let's do this."

The curtain lifts and behind them are Austin on a bass guitar and Jay on drums. There are a lot of weapons hidden in the drums, and Jay's face itself looks like a weapon—it's sharp and steely, full of hate.

They are covering a 30 Seconds to Mars song that starts off with this mellow vocal before it goes all crazy-rock loud. Nick's voice is perfect and resonates throughout the auditorium.

"Holy—" Issie almost swears. "This song?"

"It's 'This Is War,'" I whisper back just as Nick segues into the more yelling, growling part. This song is a call to war. It's about fighting to death, going to the boundaries of the earth. And then about it being a "brave, new world."

"Ballsy," Betty yells over the song. "And loud."

Ballsy and loud *and* brilliant because Nick and Astley are calling us to them, rallying us to battle without Frank even knowing. The song slows, the lights change to blue spotlights flashing on Nick and Astley as Astley back-kicks the stool and Nick tells us all to raise our hands to the sun, to warm them there, to get ready for a new world.

They are so good at this. I honestly can't believe how good they are. I'm scared of what's about to happen, but at the same time I'm just so ridiculously proud of them for working together, for their talent and their courage. They are the best of us. The spotlight stops throbbing and then the rest of the show choir shuffles onto the stage, singing backup into a crescendo, and Nick tells us that the war has been won. The war has been won . . . I wish.

And then, just as the music slows down but before we have a chance to applaud, Frank appears, like we knew he would. He is the type who loves an entrance. And Astley is at his most vulnerable now, right up on the open stage, bodyguards far away. Same goes for me, but I'm next to Betty.

He flies to the center of the stage between Nick and Astley, arms outstretched. His hands fling out and he grabs each of them by the throat. The music comes to a screeching halt.

Pretty much instantaneously, Betty turns tiger next to me, but I don't watch. Instead, I'm up on my feet, knife snatched from beneath the seat in front of me, and I've jumped onto the edge of the stage. Behind them, Jay's pulled out a crossbow from where it's been hiding in the drum set.

"Let them go," I order.

Frank laughs. "One move, I snap their necks."

"You didn't even let them finish their set," I mock complain. "You know what they were going to play next?"

"'Have Yourself a Merry Little Christmas'?" he taunts.

"'Valhalla,'" I spit back at him. It has no effect on his cockiness.

"I sent him there once. I guess it's time for him to go back."

"You can't go back, idiot. It's a one-shot deal."

Astley shoots me a warning glance. We've talked too much. I let my anger get the best of me, but I also bought us some time. A perfectly changed Betty pounces onto the stage next to me and hisses, ears back.

She gets a reaction from both the prewarned audience members and Frank. His lip actually curls in, and I can't say I blame him. Betty is an intimidating tiger.

"Call off the cat, or I snap their necks right now," he orders, and adjusts his grip.

I think for a second. "If you wanted them dead, you would already have killed them."

He laughs. "True, true. But I prefer that you all watch the end."

"The end?" Now it's my turn to laugh. "You're surrounded. It is *over*, Frank. Let them go."

Betty's muscles get ready to spring. Nick starts to turn wolf. His body shakes and his eyes close.

"You think we didn't know that you were planning a little ruse? We have *you* surrounded." Frank whistles and the back doors open. I look over my shoulder to see pixies start marching up the aisles, all blue, all deadly. They are not our pixies. Our pixies are strictly maintaining their glamours so the humans can make sure they're good ones. These pixies are his.

"Attack!" I yell. "Attack!"

Our people and pixies start scrambling over chairs, grabbing weapons. The ceiling of the auditorium is suddenly splattered with blood as teeth meet flesh, weapons slice through limbs. My stomach clenches. It has begun. The horrible battle has begun.

BEDFORD POLICE RADIO TRAFFIC
Dispatch: All available units. I have a report of criminal mischief at the Grand Auditorium. Again. All available units, please respond to a report of criminal mischief at the Grand Auditorium.

In a battle, one of two things can happen to time: it can speed up so fast that it's all over in an instant. Or time can move so slowly that you register every motion, every second—the blood and the screams, the opening of mouths, the ripping of flesh. That is how time works for me as Jay lunges over the drum set toward Frank. It's horribly slow.

Thanks to what's left of the National Art Honor Society, there are dozens of spears planted throughout the theater, taped to walls, painted the appropriate camouflaging colors. I yank up a spear that was hidden along the edge of the stage. The sound of duct tape ripping mixes with the screams. I turn to look. We are arming ourselves. Good. Issie stands with a knife, waiting for the attack that's sure to come. Others are already engaged, trying to thrust the spears and knives into the trunks of fast-moving pixies.

I turn to face Frank, but he's gone, just gone. Jay's on the stage floor, grabbing his stomach. I pound over to him. "Where did he go?"

"Through the floor. It's like a trapdoor or something. Astley and Nick and the Frank thing—they just all fell through it. And then it closed." His sentences are gasps. He struggles back into a standing position and I help hoist him up.

"Are you okay?"

"He kicked me before he went through the floor." He stands straighter. "I'll be fine."

Yanking off two cymbals from the drum set, I toss him one. We'll use them as shields. We wait for maybe a second (that lasts a year) before the pixies begin to charge up.

"In *300*, they don't stand," Jay mutters.

"What?"

"In the movie, with the Spartans, they rush to meet them." His words are fast, nervous.

"Good plan." I step forward, use my weight and momentum to help me drive the spear into the first pixie. It smashes into her chest and blood spurts as I yank it out. The pixie keens forward as soon as the spear is removed. She thuds at my feet, but I don't stop, don't look. I keep advancing, each step full of weight and purpose.

The sounds of yelling and dying, of wounding and fear, all mix into a din around me. I tune it out and just focus on the pixies. The next one I stab low and with such force that he is propelled backward as my spear goes all the way through him. I yank it out, spin, and look for attacks from behind me, all in one fluid motion, almost like I am still inhuman. Jay's battling it out with a female. I pivot back and have a moment before the next is on me. I keep moving forward to greet her with the spear. Another step forward and there is a gap, a moment for me to see the carnage below me, for me to see Cassidy being yanked backward by a pixie that is still glamoured. His mouth sinks into her neck and he tosses her against the wall. She flops to the floor.

"No!" I scream the word and throw my spear before I know what I'm doing. The shaft arcs through the air and hits the pixie right below his collarbone. The point slices through fabric and into flesh.

I grab a sword that's taped to the curtain, tear it off, and jump from the stage, but I can't see Cassidy. I'm moving forward to get to her. Pixies rush me. My sword slashes one to the right, scraping across the chest. The wound isn't deep. But the poison will kill her. I swipe one's neck as he rushes my left side, not breaking my stride, just moving forward, right slash, left thrust, over and over again until I get close enough. I am a machine. Inside, I am nothing, feel nothing. I am a death bringer, nothing like the Zara I was before.

And then I see Issie.

And I feel again.

She's flailing around. Her hair is caked with blood, which isn't her own, thank God, but she's panicky. Her eyes are wide and full of fear. Devyn's swooping around her, fending off any pixie that comes close.

"Issie, listen to me," I tell her, grabbing her wrist to keep her here, focused, listening.

"What?"

"No matter what happens, do not lose hope." I nod as Devyn starts attacking a pixie's face with his talons. "Make sure everyone takes care of each other, after—"

Cierra and Paul are hauling in a body from the side of the theater. Issie and I glance down at the same time and a pain shoots through my gut. "Cassidy . . ."

Cierra looks up at me and tells me what happened even though I already saw. "They bit her. In the neck. She bled. She's bleeding everywhere. And Austin. I can't find Austin."

Cassidy's yellow cable-knit sweater is stained with blood. A hunk of flesh is missing from her neck. I yank off my sweater, press it to her wound. "Hold this there. Keith! Keith!"

When he doesn't immediately answer I order Paul. "Find Keith. Cassidy is a priority. Hear me? Text him your location if you don't find him right now. Got it?"

I don't even give him time to answer, just take one last look at Cassidy, who seems so small now. She doesn't move. Her eyelids barely flutter.

"She must not die," I tell them and then look at Issie, whose face is red with anger—an anger I've never seen in her before. I yank her into a hug and whisper into her hair, "You don't die. *You don't die*, Issie. You are not allowed to die."

I don't know if she hears me over the screams. I break away, hack through the pixies, barge past my friends, all these students, some parents fighting as well as they can, and jump back up on the stage. I have to get to them, get to Astley and Nick and Frank somehow. The fighting continues below me. Betty tears a pixie man in half, flinging his torso into another one, knocking it down. My friends are battling so bravely in here, out in the lobby, out on the street. The sounds of anger and pain, horror and death and courage surround me. Each slash, each moan, each battle yell shoves the pain of this deeper into my heart. This is our stand. This is where we are brave.

But we are not enough. We're nowhere near enough, I realize now. We are an army that has everything to lose. I think about what Hel said and suddenly I know what to do. I take the watch on my wrist, my father's watch, and I pull out the timer. That's like sounding an alarm, right? Isn't that what Hel said?

At first nothing happens.

My dad wouldn't let me down. And this *had* to be what he meant. I double-check to make sure I've pulled out the timer. I did. I press it back in again. Isn't that how the alarm works?

"Come on," I beg. "Come on . . ."

My lungs deflate, but then they come. They come through the crazy soundproof walls in waves, old and young, whole-looking and some with their bodies a bit worse for the wear. They glow with the transparency of the dead, not quite cartoon ghosts, but definitely not normal and solid. They do not carry weapons, but my heart beats a bit harder seeing them, as more and more appear—an army of spirits, an army that has nothing to lose.

They stand there, humans, pixies, animals that must be shifters. They stand there and wait. Some of the Bedford people stop fighting—and some pixies too—mouths open, stunned by the dead.

The dead stare at me.

"Fight," I order them. "Please, I beg of you. Fight for us."

And they do.

With fists and claws and teeth, with elbows and feet, they battle, surrounding the evil pixies and pulling them to the floor, engaging them with mouths and knees. I turn back to the trapdoor that Frank pulled Nick and Astley through.

There's got to be a way to open it, but there's nothing obvious—no hook, nothing to pull, just the floorboards that are part of the stage. How did he open it? Magic? No, it's part of the theater, the human theater, so there's got to be a way that's mechanical, and it wouldn't be here on the stage, it would be on the control panel.

I rush to stage left and then the wing where all the levers and buttons are. Most are labeled, but there's one green button, way off to the side. I push it. The lights in the theater go off. It's complete blackness.

"Crud!"

I push it again. The lights fizzle and come on again. Resisting the urge to check on Cassidy and Issie, to assess the battle, I keep looking for the trapdoor mechanism. My fingers run underneath the table next to the control board and find a lever. I flip it down. The stage door opens. I rush back on stage and a pixie smashes me to the hard, wooden floor. I don't know where he came from, but it doesn't matter. His hands smash into my shoulders, holding me down. He's got a knee on my belly and I'm scrambling to find the pixie mace that's in my pocket.

He's a dark shade of blue and he laughs, moves his hand to grab mine.

"Nyuh-nyuh-nyuh," he scolds.

"What are you, one of the Three Stooges?"

He cocks his head. "Who is that?"

"Classic comedians," comes a voice from behind him, and the pixie is wrenched off of me. "That's sad you don't know that. What are we teaching our pixies these days?"

I blink hard and scramble backward. My savior cracks the pixie's neck in a quick movement, killing him, and then he tosses him to a bear, a glowing, luminous dead bear who quickly rips him in half, which is beyond disgusting but effective.

"Hello, daughter." The ghost offers me a hand.

"Hello, pixie father." I take his hand and let him heave me up. It's cold, but solid. He's here, my biological father, the pixie king is here. "Thank you for the rescue."

He shrugs and runs his free hand through his dark hair. "What are dead fathers for?"

"Hugging?" I suggest, and it's true. I really do want to hug him. I never in a million years imagined that. We pull each other close and he sighs. And it's then that I know what he wants, what he needs for him to leave Hel and to go to whatever is next. But as I start to say it, he puts a finger on my lips.

"Let me help you here first," he says. His eyes flame with purpose. "Okay?"

The bear joins us as we stride over to the trapdoor. My father guards one side of me. The bear protects the other, and I know she must be Mrs. Nix. Her fur is scorched in places, scarred in others.

I place a hand on her back, touch the bristly fur, and say loudly enough to be heard over the battle, "I am so sorry. So sorry you died, that it was a trap, that it was my fault. I am so, so sorry."

She swings her head to look at me. Huge brown eyes meet my own gaze and she winks. Then she bumps me with her front shoulder. She is so good and so kind, even in death, even in battle.

"Betty!" I call out, hoping she's nearby.

I want Betty to see her, so I scream my grandmother's name as we move.

It takes us maybe five seconds more to get to the door. Just then the air explodes. My body's thrown across the stage and my head spins into some crazy half-conscious place for a second. Part of the curtain falls on top of me and Paul's body slams down in front of me. "Paul!"

I scramble through the curtain to get to him. His eyes are glazed. His mouth is trapped in a forever grimace. Horror closes my throat as I try to see through the smoke, try not to dwell on poor Paul, try to keep fighting, keep thinking, keep going on. The explosion came from the front of the theater. A gaping hole to the outside is there now. Smoke mixes with snow. Still, even though it should be silent, the battle wages on. People cry and scream and attack. The cold rushes inside. The wind swirls programs into the stinking air.

At the center of the stage, a bruised and blood-stained tiger brushes her nose across a giant bear's muzzle. The bear lowers her head even more and nudges the tiger's shoulder.

My father grabs me by the arm. "Come on."

We scurry back to the trapdoor and look down. Below us are pixies, at least a dozen. They snarl, waiting for us to attempt to get down there too. Austin is crumpled on the ground, bitten and dead. They step on him like he's a piece of dust. Austin . . .

"There's too many," I say. "They'll tear us apart."

"We are ghosts." My father stands there, obviously ready to jump. He nods at Mrs. Nix. "We have nothing to lose and everything to gain by helping you."

Mrs. Nix rolls her eyes and plunges into the pit, snarling. She stands on her hind legs and roars. My father jumps down behind her and yells, "Give us a second."

"Zara! Look out!" some guy yells.

Arrows fling at me. I just barely manage to duck down. More arrows come, diving into the wood. Frantic, I try to see where they're coming from. It's a pixie at the edge of the theater, hunkered down behind the seats. He only pops up to shoot. Issie's parents are rushing at him, knives drawn. I can't watch. Instead, I jump down into the space beneath the stage, landing soundly by Mrs. Nix. Pixies are still fighting them.

My father, the former pixie king, yells, "Go ahead. The tunnel. I can smell Nick that way. We'll hold them off."

"Dad." I swallow. "Thank you."

He smiles a tiny bit and snap kicks a pixie. "You are welcome."

Mrs. Nix snorts.

"I love you. I love you both." The words don't seem enough.

"Zara! Go!" my father yells. "And tell your mother about this, okay? If the world doesn't end? I'd like her to think of me more fondly."

"You never give up, Dad."

"Neither do you," he grunts, grappling with another pixie. "It's in the blood."

I know it's the last time I'll see either of them, but still I run forward, down the cement hallway that leads from beneath the stage. My footsteps echo. I grab the mace I've stashed even though I know it probably won't do any good.

There's a wooden door at the end of the hall.

There's a huge six-six pixie guarding the door. His teeth are plated with gold and they glint when he smiles.

"Finally," he says, bringing his hands together and bending the fingers backward like he's some actor in a movie getting ready for a bar brawl, which is actually incredibly intimidating even if it is a cliché. "I've been waiting forever."

"You know what they say," I quip. "We girls like to take our time, get ready for the big important events in our lives—hot dates, National Honor Society induction, killing pixie kings and their thugs."

My hand clenches the pepper spray. The problem is that I have to be close to use it, which means with those long arms of his, he'll get a good hit in. And now that I'm human again I might not be able to withstand it.

He yawns like I'm too boring for any more words. He lumbers toward me.

"Gasp! Scary."

"You are just a little girl." His voice seems like it deepens with the insult.

As I try to think of some witty comeback, he makes some sort of primal noise and lunges. I lift my arm and spray right in his face. The chemicals make contact. His skin sizzles, really sizzles. The smell of burned flesh makes me gag. His huge knuckled hands lift to his face, shaking, as he screams. I take my knife and plunge it into his chest, right through his Black Sabbath T-shirt, right in between the ribs and up a little. The force of blade meeting body battles through my arm. Stabbing someone hurts. I yank the knife back out as he falls. It worked better than the spears.

"Sorry," I whisper as he thuds to the floor. "You chose the wrong side. Plus, you made 'little girl' sound like a bad thing. There is nothing wrong with being little or a girl."

Quickly, I wipe the knife on my jeans to get the blood off. The jeans are goners anyway, full of bloodstains and dirt. I can't believe I'm thinking about jeans. I can't believe I lectured him on his terminology when he's already dead. I'm a wreck.

I'm such a wreck that my hand trembles as I turn the doorknob. But there's no point in nerves, no point in trembling. Paul is dead. Austin. Cassidy is injured, and possibly dying. People are fighting out there, struggling with everything they have, doing things they'd never thought they'd do. I have to save Nick and Astley and then I have to save them, save the world, whatever the cost.

So I push open the door.

BEDFORD RADIO TRAFFIC
14: Holy God. I've got . . . You've got . . . It's a disaster down here. We have kids with weapons. Blue humanoid things. Explosions. I need backup. We need Fire to respond.
Dispatch: 10-4. Will page out Fire. All available units, please respond to the Grand Auditorium. Unit 14 is reporting armed civilians, full-scale rioting, and fire. Proceed with caution.
14: The Feds are here. At least one is down. Again. I have an officer down.
Dispatch: I need the exact location, 14. Paging County Ambulance now.
14: I have . . . Oh . . . Stand by.

The door opens to a chamber that is not a room but more like a cave, which makes no sense. Why would there be a cave under the Grand? There's no point in wondering. Wondering wastes time I don't have.

The walls are some sort of white limestone-type rock, totally not typical of Maine, which is more full of gray granite. Stalactites hanging from the ceiling form sharp, white points. Another chamber leads off of it. That one is emitting a weird pinkish orange glow.

In the center of this room is Nick, human. Nick's teeth are gritted and he's bleeding everywhere. Blood runs down the side of his face, down his arms. He is a gory, awful mess and it's so obvious that he can barely lift his head up because the effort is just that much. Still, he does. He does lift it. He mouths my name and I know it's a warning. I whirl around as the door whips shut behind me, guarded by four large pixies.

"So, you finally come to give us what we want," Frank says. He has a wound on his arm, claw marks. Nick must have fought him well.

I don't answer.

"Put down your sword," Frank says, and I guess just to prove how tough and strong he is, he pushes Nick forward and away from him. He falls on his knees and forearms in the center of the cavern. Then he flops to his side.

He reaches toward me. "Zara. Don't."

The words are all he has. His lips stop moving. The pain makes him shudder. Anger rips through me. How can I let him suffer? How can I let any of them suffer? And where is Astley? "First, leave Nick alone."

"Hardly. He is our insurance. To make sure you free the god."

Frustration gets the best of me and I roar, "I will never free the stupid god."

Frank unleashes a patronizing smile. "Oh, you will. And you will survive freeing Loki, but without your pixie blood you will never be able to survive what is required to stop the Ragnarok."

"Don't do it, Zara." Nick's words are broken and pleading. I don't need pixie senses to tell that he might be dying, that his energy is running out quickly. I can't lose him again, not because he was my boyfriend, but because he is Nick, and Nick is wonderful and imperfect and bossy and good. Maybe I can buy some time.

"What do I have to do?" My question comes out flat, almost robotic.

Frank bounces up and down with glee, stomping his heeled boot on Nick's finger.

"Stop it! Hurt him any more and I'll refuse," I yell, taking a step forward.

Frank presses his boot into Nick's finger again. A bone cracks. "I hardly think you're in a state to bargain. I truly wish my sister hadn't humanized you. I wanted you for my queen. But maybe I *could* turn you back; it might be worth the risk."

And then Astley steps into the room from another chamber. He is uninjured. He meets my eyes. "She's too puny and too easily manipulated by her heart. She is an unworthy queen, hardly worth anything, let alone a risk."

"Astley?" I gasp out his name. Why isn't he hurt? Why is he smiling like that? What is he doing?

He walks right up to Frank's side and says, "She'd be so fun to torture, though."

"You can torture her later." Frank brushes a bloodied hand against his own cheek, stroking it. "Let's bring her to Loki."

"But . . . But . . . Astley?" Pixies start grabbing and pushing me forward. I try to plant my feet, look to Nick for help, but he's on the floor, trapped and injured.

"He lied to us," Nick says.

"You think?" I snap. Astley shrugs as I say it. He motions for the pixies to let me go and they do, almost as if he's their ruler now.

"But they poisoned you," I say. "You were fighting with us. Your mother—"

"All that happened," he says. "All that happened and then I saw the error of my ways. The Council convinced me. They were on his side all along. They sent me here because they wanted to keep up appearances, make it look as though they were on the side of continuity, but Frank and my mother had paid them off, convinced them that the end of humans would be the beginning of a true pixie realm, where we would not have to hide who we are anymore, where we could take our rightful places, where love and matters of the heart are unimportant, where our needs are always met, our energy always strong, untainted by humans and iron and technology."

He comes closer to me, but not close enough for me to attack him, which is totally unfortunate because I'd really like to rip his gorgeous hair out.

"How could you do this?" I gasp and say the obvious, "I trusted you."

Nick growls on the floor, which probably means that I'm an idiot or something. My heart breaks in half.

"We were going to lose," Astley says. "The Council was on their side. It seemed— It seemed the only way. And Frank is so much more powerful with me."

"And he is more powerful with me, especially since he's lost his little queen," Frank says. "So, we made a deal. He comes to my side. I do not kill his second, Amelie. His pixies survive in a world where they do not have to pretend to be things that are beneath them."

"Humans," Nick sputters.

"And what does he give you?" I ask Frank.

"You." Frank points at me.

"Me?" Anger makes me want to tear off my own skin. "I am not a possession that someone can give." I turn to Astley and spit out, "You don't own me. You are *nothing* to me. Don't you realize what you're doing? You're condemning all of us."

Astley's face twitches and for a second his eyes almost look like they'll cry. But the moment passes and then his face hardens again, and when he speaks his voice is nasty, condescending. "No, you are the one who condemns us, Zara."

"Wh-what do you mean?"

"He means," Frank finishes for him, "that the fate of all pixies lies in your hands. You're the key to Ragnarok, pure, innocent Zara of White."

"Why me?"

Frank laughs. "It's because of the prophecy. It is because you are the child of the willow and the White, the stars. You are human. You were pixie. You are the one who changes. You are the one who would sacrifice everything so that those she loves survive. The only thing you lack to complete the prophecy is your fae blood and the magic. You are sadly without magic now. It makes you far less interesting and less useful to the do-gooders of this pathetic world."

"You tell her too much," Astley barks out.

"It matters not. She will do what we ask. I can tell her it all."

Glaring at him, I mutter, "Then do it. Tell me how to stop the end of the world."

"You have to die."

"Duh."

"You have to jump into the mouth of Hel, Zara," Astley says. "You have to sacrifice yourself."

I look around.

Frank starts laughing. "She's looking for it! How cute. It is not here yet. You have to free Loki first. Come on, idiotic Zara White. Let's go free the god."

I want to process the information Frank just gave up, figure out Astley's traitor ways, but I will myself to focus on the moment. I try to remember everything Devyn has ever told me about Loki. Different sources say different things about Loki's relationship to the other gods. He was helpful and problematic. He is the father of Fenrir, the wolf that ate my pixie dad, just swallowed him whole.

"She is thinking," Frank says as we walk through a tunnel. The surface is uneven, the stalactites are glowing orange like there is fire buried deep beneath them.

"She is *always* thinking." Astley says this scornfully, like thinking is a bad thing.

That's obviously his spiteful way of trying to make me stop thinking, but I won't. I focus. Loki. He was a shape shifter, some say the first of the shape shifters, and has been cited as being a fly, a seal, a salmon, a horse. But when we enter the second cavern, he is shaped as a man, a suffering man.

I must gasp out loud, because Frank says, "Horrible, is it not? And yet, this is what the good gods have done to him."

"For punishment?" I squeak out as the pixies pull me forward across the wet stone floor.

Frank indicates for them to let me go. They do, but hover behind me, in case I decide to make a run for it. Frank moves to my side and whispers almost in my ear, "You remember what he did?"

I can't.

"He is said to have engineered the death of the much-loved

god Baldr. So, to punish him, the other gods bound him here. Do you know what he is bound with?"

I don't say yes or no. "We should help him."

"It's with his son's own entrails," Astley says.

"That means intestines. Entrails mean intestines," Frank pipes in. He claps his hand against his chest. "Oh! She's shuddering, how delightful."

A giant serpent hangs above Loki's head. Venom drips out of its fangs but is caught in a bowl held aloft by a beautiful woman. Her really defined back muscles show via the drape of her flowy, old-fashioned dress. How long has she been protecting him?

"According to the prophecies, Loki is to fight with the jötnar against the gods. It's hard to blame him," Frank says. "He will kill Heimdallr."

"Heimdall?" I croak out. The air is so hot it hisses and I remember how kind Heimdall was when I crossed the bridge to Valhalla.

"Heimdallr." Frank flicks his finger against my cheek. "You children never get anything right. BiForst became BiFrost. Heimdallr became Heimdall. It's like you don't even hear it correctly. Honestly, it's insulting to have you as foes."

I can't help myself. "Obviously, we are pretty good foes, because you haven't actually defeated us yet."

He spins around and the pixies lift me up so our faces are mere centimeters apart and in less than a blink he drops the glamour. He's blue, and toothy, and feral looking. "You wouldn't call this defeated? After days of us destroying this pathetic little town. This isn't defeated? Your puny human 'army' is up there being slaughtered. Your good pixie king, the one you chose, the one you loved, is 'evil' now. Your wolf is dying on the floor behind us. You, no longer pixie, are about to release Loki into the world. You are alone and about to do what we want, after we tormented you for days, toying with you. I would call that defeated."

There's no arguing with that, but anger still stiffens my muscles, and pity—pity for Frank because he is so evil, pity for Loki, who is naked and tortured for centuries, and pity for Astley for giving up.

"Fine," I say.

Frank makes a motion and the pixies set me down. He starts to say something, but I ignore him and all the pixies and instead walk toward the god. The water sizzles where my boots touch it, ripples showing the displacement caused by mere forward motion. Nobody stops me.

"Loki." I whisper his name and he looks at me, turning his head and revealing eyes as blue as my biological father's. There is so much sorrow and pain in there. His mouth opens but no sound comes out. Above him the serpent's fang drips one more drop of venom. It clangs into the bowl and the sound of it makes Loki cringe. What must it be like to have to listen to that for so long?

I ask Frank, because Astley is such a waste. "He's here because he killed someone good?"

"Yes. And for mouthing off," he answers.

"But the gods are always killing each other," I say, remembering all those stories Devyn told us. The names run into each other and muddle up in my head now, but I do remember that there is a lot of death. "Why punish him like this for so long? Why single him out?"

"Does it matter?" Frank snaps. "Free him and let's begin the end of it all."

"Why can't you?" I ask. "Why do I have to do it?"

"Because only someone who knows what he has done and still feels pity can let him go." Frank groans as if I'm far too dumb to deal with anymore.

"And after I let him go, you'll take care of Nick, help him?"

"Well, we'll stop torturing him, although it is so much fun. Wolves are fun to abuse. And Astley hasn't had his turn yet."

I ignore him and step close to Loki. Despite his torture, he still has the form of a god, all powerful, chiseled muscle. I reach out and touch his arm, ignoring the jealous and/or protective hiss of the woman above him. Her arms quiver from holding the bowl. She must truly love him to hold that bowl for so very long. There must be something inside of him that is worthy of that kindness.

It's so sad and so wrong. Should one being suffer against his will just so the rest of us can survive? Who are the gods to condemn one man forever? What kind of existence is this if my survival depends on his staying here, suffering forever, wrapped in the intestines of his very own son? What does it make us that we can allow such pain? Is survival worth that?

He cringes. I'm not sure if he's cringing from pain or because his wife is hissing or because I've touched him, poor thing.

"Why can't you just shift?" I ask. "If you're a shape shifter, why don't you turn into a fly and escape?"

He blinks at me and I move my hand away.

Everyone else just starts laughing. The horrible gales of it echo around the cave. Even the snake looks as if it wants to laugh at me somehow. My hands ball into fists, but then Loki's eyes twitch and a horrible realization/sadness fills them and he roars. The primal fierceness of it vibrates against the walls.

I think I must swear a little under my breath, and I remind myself that I am doing this to save Nick, to free tortured Loki, and there's this other weird feeling like a sense of destiny. But then what about the world? What about the end of it? What about Issie and Devyn and Cassidy and Grandma Betty and my mom? What about trees and birds and flowers and puppies and— What if my need to save kills everyone else, including Nick? What if I can't stop the apocalypse once it starts?

But it's not just Nick or Loki and his wife. Deep inside, I know I need to do this. Maybe I always have.

Reeling away from Frank, I push my fingers into my eyelids, trying to think, to understand. It's hard because there's an annoying house fly buzzing near my ear. I do not want all of us to die. I do not want—

Fingers touch my shoulder, firm but not aggressive, flatly planting against my sweater. Whirling around, I make fists, even though I know I can't fight them well, not as a human anyway.

Loki looms above me. His face aches with joy. His eyes light up from within. His much smaller wife is clutching his side as if she's afraid to let go. He's so different than what he was just a minute ago.

"Y-you're free," I stutter. "Did I free you? I— I— What did I do?"

"I am free, thanks to your kindness and intellect." He shakes his head. He exudes so much power now. "Centuries I have dwelled here and never saw the logic of escape. It humiliates me. To think I could just shape shift into a fly."

"Oh . . ." I try to think of something to say, some nice platitude or cliché about not seeing what's right before our eyes, but I can't. All I can think about is the future, so I blurt, "Can you please not cause the apocalypse?"

For a second he just stares at me. Then he throws his head back and laughs. The booms of it shake the floor. Frank laughs too, but I'm not sure he actually knows what he's laughing about. His pixie minions smile. Astley's eyes are closed, like it is all too much to deal with.

When the laughter ends, Loki puts a hand on his wife's head, strokes her hair, but keeps his eyes on me and addresses me directly. "It was inspired of them to say that I would be the inciting force for Ragnarok, but, alas, that is untrue, little human. I do not incite."

"Zara," I tell him, unclenching my fists. "My name is Zara."

"Zara . . . princess." He takes in this new information.

I need to understand. "So, you aren't going to fight against Odin when the apocalypse comes?"

"Oh, that I shall, I don't doubt. But I do not cause the apocalypse."

"You don't?" I ask. "Everything I've read says that you do."

"No. It is wrong."

"Then who does?"

He points at Astley and Frank. "They do. The pixies."

NCIC TELETYPE
Attention All Bedford County Area Agencies: Please contact the Emergency Management Services immediately about sending all available personnel to assist in an event currently occurring in Bedford. See below for details.

Finding out that he is responsible for the beginning of the apocalypse seems to absolutely make Frank's day. He and Astley pretty much prance around the cavern, smacking each other on the back and bowing to their pixie minion types, who appropriately salute them and wipe the sweat off of their brows. It's really ridiculously hot in here, too hot to be cavorting, and there is a battle going on, and Nick is still injured in the outer cavern, and . . . I need to get out of here.

I am terrified of Loki, but I touch his arm. "Can you help my friend? Can you get us out of here?"

He looks at me, expressionless.

There's probably a protocol for asking this sort of thing of a Norse god, but I honestly don't have the time or means to google it at the moment, so instead I try to give him the pleading-eye look that always used to work on Nick.

"She can't leave!" Frank hisses.

Loki puts out his arm, but doesn't even look at them.

"Inconsequential little slugs," he murmurs, and then they freeze—all of them—Frank, Astley, their little groupies. Loki cocks his head a tiny bit and says, "I am still weak. You should hurry."

"Nick?" I ask.

He shakes his head. "I do not have the power to heal."

"Okay." I start to rush across the thin sheet of hot water toward the cavern opening but then think better of it. "Are you going to be okay?"

His eyebrows raise almost all the way up to his hairline. "You truly are a compassionate one, princess. Perhaps that aspect of the prophecy was true."

He hasn't answered my question, I notice. I hesitate one more time and then beg, "Please don't go on a killing spree. At least not with humans. Please . . . I don't want to be responsible."

Slowly he nods, and his wife moves to hug him fully again. He hugs her back and whispers, "I promise. I hold no ill will toward your kind. Hurry."

I have no idea if I should trust him, but right now I have no choice. So I run. Nick's on the floor, a wolf, barely breathing. Two pixies stand over him, frozen, but with lit cigarettes in their hands. They've tied up his limbs. There are burn marks in his fur and it smells of pain, burned flesh. I swear at them, and bend down and start yanking Nick backward, dragging him across the floor, but he's heavy . . . so heavy, and I am just human. It's just like when he died, I couldn't move him quickly enough, couldn't save him.

"Not this time," I mutter. The ground shudders beneath me. I turn and there is Loki and his wife. He's a wolf now, giant and huge. With one swipe he knocks down the wall. His wife rides on his back.

She reaches down. "Hand up your wolf. We will get him to safety."

"Promise me?" I say, struggling to lift Nick. I can't do it.

"I promise you. It is the least we can do for you." She reaches lower, but I still can't raise him up.

"I'm too weak," I complain.

Loki growls and turns. He reaches down and takes Nick in his mouth, gently, carrying him by the scruff of Nick's neck, as if Nick were a puppy.

"You are strong, Zara White. So strong. You should know that now." She shakes her head at me. "*Af kvöl er friðr.* From suffering, peace."

And then they are gone, leaping out of the room and down the hall. I text Issie and hope she has time to read it: Do not kill giant wolf. Good guy.

And then I have two choices. I can rush after Loki and his wife while Frank and Astley and the rest are still frozen or I can go back and try to stop them for good.

There is no choice, really.

I grab a sword off one of the frozen cigarette-holding pixies and head back down the tunnel and into the second cavern room. Astley and Frank stand where I left them. Astley's eyes reveal a near panic, and his back is hunched a little bit. I should kill him right now, drive the sword right through his heart, and then do the same to Frank. Raising the sword, my hand starts to shake. I believed in him. I believed in him so much.

The air smells like sulfur. It shimmers. It's like the entire world twitches, and I panic, scoot backward, and hide behind a giant rock formation. I don't have time to do any more because the world just starts again. Loki's power wasn't strong enough to keep the bad guys still. Frank laughs with joy.

He hugs Astley to him. "We did it! We did it!"

"There is no mouth to Hel," Astley says, deadpan. "I hardly see what you have achieved."

I flatten myself against the wall, hide partially behind an outcropping.

"I achieve it now," Frank says, raising up a sword and chanting something fast and crazy sounding. His eyes flash red and then glow a pretty sort of silver color that spreads around him like a ball of magic. A silver aura emanates from Frank and then spreads throughout the entire room, sounding with a pop. Black ooze creeps around his feet.

"Nice," I mutter, thinking this must be the worst thing that has ever happened in the history of the world and it's my fault. I was too slow. I should have killed him at least.

As I'm thinking this, Astley lunges for Frank, knocking him down. "No! You cannot! You cannot! Fool! Do not do this!"

"It is already done." Frank laughs as the earth shakes around us, and that's when I do the only thing I can think of doing.

"Astley!" I step out and throw him my sword. He catches it by the hilt and plunges it into Frank's chest. Frank gasps as blood splurts out and then begins to trickle away more slowly.

"It is too late," he whispers. His arm grabs Astley by the cloth of his shirt. "It has begun."

"No!" Astley shakes his head, yanks out the sword, and with

one smooth movement he slashes the blade across Frank's neck, silencing him forever. I turn away as he whispers, "It is never too late."

The ground continues to shake as one moment passes and then another. Astley comes up beside me. "I am so sorry."

I whirl around, stare into his grimy, grief-stricken face. His face is beautiful and so good. How could I have believed he'd betray us? Relief floods into me, pushing tears to my eyes. I rub against them with the heel of my hand. "You should have told me what you were doing. I thought—I thought—"

"That I had betrayed you all. I know. But Nick and I—"

"Nick knew!" I interrupt as the floor cracks.

"It was his idea. We thought it was the only way we could get all the information we needed. I learned how to stop the apocalypse, Zara. I learned about this room, about Loki. That's why we didn't fight him more on the stage. We let him take us here."

I swallow hard as the floor dips beneath us and slants. "I am so mad at you."

He grasps me by the waist as we start to lose our footing. "I know."

His eyes are so honest and upset. The color of them changes, but the truth of him doesn't. He is always Astley, and sometimes he does stupid reckless things, but so do I. Forgiving him, and Nick too, is easy. If we survive, I can yell at them later.

Clutching each other, we scramble toward the hole in the wall that Loki escaped through. Pixies, the bad pixies, are screaming and trying to run too. Looking behind me, I see what Frank did. There's a pit, a hole into the earth. Icy blue flames leap out of it. It's what Hel showed me before. It isn't getting bigger, but there are cracks radiating out from it. Something explodes and I stop moving, my heartbeat fast.

As we reach the auditorium, people and pixies are scrambling toward the exit doors. A curtain falls, flaming. Betty's feline form leaps over the tops of chairs and toward the outside. Then the building starts to crumble down around us. We dodge and duck and scurry, but make it to the street. It looks like it's been bombed. Buildings smoke. Some blaze. Sirens go off. With a roar, the Grand collapses into rubble.

Issie and Betty hobble from the ruins. Issie's hand clutches the fur on Betty's back. More people, survivors, teeter and moan. Some film things on their cells. Some stand and stare, sobbing. Betty sees me and howls. A frazzled-looking FBI agent makes eye contact with me. I hold his gaze for a moment, but look away. There's dead all around us. So many dead. My insides break with the loss of them, all of them, good and bad.

"Zara!" Astley orders at my elbow, trying to pull me toward the end of the street, where there seems to be less disaster. "Come."

My voice is calm, quiet. There is no more fighting, just doing. I let go of my hold on Astley's arm. "No."

Head lowered, Astley looks at me. His eyes meet mine and there's a chill inside his. He understands.

"Zara, no," he repeats, even as a piece of road topples into the slowly expanding hole. "You can't. I can't."

Orange haze from fires colors the white snowy air.

"I am the one who has to close it up, Astley. Me. That's what the prophecy said. It's what I'm meant to do."

He growls, an inhuman noise, full of fear and pain. "I cannot lose you."

"You will lose me either way. At least . . ." I stare into the pit that's growing now, growing even as we speak. It's engulfed every bit of the rubble from the Grand. It's like the theater never existed. "At least this way the world will survive."

"You aren't even pixie."

"Isla said I didn't have to be."

"You're going to trust my mother now?"

"Then make me pixie. Make it so it works. So there are no uncertainties. Just turn me, Astley."

The ground shakes beneath us. I grab him by the front of his shirt. He's so alive and beautiful. I need him to stay that way.

"I need to do this. It is my destiny to do this." I am determined even though my stomach is cramping. I can feel my expression grimace.

"Zara." His eyebrows raise up and he pulls me backward, away from the ever-expanding edge. It tugs at me, just as it did in Hel's home. Doesn't he feel it too?

From the top of the Maine Grind, two of our hunters have their rifles loaded and they are calm enough to shoot every blue pixie they see. Most of them have turned blue. Most are running away. They must feel Frank's death. They must know everything is different now. Humans scream down the street. Sirens blare. Astley and I sink to the ground, clutching each other.

"I have to do this, Astley."

"But—"

I cut him off. "You know I have to."

"I love you," he says. "You have to know I love you."

He loves me, and that is such a good, lovely thing, and it makes me happy to know, but it can't change who I am, can't change my priorities, can't change what I have to do even if I wish it. Part of me just wants to run away with him and go to that castle place he talked about—the one with the flowers and the seals. But the world will end if I don't stop it right now. There will be no more warmth, no more flowers.

"What if I survive this?" I ask, even though I know I won't. I might not be able to even stop it since I have no magic. "What if by some crazy luck I survive it and I'm a pixie? Or I don't change and I'm a human?"

He holds my shoulders in his hands. His thumbs move slowly back and forth. "It doesn't matter."

"Of course it matters."

"No. No it doesn't. Pixie or human, either is just your outer shell, Zara. It does not affect your soul—the essential thing that makes you, you. That is what I love. I love the girl who could not stand to see the enemy suffer, the girl who risked her life to untie me from a tree."

"That's not who I am anymore, Astley. I killed. I've killed pixies."

"Evil, murdering pixies who wanted to hasten the end of the world."

Good point, but still Chogyam Trungpa says an enemy should only be killed "once every thousand years." I totally didn't follow that rule. Instead I fought to become a pixie queen, killed to keep my town safe. I wonder if we could have found another way to survive, found a way to deal with my father, and then Frank and Isla, more peacefully. It is too late now to wonder anymore. What is done is done.

"Zara!" Devyn and Issie are approaching from beneath the Maine Grind. He is human again.

Holding up my hand, I try to stop them from coming any

closer. I swallow hard. Fear battles against what I know I have to do. "What if I end up in Valhalla?"

"Then I shall come to you. But you won't. You can't because you have already been there. You would end up in Hel."

"What if I just die?"

He groans. "I could not bear it."

"Yes, yes you could. People you have loved have died before."

"Not you." Desperately he looks toward Devyn. "There's got to be another way."

Devyn shakes his head. "There isn't. I wish there was but . . ."

"Zara!" Issie half sobs and half yells my name. "The watch! Look inside the watch."

What?

"Yes," Devyn says. "Remember what Isla told you. They hide secrets in timepieces."

They're right. I never thought of it. I pull up my sleeve to look at the watch my dad gave me. There must be a way to open it. I try to pry at the face with my fingers but it's no good. Astley reaches out. His fingernails have turned into pixie claws and he gently uses the tip of one to pry open the watch face, revealing a message scratched underneath: LOVE IS MAGIC.

Holy— That's it? A cheesy 1960s, hippie sort of message? Love is magic? It makes me groan. I snap the watch shut. Issie's face is full of worry.

"It will be okay, Issie," I lie. "It'll all be okay."

In her hands, she holds the branches that signify Astley's and my souls. They glow, still entwined and solid, but shaking in the horrible, hot wind that blasts up out of the hole in the earth. All this time, Issie was the guardian and she never told me. There is so much about my friends, about this world, that I will never know.

"Where did those come from?" I ask Astley.

"In a safe, at the Maine Grind. They'd been in her home, but we moved them there for—" He starts to say more but I realize it doesn't matter.

I grab Astley.

"Kiss me with intent," I order him. "Change me."

"It takes too long," he says.

Grabbing his head, I force his face to mine and whisper over the screams. "Make me like you again, Astley. Let me feel your love before I die. It is all I want. Please . . ."

And he does. His lips, his soft and amazing lips, touch mine and the world spins with a different kind of magic. This kind isn't evil or hard, but lovely and wild, and I melt into it. He melts into it too, I can tell. I can feel how much he loves me just by the touch of his lips. And it is a good love, a really good love.

I make myself move away just enough to say, "Change me."

As soon as the words mingle with the screaming air, I push my lips against his again. The kiss morphs into something different, something filled with a new kind of power. My focus leaves and it's just spinning, spinning until Issie's scream and a tiger's roar slash through the spinning, until Astley breaks away the kiss. I manage to open my eyes and see his beautiful, worried face. Blood is smeared on his forehead just below the hairline. I will miss him so much. I will miss all of them. I want so badly to have some sort of happily ever after where we don't have to battle evil or save the world, where I get to finish high school and go to college and save the world by writing letters to dictators instead of killing monsters. I want a world where my body doesn't feel like it's about to implode, where I get to love Astley and be his queen, where there's no crazy Hel pit right beside me. I want a world where I don't kill. I want a world where I can live my life with kindness.

"I love you," I say, and I'm saying it to all of them, to Astley and Issie and Betty and Devyn, to my mom safely far away, to Nick, to this crazy Maine town, to all of it, but especially to the king in front of me. "I love you and love is magic."

He reaches out to me. "No. I can't . . . You can't do this, Zara. You—"

But I scramble forward out of his reach and fall, tumbling into the flames that are fire and cold, tumbling toward death.

"I love you, Astley."

In the last second I remember my father, my pixie father, and how he came through for me. So with the last ounce of will that I have left, I whisper it, and hope that he and the higher powers can hear.

"I forgive you," I whisper. "I forgive you and I thank you, Dad."

The frosty fires of Hel wait below me. And I fall.

CNNS NEWS
Emergency Management Agencies from throughout the northeastern state of Maine responded to the town of Bedford last night when a mysterious sinkhole appeared beneath a local theater that was hosting a high school fund-raiser. Dozens were injured. At least twelve died and many remain unaccounted for today as authorities mounted cleanup and rescue operations. Bedford has recently been the site of multiple abductions . . .

I wake up. There's this smell of a man in the room—warm and crisp. The heat of a fire pushes against my skin and I can feel it against my face before I even open my eyes.

I clear my throat and then realize there are fingers touching my fingers, gently holding my hand on top of a soft, furry covering. My lungs haul in air. I manage to push my shoulders up and the fingers on mine squeeze gently, reassuring.

"How long have I been out?"

Opening my eyes takes effort, but it's worth it to see him, right there in front of me. He's so beautiful, golden. It's so hokey, but it's how he is. He is warmth to me. And he holds my hand. And he looks at me like he loves me. And he has tears in the corners of his eyes.

"You're here." My voice is hoarse and full of tears. "Are you dead too? Did the world survive?"

"It survived. The pit closed after you fell in. There's a huge hole now. They are calling it a sinkhole."

"But Issie, Betty . . . everyone else?"

"They survived."

"Cassidy?"

"She is in a hospital in Boston, but alive."

Beyond Astley is a window with an ornate gilded frame, beyond it is a world covered in ice and frost. It hangs from the trees, covers the ground. I'm in Hel.

"Am I dead?"

He moves forward, scooching up on the bed, completely obscuring my view of the world. "That's debatable. You are technically half-dead, but the rules are being broken for you because you risked so much to save us. The moment you want to, Hel is allowing you to go back. She has a soft spot for you."

That's nice to know. My lips are dry but they manage to smile. Then I realize all the possibilities.

"Wait. Are you dead?" I ask.

Astley's eyes flicker and widen and he leans forward, kissing my forehead; soft lips, cool against my skin. Then he settles back in a chair, never letting go of my hand, his gaze fixing me. One tiny tear leaks its way onto his cheek, slowly traveling down toward his lips.

"I am not dead. And this time, Zara White," he says, "this time it is my turn to rescue you."

Four Months Later

FROM AGENT WILLIS'S PERSONAL LOG

For about two months now, the town of Bedford, Maine, has been quiet. All winter it was besieged by random kidnappings of teens and eventually adults, scores of missing, and then a sinkhole that destroyed the local theater and coffee house. The snow has stopped. Incident reports are run-of-the-mill. There are no missing youths, no reports of strange whispers in the woods. Still, the place has something off about it, and my case, I fear, will never be officially closed. So many civilians and so many officers lost their lives in the strangeness that went down here. That sticks in my gut.

Spring in Maine comes with a rush of mud. Streams overflow from melting snow, and temperatures plunge back into the land of cold every night, but I do not care. Spring is spring, and my friends and I are alive, even Cassidy, although she was in the hospital for a terribly long time. The show choir is headed for Disney and the national competition. Disney is in Florida, where it's warm, even at night.

We sit on the lawn in front of the school. Seniors shuffle off to get their cars out of the senior lot. The late bus straggles up to the turnaround. Brakes squeal as it comes to a stop, the door opens, red lights flash near its roof.

Nobody is in danger.

Nothing is going to snatch anyone away.

Issie flops onto the grass, then adjusts herself so her head is resting on Devyn's thighs. His hand plays in her hair.

"Do not get me wrong," she says, crossing her feet at the ankles. "I like that nobody is in mortal danger anymore but it's . . . it's kind of . . . Well . . ."

"Boring?" Nick offers. He's plucking out blades of grass while waiting for another Amnesty letter I want him to sign.

"Exactly," Issie breathes out. "Boring."

"Boring is good," I announce, handing Nick a letter and giving another one to Astley. His eyes meet my eyes. We were talking about the same thing in the car today, about how our lives have settled into something calm. The Pixie Council has disbanded. Rogue kings still exist, but none right here, and none as bad as Frank. Amelie is in charge of the day-to-day aspects of the kingdom, and Astley, who was homeschooled and tutored his entire life, is attending high school with us, taking all AP classes. It's disgusting. And nice. And disgusting. He's as smart as Devyn. He's going to deliberately get a B in health class (totally required to graduate for some reason) just to make sure Devyn keeps valedictorian for next year. It wouldn't be fair otherwise.

"Remember when you came here?" Nick asks.

"She was all peace jeans and U2 songs," Cassidy sighs, coming toward us. She walks with a little hitch now, like she's still protecting her wounds. "And you two argued constantly."

"Not constantly," I argue, all defensive, casting a side look at Astley, but he's not jealous. He never gets jealous, which is lovely but kind of weird.

"Constantly." Nick laughs. He hands me back the letter. I pass it to Cassidy to sign. It's about the death penalty, which is ironic because we're protesting it being used unlawfully when we've used it unlawfully more times than I can count.

"And she'd always be mumbling those phobias under her breath." Issie sits up. "It was so adorable."

"Adorably neurotic," Devyn says. "I thought she'd be my parents' next patient."

"Not nice," Issie says, punching him in the shoulder.

"But true." I agree with Devyn. I was a wreck. "Now I'm just neurotic about getting into college."

"And keeping the world safe from those who don't care about human rights," Issie says.

"You will be accepted," Astley says.

"That's what Betty says." I touch a tiny blade of grass. It's so different from the grass in Charleston—thinner.

Cassidy looks up from signing her letter. "How's Gram doing?"

"She still misses Mrs. Nix but is pretending not to. She's taken over Mrs. Nix's honey hives. It's sweet and sad all at the same time, you know?"

For a minute we're quiet. There have been so many funerals and wakes, in-school service days with counselors that they've shipped in so that those of us who are left can handle our post-traumatic stress and survivor guilt. The town has lost so many people.

There's a little wind. Dandelion weeds are starting to poke up through the grass. Soon they'll grow pretty yellow heads. Then they'll turn to skeletons of themselves, and the wind will blow their seeds away, spreading them everywhere. Part of me wonders if that's what the evil pixies are doing, waiting, ready to burst from the ground and spread everywhere. Part of me thinks I'm paranoid.

"So, spring break . . . ," Issie prompts. "How awesome."

Cassidy eases herself to the ground next to us. "It will be."

Cassidy is going on the show choir trip, as are Devyn and Nick. But Astley, Issie, and I are headed to Europe, to go to that villa Astley promised. We will see seals and flowers. We will be free of Bedford, no offense to it. It will just be nice to go someplace that wasn't the site of massive deaths and evil.

When I first got to Bedford I was so full of fear that I had become nothing. I hardly felt anymore because feeling hurt too much. And now? Now I think of a quote my stepdad used to say. It was by Anandamayi Ma: "Be anchored in fearlessness. What is worldly life but fear!"

I have no idea who Anandamayi Ma is. I should probably look her up, but not now, because right now I am so happy that I am not the only one who remains, that I am the one who risked everything so the world didn't end, that I get to hang out on the grass and feel the sun and let Astley rest his head against my hip as he sprawls out and stares up at the sky. Most of Frank's pixies are ours now, assimilated into the fold, contrite and upset about what they had become, and working toward redemption.

Winter is over. My friends and I own lives where we can all exist without constant fear. It's a life where I can be proud of being half pixie, proud of who I am, who we all have become.

Acknowledgments

Thanks to my mom, Betty Morse, who has been battling sickness after sickness and staying alive despite everyone's doubts. She personifies fierce and good. I love her the whole world. And thanks to Lew Barnard and the rest of my family for not disowning me yet.

Thanks to Emily Ciciotte, who proves that you can be glorious even when watching TV.

Thanks to Shaun Farrar. You have taught me to be brave and to have hope. I am so sorry that you have to keep teaching me that over and over again.

Pixie kisses to Alice Dow, Lori Bartlett, Marie Overlock, Jennifer Osborn, and Dotty Vachon; to Laura Hamor, Kelly Fineman, Jackie Shriver Ganguly, Tami Brown, Melodye Shore, and Tamra Wright. You have all been so patient with me and so wise.

Thanks to Jim Willis, Ken Mitchell, and the Mount Desert Police Department for letting me write and dispatch and for all of you offering to be in my books numerous times. You are.

This series would not have existed without the guidance of Michelle Nagler. She is a rock star of an editor and I am so lucky that she was there to make Zara as tough and awesome as possible. She and the rest of the amazing Bloomsbury crew—including, but not limited to, Melissa Kavonic, Alexei Esikoff, Jill Amack, and Regina Castillo—make it wonderful to be an author. Thank you. They don't get the fan mail, but they deserve it more than I do.

And all my thanks to Edward Necarsulmer and his mighty assistant, Christa Heschke. There can be no better agent and no better friend. I am so sorry I always pocket dial you when I am in an airport and disconnect you when I drive. Some day I won't. I swear.

Finally, thank you to all the awesome people who send me e-mails and comment on Facebook and Twitter and all the random social network places I appear. You have no idea how much you help me believe in the goodness of people. Thank you so much for being goofy and supportive and . . . well . . . yeah . . . awesome.